Terry,
Thanks J
Hopefully one
can visit your
club in sunny CA.

TEMPERANCE RIVER

by Jason Holscher

Temperance River

Copyright © 2010 by Jason Holscher

All rights reserved. No part of this book may be
reproduced in any form or by any electronic or
mechanical means, including information storage and
retrieval systems, without permission in writing from
the publisher, except by a reviewer who may quote
brief passages in a review.

First Edition: May 2010

Manufactured in the United States of America

ISBN-13: 978-1450581202
ISBN-10: 145058120X

TEMPERANCE RIVER

The truth is often a terrible weapon of aggression. It is possible to lie, and even to murder, for the truth.
 -ALFRED ADLER (1870-1937),
  PROBLEMS OF NEUROSIS

OCTOBER 2007

Chapter One

Dale Jacob stood at the window listening to the melancholy lowing of a ship's horn out on the lake; the uppermost trellis of the lighthouse bridge, caution lights blinking like stars through the mist.

It was gray and ominous. Hell, Dale thought, it's always gray in Temperance. Nothing ever changes about that. Temperance River. A place so inhospitable and vague Dale wondered why he never left.

Lightning spilled through the window in a brief blue-white glare. Little Rose was crying in the back bedroom and Michelle wasn't doing anything about it. Lazy slob of a mother she was.

He was stuck here, that's why. He couldn't leave. It was the end—the end of the world.

Rose was crying even harder now. Why didn't Michelle get her lazy ass out of bed and tend to her? He had to go to work for Christ's sakes; he couldn't be taking care of Rose right now.

Dale looked around for the keys to his pickup truck.

The Airstream was a goddamn pigsty. No rug on the floor, dirty dishes in the sink, empty beer bottles on the counter left as a gift last night from his freeloading friends. The mirror on the wall had a crack in it and the TV was going on the B.O. again. A person could commit suicide in a place like this.

Rose was crying like crazy.

"Shut that kid up!" Dale hollered, but he figured Michelle was still sleeping off last night's drunk.

Why the hell did she get to sleep when he had to wake up and go to work?

He should dump the bitch. He'd wanted to do just that plenty of times, but then she went and got herself pregnant and had little Rose. Now he'd never be able to leave. Michelle had even started bugging him about getting hitched. Hell, he didn't want to be tied down to one woman like that. It would be like waking up and having Cheerios for breakfast every morning for the rest of your life.

Who needed that?

Rose was *screaming* now.

Dale went down the narrow hallway to the bedroom and found Michelle still sleeping on the sloppy bed. Her naked body filled him with disgust. She used to be cute when he first started dating her, but she'd really let herself go after having Rose. Her cute little ass had all but disappeared and was now a flabby and white dimpled thing, and her pear-shaped tits were mushy and limp.

"Can't you hear that goddamn kid?" Dale screamed at her. "She been cryin' all mornin'."

Michelle tried to pull the covers over her head, but Dale grabbed them and threw them on the floor.

"What the hell, Dale?" she said, her voice thick with last night's booze and cigarettes.

"Don't what the hell me, girl. Get up and see what's wrong with Rose."

Michelle stumbled from the bed and went past Dale into the bathroom. "Do it yourself, asshole," she mumbled at him.

He tried to go after her, but she slammed the door in his face.

"Fucking bitch!"

A flare of anger shot through him, seemed to explode in his brain. He slammed the flat of his hand on the bathroom door and went down the hall to Rose's room.

She was sitting on the bed in her pink Barbie pajamas. Her favorite teddy bear, Mr. Honey, was in the crook of one arm, and she was wiping tears away with the other.

The loudest crack of thunder yet broke overhead, loud enough to make the trailer's tin roof vibrate.

"What the hell's wrong wit 'chou?" Dale said, picking Rose up off the bed.

He almost dropped her when he felt the bottom of her pajamas. They were soaked.

"What the hell you do, girl? How many times do I gotta tell you not to wet the bed? Huh! If I've told you once I've told you a million times. If you gotta go, just get up and go. What's wrong wit 'chou, girl?"

"You're hurting me," Rose cried.

Dale didn't even realize that he had her by the arm and was dragging her across the floor.

She was pitiful in her wet pajamas, crying like a goddamn baby. Her goddamn fat mother spoiled her too much, that was the problem.

"I just couldn't hold it. I just couldn't hold it, Daddy."

Daddy!

He hated that word. He was too damn young to be a daddy.

He picked Rose up under her arms and carried her down the hall.

"You're hurting me, Daddy," Rose cried.

"You think I'm hurting you now," he screamed at her. "Just wait and see what happens if you piss your bed again, girl!"

Michelle came out of the bathroom then, wondering what all the hollering was about.

"None of your business!" Dale shouted.

"He's hurting my arm, Mommy!" Rose cried. "He's hurting me."

"Dale—"

"She pissed her bed again," Dale said in a low, hoarse voice. "I'm gonna show her what happens to little girls who piss their bed."

"Dale—stop it!" Michelle screamed. "Just stop it. She didn't do it on purpose, you know."

Dale carried Rose into the bathroom and slammed the door. Michelle tried to open it, but he'd locked it from the inside.

"Dale! What are you doing to her? What are you doing?"

"Stay out of this, Michelle," came back Dale's muffled voice through the door. "If you would have disciplined her more when she were little, she wouldn't be in this mess."

"Mommy—" Rose screamed out. "Mommy—"

Michelle pounded on the door.

"Dale!" she screamed. "Stop it, Dale. Dale—"

Chapter Two

"I'm gonna come! Oh Danny, I'm gonna come!"

BCA Special Investigator Danny Pierce was screwing the socks off Heidi Voss, the pretty little blonde waitress from the Loon's Nest. He had her on all fours on the bed, her face buried in the pillows, her bony behind up in the air, waggling at him like a hardboiled egg. She liked it rough, and by god, he was giving it to her the way a bad-hearted man with a greenwood stick might drive a lazy horse.

He didn't hear the phone ringing, what with the way Heidi was screaming and with Homesick James blasting out of the stereo singing about how he was going to dust his broom.

The telephone kept ringing until Danny came up for air.

"Goddamn it, Danny," Heidi said, looking over her shoulder at him, blowing a strand of dirty blonde hair out of her face. "I was just about to come that time."

She lay back against the pillows and sighed as if she'd just had a big meal.

Danny reached across the bed and hustled the phone to his ear. He said in a low voice, "Pierce."

And a lion's voice replied: "E-yellow, Pierce."

The voice belonged to Michael O'Malley, Chief Superintendent for the Bureau of Criminal Apprehension. The BCA was a state-funded organization that assisted law enforcement agencies throughout the state of Minnesota in solving local crimes and apprehending the state's most dangerous criminals.

Danny grabbed a pack of Marlboros off the bedside table.

"What do you want, O'Malley?"

"Just cut to the chase, right, Pierce?" O'Malley said. "Don't believe in beating about the bush, eh?"

Danny could visualize O'Malley, who was fifty-five, bald, and barely five feet tall, with a pot belly the size of a bowling ball. He always reminded Danny of an enlarged, elderly, bald rendition of the village fat boy.

"That's right, sir" —Danny sighed— "I'm a little busy."

Heidi turned over on her side and snuggled up close to him, tracing her fingers through the hair below his navel. She had no make-up on and her lips were full and pale red, her eyes large and deep and chocolate-colored; her skin warm-looking and tanned. Her body, outlined beneath the sheet, was full and soft and curving.

Danny heard O'Malley chewing something on the other line. "Right, right," O'Malley said. "I understand. A bachelor like you. Well, all right, Pierce, I'll get down to it. Here goes. I thought you might be interested in working a new case. Now, I know you're supposed to be on vacation, but..."

"I'm not interested."

"You didn't even wait for the pitch, Pierce."

"That's because I know I'm not swinging, sir."

Some more chewing came over the line. "You might be interested in this one."

"Why's that?" Danny asked, not really interested, but wanting to get O'Malley off the line as quickly as possible so he could crawl under that sheet beside that warm soft body—

"A little girl is missing," O'Malley said.

"So," Danny sighed. "Little girls go missing all the time. What's so special about this one?"

O'Malley was still eating. Danny listened to him chew.

"It happened in your hometown," O'Malley said between bites.

Danny shifted the phone to his other hand. "Temperance River?" he asked.

"Yep," O'Malley replied. "Ever heard of a bim named Michelle Violette?"

"She graduated a few years behind me."

"Her six-year-old daughter is missing," O'Malley said. "It's been three days now and the law up there has come up goose eggs."

"What happened?"

"Well, it appears this Michelle Violette woke up one morning and the kid was gone. But there's some suspicion about her and her boyfriend."

"What's the boyfriend's name?"

"Hold on." There was a pause and Danny could hear O'Malley shuffling some papers around. "Here it is. Jacob. Dale Jacob. Know him?"

"Yeah, I know him." Danny rubbed one eye with his fist. "Jacob's a drunk yokel from the sticks. Been getting in trouble his whole life. Why is there suspicion about them?"

"Well, for one thing, they never joined in on any of the searches and they've never inquired about the investigation after their initial report to the local police." O'Malley paused. "I'd called that suspicious, wouldn't you, Pierce?"

"Who's the local police up there anyway?"

"Says here it's one Sheriff Garski."

Hearing that was enough to knock the Kiwanis out of Danny's soul. "J.P. Garski?" he asked.

"Yeah. Sounds like a Polish cowboy to me. Why, you know him?"

"Yeah, I know him. He was my best friend when I was a kid."

"Isn't that cute," O'Malley said. "So do you want the case; or am I going to have to give it to someone not as gifted as the great Danny Pierce?"

†††

When Danny hung up with O'Malley he was quiet for a long while, blinking hard against the burning in his eyes. He could have killed O'Malley. He could have reached through the space to strangle him with the phone cord. The last thing he wanted to do was go back to Temperance River. His hometown. A place that never forgets and never forgives.

What was it that old writer once said? You can't go home again. Well here he was, about to do just that.

Danny looked over at the waitress, lying on her back now, her perfect pink nipples pointing arrogantly up to the ceiling. She smiled and reached over, and her hand wandered slowly down his belly, touching his cock lightly and lovingly.

"Want to fuck some more?" she asked.

He got out of bed and went around the corner to the kitchen for a pint of Scotch and a fresh pack of smokes. After dropping a quick line of coke off the dirty kitchen counter he went back to the bedroom and fucked what little brains were left in Heidi Voss's cute little blonde head. He could feel her there, beneath his weight, moaning like there was no tomorrow, and all he could think about was how long it had been since he'd been home.

That one word terrified him.

Home.

Chapter Three

The next morning Danny got out bed and staggered into the bathroom, holding himself upright with one palm against the wall as he urinated, staring at his red-eyed image in the mirror. Heidi was sleeping soundly, her lips slightly parted and her bare back exposed to him. He raised the blind and the room flooded with bright sunlight. He shook her gently by the shoulder and she opened her eyes quickly, blinked them against the shine.

"Time to go," Danny said.

She sat up in bed. "I don't even get breakfast?"

"Nope."

"Well, geez. Will I at least see you at the club next week?"

He didn't make her any promises. When she left he ate some Wheaties and a chocolate doughnut. Breakfast of Champions. His nose hurt from all the coke he did last night, and it didn't help any that his head was throbbing with guilt. Every time he did coke, the guilt would eat him up like a cancer the next morning. Eat him alive. But he knew he couldn't quit, even if he wanted to. Why even bother trying anymore? That biting electric edge would always be there, calling him, taunting him, seducing him. He'd start out clean each morning, but the day would soon take chunks out of him, begging him to take her. That's the way he looked at coke—as a distrustful lover, irresistible, yet despised, demanding that he fuck her. And after each fuck, the guilt was always inevitable.

After popping four dry Advils, Danny quickly packed his suitcase and locked up the apartment. The hallway stretched wide and dark and empty before him. From behind a closed door came the low-voiced moaning of a lonely rap song, that, and the pungent smell of some kind of weed.

He got on the dim crimson elevator and plunged down twelve stories, turned to the right as the doors spread open, and went outside into the deafening chaos of cars and busses and people screaming at each other. The chaos of the city. All the sights and sounds of modern man—the background of our lives.

Some days he hated the city. He felt sorry for the hordes of unburied dead that lived in it, fumbling blindly and dolefully about, eking out from one day to the next the flaccid sustenance of abject lives, punishing themselves through their endless cravings; seeking satisfaction but finding despair, like monkeys snatching at moonlight on water.

He went into the underground garage and found his car, a convertible Cadillac XLR. He had a lot of vices, but the car was his biggest. He bought it for seventy-seven five from a dealer in White Bear Lake and every time he slid behind the wheel he felt a little ostentatious. An innate reticence about it, like being caught in public with your pants down. Nice car on a cop's salary. But he didn't have anything else to spend his money on except booze and women and a little blow now and then. No wife, no kids, no big mortgage hanging around his neck like a millstone. All he had to worry about at the end of each month was if he had enough money to cover food and rent for his crappy one bedroom apartment in the muck of the South St. Paul stockyards. And usually he did.

He drove the Caddy out of the dark garage, turned onto 7th Street and followed the exits for I-94, through Dogtown and what was commonly referred to as Spaghetti Junction. There was a weird white blimp hovering above the city with the words ENOUGH IS ENOUGH painted in big red letters on one side of it. That was weird; he'd never seen a blimp in the city before.

Danny inched the car onto 94 and immediately got stuck in traffic. The horizon shimmered and danced with car exhaust; the air stank of hydrocarbons. He felt like taking out his service revolver and letting everyone else on the road have it. Instead, he slipped a compact disc into the Caddy's expensive Bose stereo—250 watts of total audio power with a convenient six-disc changer and nine speakers—and a few seconds later Bruce Springsteen started singing about riding through mansions of glory in suicide machines. Danny didn't know what the hell that meant, but right now, stuck in traffic like he was, he sure liked the sound of it.

When he finally broke out of the gridlock, he accelerated off 94 and merged onto Highway 61—the same 61 Bob Dylan sang about—and headed toward Duluth and then further, to the edge of the deep north, to a place called Temperance River.

Danny abandoned himself to the music, allowed it to invade his consciousness more and more completely, till at last there was nothing left in the world but that one deep catalyst of sound as the twin cities of Minneapolis and St. Paul began shrinking in the rearview mirror like two cranky and weary sisters. He never got to see what was painted on the other side of that weird white blimp.

The Caddy handled like a gift from heaven. Made him feel like he was sixteen again. The speed limit out here on the highway was seventy, but he had the powerful Northstar V8 engine doing a steady eighty-five. Cars were dropping past him like flies. He wasn't wearing his seat belt. He never did. It wasn't that he didn't believe they worked. He just didn't like the government telling him what he had to do to protect himself. It wasn't your typical *modus vivendi* for a cop, but Danny stuck to it like a monk sticks to the Eightfold Path.

He drank black coffee out of a thermos and resigned himself to the long drive ahead. It was going to be about three hours to Duluth, and then another couple hours up the North Shore of Lake Superior to Temperance River, a gatehouse pimple on the butt-end of Canada.

He went through three more Springsteen CD's and four more cups of coffee, and pretty soon the highway stretched out like an elastic band and there was nothing out here but farm fields and Burma-Shave wisdom on the side of the road: EAT AT EARL'S; SEAGREM'S 7...IN-LAW TONIC; LUNCH SPECIAL WE HAVE WORMS SOFT PRETZELS & ORDERS 50¢ POWERBAL 55MI. It was like being in a different fucking country.

Then something magical happened. The billboards disappeared and the woods started creeping closer and closer toward the highway like lost souls in a Fellini movie. The temperature dropped about ten degrees, and then he saw the lake—Lake Superior, the largest lake on the planet; a huge, rock-bound basin where big ice crunches ashore in the wintertime, some of it pale blue, some pink as if it had been bled upon—the watery grave of more than 325 ships, better than thirteen hundred feet deep in some places. Some of the local Indians have been known to claim it is bottomless. There was a story Danny's father used to tell him about the Ojibwas that used to live on the lake's shores. Before they were married, an Ojibwa couple would cut off a strand of their hair and braid it together into a cord. On the morning they were wed, they tied the cord around a stone, took a canoe out into the lake, and dropped the stone into the water. The stone plummeted down forever, the Ojibwa believed, its spirit hand-in-hand with the braid of hair, and for eternity there would be a life force that joined them together forever.

The nearer Danny got to the lake, the more fabulous it seemed. He could smell it and feel the cool cat's-paw breeze blowing through the convertible. The road curved up ahead and slowly rose in altitude. He had to press hard on the gas to even the car out with the higher elevation, and then the city of Duluth commenced the skyward climb, appearing out of the clouds like a mirage of some fabled and magical city—a Midwest Shangri-la straight out of a book by Fitzgerald or Sinclair Lewis.

A long time had passed since Danny had last seen the old city of Duluth, and every time he came back he was amazed at how breathtaking she was, like a friendly stranger who smiles at you when she passes you on the street.

It was a classic afternoon of turning leaves and crisp clean air. Classes over for the day, the town teemed with UMD students, hanging around in groups, in pairs, alone; the frat boys and the stoners, the hippies and the beautiful sorority girls walking around in tight sweaters. The lake was spackled with sailboats and patrolled by swooping seagulls, the treetops surrounding it alight in fiery hues, the maples orange, the oaks a soft tint of raspberry.

He passed slowly through Duluth and out the far side with the lines of traffic, pointing the car north on Highway 61 again, taking the old lakeshore road instead of the new expressway. He got caught in a brief traffic jam just outside of French River, due to an auction, it appeared. Most of the vehicles in this parade were mastodonic RV's which looked big enough to transport entire football teams.

The road hugged the rugged shoreline and served up some of the most spectacular scenery in the world—Hansel and Gretel forests, pine-studded hills, rock-bound bays and inlets, lighthouses and waterfalls, and always the limitless horizon of the lake, vast an very cold. The waves coming in, coming in, coming in; boundless, clean and deep. You always knew there was going to be another wave. The lake had always been there, and more than likely it always would.

Danny proceeded another thirty or forty leafy miles, and when his belly started begging, he stopped at a greasy truck stop called *The Red Shed* in the small town of Castle Danger. The food in this type of place was always greasy and so were most of the customers. The greasy spoons drew a greasy crowd in every big city and small town Danny had ever been in.

There were several truck drivers in the place and a bunch of gray-haired Red-hatters traveling the North Shore, and a crowd of students from UMD who were either homosexuals or dope heads.

Sometimes you needed a scorecard. Everything looked the same these days.

The coffee wasn't too toxic though. A waitress—who was a few years past her use-by-date with an Iowa accent—brought him more of it. She was a long way from home.

He asked her what was good to eat and she suggested the Rueben. It was an odd choice, good and not too hard on the credit card. He washed it down with another cup of coffee and a third cup of coffee. Then it was back on the road. There was still a long stretch of empty highway between him and Temperance River.

†††

Danny pulled out of the parking lot and felt the wind blowing through the car and he inhaled a nose full of that tangy, sweet smell of fish emanating from the cerulean waters of Lake Superior. It was chilly now, but he liked driving with the top down.

He drove another hour and when his knee got stiff—an old football injury—he pulled over on one of the winding subalpine roads and parked the Caddy behind a stand of birch trees at a small roadside picnic area overlooking the lake.

There were no other vehicles and no other people around. In every direction was a picture postcard vista of endless sky, blue water, rocky cliffs, towering pines, rivers and streams and thundering waterfalls all emptying into the lake.

The wide open spaces freaked him out a bit. He wasn't used to it any more. He'd gotten too accustomed to City Life down in St. Paul.

He stretched his legs and took a deep breath, watching a giant freighter weighted down with a belly of iron ore out in the vast blue distance. The mournful cry of the freighter's foghorn came and went like the voice of some ancient beast. Sorrowful. Lonely.

Danny reached into his pocket and took out the clear plastic sandwich bag. He stuck his pinky in and dipped it gingerly into the white powder and licked his pinky, feeling the blood rush to his face, up through his chest, and he felt the ease. It was always the same with the day's first taste of coke, his head a little light and a little dizzy, like the way he felt when he had first taken a lower lip full of Copenhagen when he was a kid.

He stuck his pinky back in and inhaled a clump of powder.

Repeat. This time in the other nostril and with a bigger clump.

Light flared—blinding white light that filled the void. Then it was dark.

He blinked his eyes and the red fog went away and he looked out across the big lake, at the mournful freighter, a big inky patch against the shimmering water, growing smaller and smaller, dwindling stealthily into the horizon, until it tapered into extinction and was there no more.

Chapter Four

Danny got back in the car and drove north. Always north. He could feel the town—his hometown—getting closer, pulling him like a giant magnet. He thought about the day many years ago when he'd left, working it back to the beginning, like tracing a river to its source. When he was in high school, he always dreamed about leaving— *flee the cows,* as the saying goes. He'd been going steady with Sadie Petersen for about a year back then and they talked about going off to college together. He had a few schools looking at him to come play football, but then he blew out his knee and the recruiters all but disappeared. He was a straight-A student, but all the good schools turned him down—Hamline, Bethel, St. Thomas. You needed old money and family connections to get into those schools, grades alone just didn't cut it. Sadie went to UMD at her parents' urging, and Danny ended up down in the Twin Cities with the rest of the driftwood at the University of Minnesota.

"I think we'll grow to love each other more that way," Sadie said about their separation.

They promised to stay together no matter what, but they had been too young and did not yet know that most long-distance love affairs seldom work, and in their case, the odds played out against them. Within a year, they had split-up.

She still loved him, he could tell. She'd never say so, any more than he would have told her. What a weird thing that was. When it was all said and done, Danny realized that he really did love Sadie, but in the end, it was too late. She had already moved on without him.

He ended up coasting for most of his four years at the U. He didn't remember most of the courses that he took. He was enrolled in the College of Liberal Arts, but that generally leaves you a lot of room. His father and mother didn't believe in college, more specifically in paying for college, so he had to scrimp and save every penny he managed to come across. During his third year there was another girl and they had talked about getting married after college, even though Danny still harbored some of those old feelings toward Sadie. Then the shit really hit the literal fan. He started partying a little too much, the other girl missed her period and they both agreed on an abortion. That managed to kill things for them. The girl dropped out of school with less than a semester to go and moved back in with her parents on a farm somewhere in Wisconsin. Danny never saw her again, or if he had, he didn't recognize her. He went on a three-month drinking binge after that and missed the majority of his final exams. Truth was he didn't care much anymore. He ended up graduating with a mediocre GPA, a degree in Speech Communications, and no idea what he was going to do with it. He took a few menial jobs—hotel clerk, garbage man, loan officer—and then ended up joining the Minneapolis Police Department on a whim, right smack when the city acquired the dubious nickname "*Murderapolis.*"

He didn't like being a cop much. The filth he saw day in and day out. The reek of the city, the dry rot of its denizens, the violence and the suffering and the waste of humanity. After two years he was ready to quit.

He could have gone home then, back to Temperance River, but he didn't want to go back home, like a dog with its tail between its knees; back home to his family and friends and the rest of the fools who never had the courage to leave. He didn't want to have to make up some bullshit story and have to look at their faces and wonder whether or not they believed it. It was like being in a forest where you look over your shoulder and see that the path has disappeared behind you. So he endured the proclivities of being a cop, and soon realized that being a cop meant having to deal with yet another form of bureaucratic bullshit, so he quit and took a job with the BCA and soon realized that bureaucracy was everywhere, like taxes or the flu or global warming.

It was like he had missed the boat somehow, like he had been born in the wrong era or miscast in the wrong movie and within the past year or two there had come over him an unsettling sense of failure and frustration, a remote but powerful feeling that his life was somehow growing fruitless and sterile, a sense of having missed something beautiful and brilliant in life, without knowing at all what it was. His life was all right as long as he lived it one day at a time. A man can endure many things day by day that become self-contradictory when seen as a larger chunk of time. See it as ten years of the same thing, with Superintendent O'Malley pimping his ass out to every five-and-dime case from Faribault to Thief River Falls, and the windows grow bars and the doors of opportunity lock themselves and the job becomes just another cell. Everyday existence is the hardest thing of all to change—all the great leaders, the monarchs and kings have found that out. The path you are destined to follow is the path you have to follow. There are no detours permitted to you, even though you think there are.

Danny had always had that trapped feeling, like some sort of a panicky insect that you've put inside a down-turned glass, and it tries to climb up the sides, and it can't. And now he was going back to Temperance River after all these lost and forgotten years. Temperance River. A charming little town, where everyone got along with everyone else, the kids didn't have drug problems, and the streets were safe at night. Church suppers, walks along the lake, hard work, goodnight-kisses in bed. The kind of small town that George Bush always talked about, but hardly exists anymore. Temperance River. A town of a few thousand, set like a jewel in the rolling hills of the Pincushion Mountains, in a region of wheat and corn and wild woodlands and little groves. A land of exquisite forests, clumsy speech, and a hope that is boundless. A place that is merely an assemblage of pretty surfaces, strung together and ultimately empty.

Danny often wondered what had happened to Sadie. Had she wandered home to Temperance and was she there now? If he closed his eyes, he could almost see her with the distinctness of a good photograph, looking over her shoulder at him, laughing; her pom-poms held in her hands like big blue-and-gold mulberries. The thought of her was like a real presence, naked and tangible, right down to the little brown heart-shaped birthmark on the back of her left calf, the freckles on her nose that turned red whenever she got angry, her green-blue eyes and brown hair and the way she smelled of Sung perfume and the small sounds she used to make when he kissed her. He could almost hear her giggle, like she had when they washed her father's Suburban on a warm spring afternoon so long ago and he sprayed her with the hose, the smell of lemon dish soap and the taste of water on her lips. But over time, the picture had lost a little of its focus. It wasn't a close-up anymore. It was a snapshot, getting farther and farther away.

Thinking about the past gave Danny a feeling like there was ghosts around him, tickling him with fingers he couldn't quite see. Memories, that's what ghosts are.

He hardly seemed to be driving at all now—it was more like he was floating, the lake and the pine trees just rolling past him on either side of the highway, movie props on hidden wheels.

The Caddy was eating the road between Castle Danger and Lutsen in great gulps, and as he came through Grand Marais, a sharp, resinous tang of burning was in the air, the day slowly dying in turns.

And then he saw the town of Temperance River, hugging the shores of Lake Superior like a long-lost lover, drowsing in tranquility in the deep solitude of a hilly and woodsy isolation where news from the outside world hardly drew close enough to disturb its slumber.

Founded by exiled Germans in 1851, the town's settlers came to Minnesota to create a Utopia which emphasized communal property, wealth redistribution, and religious sovereignty. They supported their own churches and schools; they were their own courts, judges and executioners. One hundred and fifty years later, the town still reveled in its Germanic origins. The town's unofficial slogan was: "When you're surrounded by 4,000 thirsty Germans, you'd better bring darn good beer."

At the town's front was the restless lake, its surface painted with cloud forms. Behind it rose the tall, rounded mound of birch and red shale cliffs that make up the summit and face of the Pincushion Mountains, with the river running out of the mountains and along the southern edge of town and finally dumping itself into the covetous lake.

Danny pulled the car over on what had once been an embankment of a railroad trail and stared down at the old town, and he had an instant sense of something refound that he had always known—something far, near, strange, and so familiar—and it seemed to him that he had never left, that all that had passed in the years between was only a dream.

He was home. Goddamn. He was home.

†††

He got into town at sundown, where the quiet-colored end of evening smiles, and all that was left of the day was a pale streak at the horizon. He had been on the road for more than five hours. When he pulled into town, he switched off the CD player and listened to the local deputies on the RF talking about him:

"Has he got jurisdiction up here? Come on?"

"Hell if I know."

Danny smiled as he turned the police radio off and pulled into the first motel he saw, the Aurora Bora Palace. It consisted of a dozen identical rooms and it had an outdoor pool which was useless in October, but overall, the place looked clean and well-kept.

He parked the Caddy and got out and walked into the front office. A woman with a round face like a bird's was sitting behind the desk watching the local news on a small black-and-white TV. She didn't even look up when he walked in.

"Do you have a room?" Danny asked.

"I've got more than one," she said, her eyes never leaving the news. Her voice was slow and her words seemed to possess an extra syllable, an accent that was virtually indecipherable to anyone outside of Temperance River. "How many nights, hon?"

"At least a week, maybe more."

She looked at him then.

"We got a weekly rate. A hunnered and thirty-five dollars plus twenty percent tax, that's $162."

"One hundred and sixty-two..."

"Yes, sir."

"For the week?"

"Yes, sir. For da week."

"Is that your best rate?"

"Yes, sir. There's not no Triple-A discount on da weekly rate."

Danny took out his wallet, charged it to his credit card, got the key from the clerk, and walked down the long dark hallway to his room. He went in and shut the door and set his bags on the bed. He went over to the window, opened the heavy curtains, and stood there looking out at the empty highway and across the harbor at the bay. At that hour, the town looked like any other small town in America with everything closed or closing except for a few bars. There were two video stores, the Hollywood and Valu Plus, and one had already turned off its marquee.

Danny closed the heavy curtains and went over to the bed. He unzipped one of his bags, and took out his Sig Sauer P-226. It was an ugly black gun, but he liked its performance. Some handguns are loaded with charm, appeal and pizzazz—the Luger is one such gun that comes to mind, the Colt Python another—but the SIG was built strictly for killing. An extremely accurate, tough and reliable service auto.

Danny put the gun on the thick bedspread, propped a few pillows on the headrest and sat up on the bed. The enticement of coke was whispering sweet-nothing's in his ear again. Reluctantly, he took out the plastic sandwich bag and quickly snorted two full hits. Immediately he could feel the blood in his veins begin to boil and his heart was pumping thank-you's into his chest. He coughed once; picked up the archaic remote control for the TV and caught the tail end of the original *Phantom of the Opera* on PBS. It was the final scene where the angry mob of villagers was chasing Lon Chaney through the streets of Paris and finally had him cornered on the banks of the Seine. In a final little dig the Phantom holds the crowd at bay, pretending to hold a grenade. He raises his fist high and the crowd all gasp and jump back—but then he opens his fingers one at a time and there is nothing. In a final hideous moment of triumphant laughter, the Phantom plunges into the darkness of the river and disappears.

Andrew Lloyd Webber, eat your heart out.

When the movie ended and the TV went fuzzy, lending weird shadows against the walls, Danny closed his eyes and listened to the occasional semi traffic outside on the highway. The screen on the window was open, and the breeze was blowing through, rich with the promise of storm; that sweet electric smell of autumn.

He shut the TV off and threw the clicker on the floor. The bed was surprisingly soft and high and the dingy multi-colored comforter was like warm snow. He fell asleep almost at once and slept like a dead man.

Chapter Five

The roosters up on Skunk Hollow Trail had been crowing for a long time and he had heard and not heard. The morning was dull gray. Fog. Danny looked at his watch. Seven-thirty. He stayed in bed another ten minutes, staring at the stained asbestos ceiling, and smoked a cigarette. The first one of the day was always the best.

He took a cold shower and shaved and put on his starched white shirt, tied the small knot in the austere tie, and worked his way into the conservative suit the way an actor puts on a costume in his dressing room. The disguise was beginning to make him ache after ten years. He thought about what Tolstoy said: You play a role long enough, you start becoming the character.

The SIG Sauer was still on the bed. Danny looked at it lying there; then he picked it up, tucked it into his shoulder holster, covered it with his dark blue sport jacket and a tan trench coat, and walked out of the room, the heavy door slamming hard behind him in the dimly lit hallway.

He went to the front desk. The same woman from last night was sitting there reading the daily local paper. He wondered if she ever slept.

"Anything good in there?" he asked her.

She set the paper down on the counter. "Nope. Nothin' but crime and sex and violence. Makes ya think sometimes what kinna world we've made for ourselves." Her teeth were slightly yellow and her voice was raw. "How'd ya sleep last night, sweetie?"

"Great. You've got a nice place here."

"Thank you. I sorta inherited it when the mista passed on."

"I'm sorry to hear that," Danny said.

"Don't be. He was one of those prickish things. Always screamin' his friggin' head off alla da time. Seemed fit as Arnold Swartzawhatever, but—" She tapped her chest with her palms. "When he finally gave over, I hiked up my skirts and tap danced on his grave."

Danny smiled a genuine smile. "Know of any places around here that serve up a good breakfast?"

"Well, you could go to one-a those tourist traps that line da harbor nowadays, or you could give Victoria's a try."

"Victoria's?"

"You bet your bobcat! Victoria's Bakehouse and Deli. Got da best break of fast in town. Cheap, too. It's over on Gunflint Avenue. Just follow 61 die-rectly to Gunflint and take a left. Can't miss it. You tell 'em Millie Hjermstad sent 'cha."

"Thanks, Millie. I will."

It was a cool morning. The fog hung heavy, smelling of the lake, quiet and deep. The pavements still showed traces of last night's rain and a raw light fell from a sky that was like a dirty ceiling. The passers-by on the street had the resentful look of people who were not yet used to the idea that summer was over.

Danny pulled out of the parking lot and got on 61 and headed north down the hill toward Main Street, past the harbor lights and the Temperance River Rec Center where he used to play basketball as a kid.

Glancing through the Caddy's fly-specked windshield, he furtively took in Temperance's Main Street color guard of classic brick storefronts: The Attic Gift Shop, Crystal's Log Cabin Quilts, Gergen's Home Cafe, Harvey's Barbershop, Flom's Skogmo store, the C&M Tap, the Corner Café, Mox's Lunch, the Friendly Bar. Temperance River used to be a sleepy little fishing village, until the fish dried out and the tourists and expats from Minneapolis and St. Paul started drifting in. Now everybody made their money somehow off the day-trippers coming up from the Twin Cities.

Danny followed Millie Hjermstad's directions and took a left off Main Street onto Gunflint Avenue. Victoria's Bakehouse was one of those quaint little hash houses you find in any small town. The one that caters mostly to the local clientele.

There was an early breakfast crowd, about twenty locals and a scattering of tourists who possessed enough intestinal fortitude to venture off the main drag. The air inside smelled of things fried and greasy. Always greasy. There were large black-and-white photographs on the wall. Old Temperance River. Women in dresses and shawls. Longshoremen and fishermen in cloth caps, smiling and holding up the innumerable quantities of fish they had taken out of the lake.

Music was piping out of the jukebox, Tammy Wynette singing about D-I-V-O-R-C-E; but the people at the red-and-white-table clothed wooden tables paid no attention to her. They talked—mostly about the Vikings or the Twins not making the playoffs—ate, laughed and raised monotonous, thick, emphatic voices:

"The odds are ahhunnerd to one da Wolfies don't make da playoffs neither!"

"I'm not gonna debate you, Howard. I'm not gonna sit here and debate."

"Ah g'wan..."

They all spoke so slowly, dragging out every word with a drawl almost too hokey to be real. And they moved slowly. They even ate slowly.

The only one moving was a breathless waitress, thin with long blonde hair tied back, rushing from table to table taking orders, delivering orders and giving orders to the fry cook in back. She had a pile of dirty dishes cradled under her thin arms and a wisp of that long hair kept escaping the band that touched the nape of her bronze neck. She brushed the strand away with her left hand and continued to take orders. She looked tired, satisfied, young.

"Sit anywhere," she told Danny with a gum-popping smile.

He made his way through the crowd, careful of people's feet. He was out of place here, in his expensive sport coat and city shoes. They know I'm from the city, he thought, feeling them watch him as he passed.

He took a table in the back of the room. A few minutes later the waitress came over and smiled down at him.

"What can I get you?"

Her voice was like liquid sunshine, captured and put into a bottle.

"You're not from around here, are you?" Danny asked.

She glanced at him suspiciously. "No. I grew up in the Cities. How could you tell?"

"By the way you talk. And move."

She smiled at him like she didn't have a clue what he was talking about.

Danny glanced at one of the greasy menus. "Is the All-American breakfast any good?"

"You bet."

He ordered the All-American, with a large orange juice and a side of cheese on his browns. The pretty waitress took his order with another smile and then shuffled off toward the kitchen in a pair of bleached white sneakers with rundown backs.

The food was good. Real good. It tasted the way food should taste. Danny almost wanted to cry with gratitude, it tasted so good.

When he finished, he got up and waved to the waitress, making a √ in the air. She followed him to the register at the front of the room. He paid the bill, making sure he gave the young waitress with the rundown sneakers a good tip.

Outside, the fog had lifted some, but the oily sun had brought the cold, the kind where the wind rips right through you. Danny rushed back to the warmth of his Caddy. He was looking forward to seeing his old friend J.P. again. What had it been? Fifteen years? Goddamn. Time passes in a blink of an eye. He wondered how J.P. had ever become sheriff of this old town anyway. Back in high school, all J.P. ever wanted to do was play football and drink beer and smoke reefers down at the trestle.

The Public Safety Building was on the corner of Cutoff Road. It was a white wooden building, stark in the northern Minnesota style, with a four-faced clock on the roof peak, which in theory gave the time to every person in town, though it was often broken. The front of the building was like a castle, with two imposing turrets like chess bishops flanking a solid double door.

Danny parked the Caddy in a slot marked RESERVED FOR TOWN BUSINESS and went in.

The lobby was large and deep, the U.S. and Minnesota state flags hanging limply from two poles in one corner of the room. A stuffed bear stood on its hind legs in the other. In the middle of the room there was a waist-high circular counter surrounding two faux-wood desks. Standing behind the counter, instead of the usual bald-headed police sergeant, was a pink-faced woman with a build of a lady wrestler and blonde hair cut short like a man's.

Danny crossed the room to the counter.

"Hello," he said tentatively to the lady wrestler's unsmiling face. "I'd like to see the sheriff."

"Do you have an appointment, sir?"

"Do I need one?"

"Well that depends."

"On what?"

"On whom *you* are."

"Tell the sheriff it's Danny Pierce."

The woman looked at him for a second, then picked up the phone and started pushing buttons. Danny looked around the room. It was very bright and sunny; the whole of the southern wall was a single window and provided a stunning view of the lake. On a clear afternoon every dock and fishing boat on the other side of the harbor stood out brilliantly. Danny could read the sign for the West Bay Diner as clear as crystal and he could see a boy in a Vikings jersey fishing from the shingle below Zurbey's Bar.

"He'll be right on out, Mr. Pierce," the lady wrestler said after a minute, then she sat down behind one of the desks and started clacking away on her computer and Danny waited. He felt sorry for her, clacking away at her computer all day, and he felt sorry for all the people in the world who are chained to desks and locked in 6X6 cubicles all morning and all afternoon, every morning and every afternoon too, sitting on their wrinkly asses getting older with each passing day as if their legs were made to sit upon, and not to stand or walk upon, and he thought that they deserved some credit for not having all committed suicide long ago. God knows he would have.

A few seconds later, his old friend J.P. Garski rounded the corner, a big shit-eating smile on his face, like a cat with a mouthful of canary.

J.P. hadn't changed much—he was lean as a fence rail and twice as long, with small blue eyes that twinkled with the unconscious humor of the born practical joker. His hair had gone gray though, where it hadn't just gone, and dark circles cupped his eyes, his lips faded thin.

"Look at you!" J.P. said, pointing a finger at Danny. "All grown up. You haven't changed a bit, Danny Pierce."

"I'd like to say the same thing about you," Danny replied with a smile of his own. "What happened to all that long hair of yours?"

J.P. dragged a hand over what remained of his once proud locks and took Danny into a big bear-hug.

"I heard they were sendin' you up," he said, grinning more widely than ever. The grin took years off his face, and Danny could almost see the kid he once was.

"What happened up here, J.P.?" Danny asked, rather heavily.

J.P. grew serious and the kid Danny briefly saw disappeared. "C'mon," he said, "I'll fill you in on it back in my office." He turned to the pink-faced dispatcher. "Davina, hold my calls, will you, honey? We might be a while."

"You betcha, Sheriff."

J.P. took Danny down the hall to his office. It was a small room with a big window overlooking the bay and a large desk that mirrored his personality—cluttered, stormy and forthcoming.

J.P. sat in the big leather chair behind the desk and nodded at one of the chairs across from him. Danny took off his trench coat, draped it over the arm of one chair, sat in the other.

"Want some coffee?" J.P. asked.

"Is it any good?"

"You're darn tootin' its good!"

He went out into the hall and returned with two Styrofoam cups. It was a small-town police station, and for the first few hours of the workday, the entire building smelled like Folgers. Danny accepted the coffee, burned his tongue on it, and set it aside.

"I don't like fancy coffees, you know," J.P. was saying. "Espressos and cappuccinos and frapp-pewhatevers. Just give me plain, old-fashioned Folgers any day. So, where ya stayin' at while you're in town?"

"Over at the Aurora Bora Palace."

J.P. waited a moment; then said, "How do you know when you're staying in a Temperance River motel?"

"I give up. How?"

"When you call the front desk and say 'I've gotta leak in my sink' and the person at the front desk says 'go ahead.'"

"You're a regular Rodney Dangerfield."

"Yep. I'm a jokey old bird," J.P. said, moving his eyebrows up and down like Groucho Marx. "People should laugh more. There's too much seriousness in the world. Don't ya think that the most essential quality for a person to have is a sense of humor?"

"I don't know. I really don't have one."

"Boy, Danny, you'd be a lot of fun to hang out with. When did you get so serious?"

"When I grew up," Danny quipped. He took another sip of coffee. J.P. was right. It was good. Darn *tootin'* good.

"So what the hell happened up here, J.P.?"

All the smiling good humor went out of J.P.'s face and his voice dropped, the way people's voices do when they enter a big church where even the silence seems to whisper.

"Here's the situation we got goin' on. We got a missing little girl. Rose Violette. Michelle Violette's kid. You member Michelle?"

Danny nodded.

J.P. went on. "After high school she hooked up with that deadbeat Dale Jacob. They had Rose six years ago, but never got married. Dale didn't want to."

J.P. paused and ran the fingers of his right hand through his thin hair. Danny could see the tiny cylinders clicking inside his head and he began to notice how tired his old friend really looked. The clear-cut lineament of J.P.'s face seemed blurred and his head hung down on his shoulders. All the jokes in the world couldn't hide that.

"What about the pervs in the area?" Danny asked.

"We got four level-three sex offenders up here from Croftville to Dulut'. A half a dozen ones and twos. We checked 'em all out and came up with squat. Thought we had one to pin it on. You might member him? Tommy Bayliss?"

"Yeah, I remember," Danny said. "Ain't he the guy who always bragged he had a tattoo on his johnson?"

"Yeah, 'Mother.' But he's got an air-tight alibi for the night of Rose's disappearance."

"What's his alibi?"

"Spent the night in the Cook County jail on a drunk and disorderly charge."

"What about the state police?"

"We faxed Rose's photo and info to the highway patrol and to police throughout the state and in the border states as well. We asked the State Bears to check every service station and convenience store and fast food restaurant along the highway. But we still came up nada."

"Did you issue an AMBER Alert?"

"Yah, we did that, too."

J.P. took a manila folder out of his desk and tossed it to Danny. Inside, there were several typewritten forms and a photograph paper-clipped to the top of the folder. In it, Rose Violette was centered and solemnly meeting the camera's gaze. She was blonde and cherubic with wide blue eyes and a pink bow sticking out of the back of her hair.

"She disappeared on the mornin' of October Twenty-Fifth," J.P. went on. "Four days ago. Cute girl, ain't she? Michelle called in and said someone stole her. Unfortunately the facts don't jibe with the fiction. We went out there and found more than we bargained for, that's fer sure. There's a shitload of unanswered questions and inconsistencies that all lead back to Dale. We found some pajamas of Rose's in Dale's car and we're not satisfied with his account of his activities and his location and movement that mornin'. We know he left their trailer at about 7:25, and arrived at work in Croftville at about 8:12—elapsed time of about forty-seven minutes for a trip that should have taken approximately twenty-six minutes at most."

J.P. wanted to cover every angle of the case to make sure they were on the same page, rolling free and easy. He didn't have to bother, it was all in the file, but he didn't have anything else to do and it's hard to do nothing day after day without any results, putting in your time behind a desk and waiting for the game to catch up with you. They always say that the waiting is the hardest time. But Danny knew *they* are always wrong. The hardest time is when you walk that little tightrope that stretches from just before you bring the perp down until you get a conviction. That's the hardest time. The hardest wait. That's the hardest time because it's the only time you can get hurt. If things get fucked-up before then, you pick up the pieces and start over. But if they go bad after that, you've got everything on one horse and if she pulls up and bucks you off, you bring down the whole fucking house.

Danny filled his cheeks with air and let it out. "What do *you* think happened, J.P.?"

"What do I think?" His words were a whisper. "I think Dale killed Rose after some sort of dispute with the girl and then dumped her body on his way to work. But we can't find her. We've had a helluva time searchin' the thousands of acres of woodland between here and Croftville. We've resorted to askin' people in that area to search for anythin' wrapped in sheets or in plastic, or to be on the lookout for any freshly-turned earth. Do I know for sure Dale did it? No. Some of the details might be wrong. But in my gut—I know he did it. Bits and pieces put together to present a semblance of a whole. There's a rumor that's been circulatin' around town that started from day one, about a party the night before Rose disappeared, but to date we cannot substantiate that at all, because Michelle and Dale have stopped cooperatin' with us. The girl's own parents. They never even inquired about the investigation after their initial report. Not once. Can you imagine that?"

"What about a stranger abduction?"

"Nah. That just doesn't happen up here. Even with all the tourists. We interviewed a hunnerd people in those first few days, but nothin' surfaced."

"You've received no contact of any kind that would lead you to believe Rose has been abducted by a stranger?"

"Nothin'. Not even a prank call."

Danny's eyes narrowed slightly. "Where can I find Michelle?" he asked.

"She's livin' over at the Big Timber Trailer Court. It's over by the marina. Me and my deputies are always headed over there on Friday and Saturday nights with our sirens screamin' and our blue lights flashin'. Real classy place, if ya know what I mean."

Danny took down the address.

J.P. stretched with his fisted hands in the small of his back. "Do you still smoke?"

"Yeah." Danny rubbed his hand over his eye. "Been trying to quit, but it always seems like I'm never more than one nasty night away from my next cancer stick."

"Yah, me too," J.P. said, taking a pack of Marlboros out of his desk. "The libbies on the town council say we can't smoke in public buildings anymore." He smacked out a cigarette from the pack and then handed them to Danny. "Fuck 'em, is what I say."

Danny smiled and took a cigarette. J.P. flipped a battered silver Zippo, lit his cigarette and handed the lighter over the desk to Danny.

"You been by to see your mom yet?"

Danny blew smoke out his nose. "No. I just got into town last night."

J.P.'s voice lost its cynical drawl and became serious again. "I was real sorry to hear about your dad passin'."

"Yeah.

"He was a good man."

"He was an asshole."

"C'mon, man, he was your father."

"He was a drunk."

"He worked hard," J.P. said. "Everyone can claim credit for at least one thing, one good point. Everyone has one. Even a drunk."

"My dad can claim credit for at least one thing," Danny agreed. "Self-honesty. He knew he was a drunk and he never lied in all his life, not to anyone, and not to himself. He was a brilliant alumnus of what's termed the school of hard knocks, toughened up by years of wresting away every hard-fought buck from a reluctant world. I'll bet he's standing on a street corner in hell right now, making suckers of the damned. He was a tough-ass, real old school, and he bought himself a case of cirrhosis of the liver and died of it. You know that he never once came to see me play football? What kind of a father is that?"

J.P. waited. Finally he said, "It's hard for any of us to think of our parents as just people. You ever miss playing ball?"

"All the time."

"That was about as good a time as I've ever had. It's too bad you blew out your knee. You could have played college."

Danny shrugged, as if it were a matter of no consequence.

J.P. took a long puff on his cigarette. "So I assume you haven't seen Sadie yet?"

A different look came on Danny's face now, hackles up, nerves extended. *Sadie.* Oh Christ, Sadie.

"She around?" he asked, deliberately incurious, his mind racing in all directions.

"Yah."

"I thought she got married and moved to Washington or something?"

"She did. But she moved back to Temperance a few years ago."

"What happened?"

"After college she moved to Hawaii of all places and met a soldier. They moved around a bit; then settled down in Washington D.C. She had a few kids. Three to be exact. Her husband was a helicopter pilot in Iraq. It went down. Everyone on board died. After her husband died, Sadie moved back here to Temperance. She's livin' with her parents in her old house over on Benjamin Street. She gets a severance from the army every month, but it's not enough to live on, much less to raise three kids on. Damn shame. Last I heard she's waitressin' over at Apache Wells."

"That fucking dive?"

"Yep."

"What's she doing working there?"

"She don't want to put her kids in daycare, I guess, and she can make a go of it waitressin' at the Wolf because summers are a little fatter than the winters are lean." J.P. looked over at his friend. "You think you might drop in and see her sometime?"

"What the hell for?"

"Don't tell me you don't have any of those old feelin's left for her? What's a matter, don't you believe in true love anymore? Fallin' in love feels the same at fifteen or forty."

Danny gave him a look. "No, I don't believe in true love. Do you realize, J.P., that humans are the only animal to make love face to face?"

J.P. kind of barked and laughed at the same time. "What the hell's that supposed to mean?"

Chapter Six

He was on the street again, and suddenly it was freezing. The wind had picked up while he was in J.P.'s office and Danny could feel it through his clothes. Autumn trembled on the edge of winter, and in Temperance River, winter was the ruler of the inverted year. With shivering hands Danny buttoned his trench coat against the cold and pulled it closer around him, feeling the weight of the Sig Sauer inside its shoulder holster. He wished he had a pair of gloves, but he hadn't thought of it when he'd left St. Paul. He stuck his hands in his pockets now instead.

The earlier sunshine had evolved back into a threatening overcast, and the air smelled like rain. The smell of leaves and loam was heavy, and permeating over everything was the crisp, penetrating smell of the lake. Always the lake.

He crossed the street and got into his Caddy and tossed the manila folder on the seat next to him. He drove down by the harbor and took a left on Eighth Avenue, and swung around the peninsula. The way led along what had once been the embankment of a railroad but long ago had been turned into Sweetheart's Bluff. He remembered coming here on warm summer nights in high school with Sadie.

As he crawled along Eighth Avenue, rain dotted the windshield, turning everything into a blurry, Dali-like aquarelle. Finding the Big Timber Trailer Court was easy. Getting Michelle Violette to talk was going to be much harder.

Danny parked the Caddy on the street next to a weed-filled lot with a sign on a stick saying the lot was for sale and crossed the street to the trailer park. It was raining harder now—wet and raw.

Dale and Michelle's trailer was silver and rusty, the front yard littered with empty beer and soda cans (apparently they had no interest in Minnesota's bottle-and-can-deposit law). A lopsided swing set, with one swing missing, stood near the back of the trailer.

Danny went around to the front door. A cluster of Harley-Davidson stickers were plastered on the storm door along with a sticker of a black face with a red line through it.

He rapped on the door. He could hear a television playing loudly inside. After a few moments, the door opened a crack and a white face peered out at him, a Viceroy cigarette sticking out of the side of its lips.

"Who the hell are you?" the white face asked.

Danny flashed the leather billfold with his badge pinned to it. "Special Agent Pierce, BCA. I'm here to ask you a few questions about Rose."

"You got a warrant, cop?"

"We don't need a warrant to talk," Danny said. "But I can get one if that's what you really want."

"Hold the friggin phone!" the white face suddenly shouted. "I know you. Ain'tcha Danny Pierce? You played quarterback in high school. I graduated a few years after you. You member me?"

"Yeah, Michelle, I remember you," Danny said. "Now can I come in? It's cold out here."

Her eyes narrowed. "I already told that dipshit town cop everything I know."

"Can I come in?" Danny asked again. "Five minutes is all I need. Besides, it's raining out here. You wouldn't leave me out here in the rain, now would ya, Michelle?"

She was wearing dirty sweatpants and an old Minnesota Twins T-shirt from when they won the World Series back in '93. Her penny-colored hair was pulled back in a loose ponytail and she had small blackheads on her greasy forehead. She used to be somewhat pretty back in high school, Danny remembered; now she was just another white-trash trailer fuck.

"Okay," Michelle finally said; her voice low and distrusting. "You can come in. But five minutes is all ya get."

He followed her inside. The trailer was dirty and had an unpleasant smell; low and ripe, like slowly spoiling meat. It was cluttered with old magazines and newspapers, clothing left where it had been dropped. Thick drapes masked the windows and the carpet was stained yellow and brown in some spots. Danny shuddered. The clutter alienated him; the squalor made him wary. How could someone live like this? It was not a place to live in, not possibly, not conceivably, especially for a six-year-old little girl.

"You want something to drink?" Michelle asked, but speaking in a tone which still had something of contempt in it. "I got coffee."

"Sure," Danny said, not really wanting any. He didn't want to put his lips to anything in this place, but he didn't want to offend her either. She wouldn't be any use to him if she were offended.

Michelle went into the kitchen and returned a few seconds later with a cracked cup that had TEMPERANCE RIVER VOLUNTARY FIRE DEPT stenciled on it.

Danny sipped the coffee. It was barely warm. Hell, it was barely coffee.

Michelle gulped at a can of Diet Coke; sat down in an old brown recliner and glanced at something on the television. Danny didn't know what it was. He didn't own a television. Nothing on it these days but violence and sex and stupidity, and he got enough of that just dealing with these assholes in his real life. What the hell did he need a television for? Major Nelson had a Jeannie, but he didn't.

"So what happened, Michelle?" he asked, shooting from the hip. "What happened to Rose?"

"I already told the sheriff everything I know."

"So tell me."

Danny watched her face, trying to see a flicker of a lie, but her eyes behind their whiskey veil were almost impenetrable.

"I went to her room to wake her up for school and she weren't there. The window was open and someone had took her. Probably one of those niggers or Mexicans they got movin' into town nowadays."

"What makes you say that?"

"I got TV. I watch the news. Every time you turn around one of those friggin' people are getting arrested for something. The United States is like a big boiling pot of shit all stirred up by the minorities and the liberals."

She was trying to be funny, but she was also scared, which meant she was trying to hide something.

Danny shot his next question in quickly: "Was Dale here when it happened?"

"No, he-he a—already left for work."

"He already left for work?"

"That's what I just said, ain't it?"

"Where does Dale work?"

"He work for the taconite factory up in Croftville," she said in a childishly whining voice. "*Hupp,* some dream life we got here, ain't it?"

"What did you do when you discovered Rose wasn't in her room?"

"I called the cops. That's when that dipshit sheriff came around and insulted that Dale and me knew something about Rose being gone."

Despite himself, Danny chuckled sardonically. "You mean, he *insinuated* that you and Dale knew where Rose was?"

Michelle glared at him. "I don't get the words right alla da time, but that's what he did, mister."

Danny held up a conciliatory hand. "Okay, okay. I'm sorry, Michelle. You know I'm going to have to talk to Dale, don't you?"

"Well, you can't do it at work," she shot back quickly. "Dale's boss don't like no one lollygagging around on the job. His boss is a real cunt, and Dale can't afford to lose his job."

"What time does Dale get off work?"

"Four-thirty."

"Maybe I'll swing by then."

"He won't be here."

"He won't?"

"Nope. He plays football with his buddies on Monday nights down at the municipal fields behind the high school. They get together and drink beer and shoot the shit. It's good for Dale to get out once in a while."

Danny stood up and set the dirty coffee cup on a cluttered nesting table.

"Is there anything else you might want to tell me, Michelle? Anything that might help me find Rose."

"Shoot," she said. "Rose been gone four days now. Whoever got her got her good. She ain't never coming back. I just have to resign myself to that. Is that how you say it, Mr. Pierce, *resign?* I just got to resign myself to the fact that Rose ain't coming back."

†††

Danny crossed the street to his Caddy. It was raining hard now, as if the world had been somehow squeezed and made to sweat, minus the heat. He got in the car and drove back to the Public Safety Building.

"Back so soon," the lady wrestler/dispatcher said.

"I missed your pretty face."

She gave a *humph!* sound at that.

Danny nodded over her shoulder toward J.P.'s office. "He still here?"

"Just a sec. He's got company." She picked up the phone and said something into it. Then she hung up and said to Danny, "You can go right on back, Mr. Pierce."

"Thank you, sweetie. And, call me Danny."

She gave another *humph!*

Danny went down the hallway, knocked on the door, and opened it when he heard J.P. grumble to come in.

J.P. was sitting behind his chaotically muddled desk, but this time there was a man standing in front of him. He was a huge brick colored Scandinavian with a black Stetson hanging low on his forehead. His face possessed the tan and sharp wrinkles of a man who spends a lot of time outdoors.

"You have no call to get snippy with me, Babe," J.P. was telling the man. "I'm just tryin' to do my job here."

"Well, maybe you ain't doin' it good enough. Goddamn it, Garski, this sort of thing scares the tourists."

J.P. looked sour. "We wouldn't want that now."

When Danny walked in, J.P. looked up and smiled, like he had just been saved from being thrown to the lions.

The brick-colored man turned his head and stared at Danny. He had deep blue eyes, the color of flames on an oven, and when he looked at you, you felt like he was staring right into your head and putting the thoughts he saw there in numerical order.

"Danny," J.P. said. "This is Babe Gorman, our beloved mayor."

Gorman flashed J.P. another nasty look. "Don't get snotty with me, Garski. I'll have your Polish ass thrown out of here so fast it'd make your wife's head spin." Then to Danny: "Your name's Pierce, ain't it? Danny Pierce? I remember you from when you were a kid. I used to go huntin' with your ol' man. He was a real corker—not a better man in town to go huntin' with. Sorry to hear about his passing."

"Thank you," Danny said.

"You used to play football, didn't you? A fairly damn good quarterback, if I'm rememberin' right." The Mayor paused, making eye contact with Danny, then switching his gaze back to J.P. "A lot better player than this piece of shit here."

J.P. smiled. "Sticks and stones, Mayor. Sticks and stones."

"Ah—"

"Danny works for the BCA," J.P. told Babe.

Instantly Babe squinted. "The BC-who?"

"The BCA," J.P. said, grinning. "The Bureau of Criminal Apprehension. He's been sent up here to help us find Rose."

Babe turned to Danny. "Well maybe you can do a better job of it," he grumbled with a low callous voice. "And I hope you find something fast. The natives are getting restless."

"They usually do," Danny replied.

Babe Gorman shifted his gaze. "So when are you going to bring in Jacob?"

"What makes you so sure Dale had anything to do with Rose's disappearance?"

"Oh, come on," Babe said in a rough, loud voice. "If you tell me you don't think Jacob had something to do with it, then I'm gonna start thinking you're about as incompetent as our *beloved* sheriff here. I know almost everyone in this town. And you know what? On the whole, they're some good people. Once in a while someone will get drunk and start a fight or crash a pickup or somethin'. But Dale Jacob is just plain bad. He's like a stain on the collective psyche of the whole town."

"That doesn't make him guilty of filicide," Danny said.

"And what does? Finding a body? Then find one!"

Danny went over to the window and stared out at the big lake. "Dale looks good for this right now, Mayor, but we need to keep checking all the possibilities before we bring him in."

"Look—" Babe said. "I know some people might find it hard to believe that Dale and Michelle could have killed their own, but the truth is man has a long history of brutalizing the ones he loves."

Danny turned around and stared hard into Babe Gorman's eyes. "I'm well aware of that, sir," he said, a cold edge rising in his voice. "I've seen that kind of brutality first hand. And I'll admit there's a lot of things pointing to Dale right now, but we don't want to make a move without having enough hard evidence to put him down."

"Oh, just bring 'em in," Babe said, waving his hand in dismissal. "Him and that tub-of-guts girlfriend of his. And get 'em darn quick, before we have a riot on our hands."

Having spoke his piece, Babe Gorman turned and staring straight ahead, his insipid eyes set into his wooden face, he crossed the room in three strides, and walked out with the rigid gravity of a cigar-store Indian.

When he was gone, J.P. let out a deep breath and lit a cigarette.

"You want one?" he asked.

"Sure," Danny said.

J.P. tossed the pack over. Danny took one out, lit it, and sat down in the chair facing J.P.'s desk.

"See what I have to put up with?" J.P. said. "The whole town wants Dale's head in a noose, and I can't rightly blame 'em." He took a long drag off his cigarette. "Well, now that our little *Robespierre* has got his daily rationing of guillotining off his chest, tell me what you found out over at Michelle's place."

"She's definitely not telling the truth," Danny said, in a low, sort of anxious voice. "She lies about as well as old people fuck."

"She's a real piece of work, ain't she?"

"Yep. Piece of something else, too."

"So what now?"

"I was thinking about paying Mr. Jacob a little visit. He plays football over at the municipal fields every Monday night. Care to join me?"

"You betcha," J.P. said, without even pausing to consider. "What time?"

"Around six."

"I'll be there with bells on."

Chapter Seven

Danny had the rest of the afternoon to kill, so he drove down to the lake and sat in his car at Artist's Point and read the file a couple hundred more times. He wanted to find something—anything—that was missed the first time he read it back at J.P.'s office. But if there was any other angle to the Rose Violette case, he couldn't find it. J.P. and his staff had done everything by the numbers. They interviewed the missing child's extended family and neighbors, retraced all possible routes, commissioned aerial photographs of the area, gave statements to the local television station and newspaper, and Rose still hadn't turned up.

Danny took the picture of Rose out of the file and stared at it.

The snapshot showed a girl with freckles in a white dress and Mary Jane sandals in the sunlight in front of a swing. Her eyes were squinted against the sun and she stood pigeon-toed, with her hands behind her back.

"Face of an angel," Danny whispered, tracing his fingers over the photograph. "What am I missing? What am I missing? What am I missing?"

He was almost positive Dale was guilty. About ninety nine percent positive. Which wasn't positive at all. But it was enough to make the odds that Dale didn't do it sufficiently small.

Who else could it have been?

Danny kept looking for holes in that reasoning. In the end it was all guesswork. It always was. Speculation, supported by circumstantial evidence. And all the speculation was pointing to Dale.

†††

Danny skipped lunch. He always did. It kept him more alert that way. At quarter to six, he drove over to the municipal football fields and he saw his old high school standing there like a nineteenth-century Spanish prison or an asylum you might find deep in the forests of France. It was an impressive six-sided brick stronghold built to scare off invaders. The classroom wings were dark and silent and deserted at this time of night. The lobby glowed with a yellow, ethereal, almost vaporous light. It had a forlorn, haunted feel to it, which seemed fitting. Many memories, many ghosts.

He hadn't been back here since he graduated. Not once. No homecomings or reunions. Now, as he looked up at the old school, a rush of memories hit him and it was like he'd broke the lock on some dust-covered toy box and scattered its contents across the floor—the football games, the dances, the parties, the small flirtations, the smell of chalk and floor-varnish the janitors put down at night after all the kids had gone home.

He parked his Caddy behind the high school and waited for J.P. The sun was entirely gone from the bay, but its traces were still visible on the

Pincushion Mountains in the east. In the distance, the siren at the fire hall screamed to life, signaling the six o'clock hour. A few moments later, J.P.'s prowler pulled up behind Danny's Caddy. They got out and together they walked over to the football fields where a group of men were hanging around under the lights, digging into coolers, tossing a couple footballs around, smoking cigarettes and drinking beer.

Danny recognized Dale Jacob right away. What he saw was the face of an animal. Not an intelligent animal, but one filled with cunning and meanness; all long-haired and wild-eyed.

The lights on the football field were bouncing off Dale's eyes in a way that made him look slightly deranged and a little high. He walked with a tough, truculent swagger and his ramping face was set in sullen suspicion.

"Well, lookit here," he said when he recognized Danny, cold vapor puffing from his mouth in a white cloud. "If it ain't the famous Danny Pierce. Big as life and twice as ugly. I thought you joined the CIA or somethin'?"

Danny cracked a condescending smile. "Or something."

"Whatchou doing back in Temperance?"

Danny's smile widened, but became no less condescending. "Trying to find *your* kid."

Dale looked at J.P., all his hatred of him coming out in a derisive stare. To Danny he said, "Well I hope you're a better cop than this cocksucker. He couldn't find his ass with both hands and an ass map."

Dale's voice had a forced quality of comic seriousness and his companions laughed.

J.P. stared at him, seemingly incapable of moving or speaking, almost the way a child looks at something that he fears will jump and bite him if he takes his eyes off it.

After several dead moments, Danny broke the heavy silence. "We'd like to ask you a few questions about Rose, Dale."

Dale was sucking the guts out of a dying cigarette. "Well—we were just getting ready to play us a little football, ain't that right boys?" he called out, to general murmuring and gurgled support from his companions. "You remember what that is, don'tcha, Mister Star Quarterback? Maybe you'd like to join us?" He spread his arms out to the rest of the group. "You boys remember the Star Quarterback of the Temperance High Tommies? Mister Danny Pierce. All-Conference, All-State. He even had himself a scholarship to college waiting for him, but then he got a boo-boo and couldn't play no more."

"He tore up his knee," J.P. said. "He would have played if he could have."

"What are you, his mama?" Dale said, glaring back at J.P.

"Give me your gun," Danny said to J.P.

"What?"

"Give me your gun."

J.P. took his service revolver out of its holster and handed it over. Danny took off his suit jacket and his shoulder holster. He could see Dale staring at the big Sig Sauer out of the corner of his yellow eyes.

"That's a nice looking piece," Dale said in a whisper, but a whisper, somehow, more penetrating than the loudest shout. "Where can I get a gun like that?"

His cool, smiling face congealing, Danny said, "You couldn't handle a gun like this, Dale."

He walked over to the Caddy and locked the guns inside, then he walked back and stood directly in front of Dale.

"Let's play."

"Whoo-eee!" Dale snarled in his comically tense, crazy whisper. "Let's get it on!"

They chose sides, Danny and J.P. and some of Dale's friends on one team, Dale and the biggest of his friends on the other. Nothing but a bunch of beer-guzzling fat-fucks that won't be able to keep up with me anyway, Danny thought.

Danny's team got the ball first and the very next play after the kickoff, he hooked up with J.P. on an eighty-yard bomb for a touchdown. Just like the old days.

They kicked off and Dale got the ball and sprinted up the sidelines, his hips narrow, moving, still, Danny thought, like some kind of animal, easy and swift, not old yet. He got all the way to the fifty before someone touched him.

He was a fast little fuck, Danny had to admit that. Back in high school, Dale was a wise-ass, cigarette-smoking, smacked-around-by-his-father fuck-up who hung out at the freak doors and, quite incongruously, was a pretty good tailback on the football team.

On the next play, Dale caught a screen pass from one of his buddies and took it up the sidelines all the way for a score. He was too fast. No one could catch him.

"How'd you like that, Mister Star Quarterback," he said to Danny, striking a Heisman Trophy pose in the end zone. "I still got my wheels!"

On the next series, Danny dropped back in the pocket and was looking for J.P., when Dale came out of nowhere on a blitz and put his shoulder into Danny's back, driving him face first into the dirt.

Danny could feel blood trickling from his eye as he lay there on the cold, hard ground.

"Goddamn it, Dale!" he heard J.P. screaming. "It's only supposed to be touch!"

Dale raised his hands to his shoulders and grinned his dank grin. "What's the matter, can't the Star Quarterback take it?"

Danny used both elbows to push himself off the ground and used the back of his hand to wipe blood from his eye.

"I can take it, you little fuck," he said to Dale.

He picked the ball up out of the mud and on the very next play he hit J.P. for another score.

"14-7, asshole," he said in Dale's ear.

They kicked off and some guy caught it, but Dale was screaming at him: "Toss it here! Toss it here!"

The guy tossed it to Dale and he took off running down the sidelines again. J.P. dove for him, but missed. Danny was on the other side of the field and couldn't get to him.

Touchdown. 14-14.

They went back and forth for a few series with nobody scoring. J.P. was starting to suck air, puffing away six licks to the dozen. But Danny was loving it. Playing ball got his old competitive juices flowing again; after all these years. Hell, he didn't even know he still had it in him.

Dale's team had the ball now on their twenty.

"Let me take him," Danny said to the fat guy who was covering Dale.

"Whatever, dude."

The quarterback snapped it. It was supposed to be a post to Dale, but when he laid out for it, Danny blindsided him with a forearm across

Dale's face. Dale's feet went straight up in the air and he landed on the back of his head.

A chorus of *O-o-o-h's* traveled around Dale's companions. No one was laughing now.

Dale lay there for a while, covering his face. He tried to say something, but it came out in a grunt that sounded like a kicked dog. He rolled over a couple of times in the dirt and mud, then he got up and stormed after Danny, his nose a mess and the lower half of his face gushing blood.

"That was a goddamn cheap shot!" Dale hollered in a wet, whiny voice.

"What's the matter, Dale?" Danny said with a big smile. "Can't you take it? I even held up a little. If I hadn't you'd be spitting out your teeth like corn."

"Fuck you, cop," Dale said, his voice trembling. "You broke my fucking nose!"

He went after Danny again, but his companions restrained him.

"Let me go!" Dale screamed. "I'm gonna teach this pig somethin'."

"You'd like that, wouldn't you, Dale?" Danny's voice was choked with rage. "I'd kick your ass up and down this field and then you'd call a lawyer. That's just the kind of pussy you are. Always have been."

"Fuck you, cop! I'm gonna kill you!"

Danny and Dale stood glaring at each other for a few moments, like two eighth-graders in a schoolyard fight who won't back down.

J.P. grabbed Danny's elbow and pushed him away.

"C'mon, Danny, let's get the hell out of here."

"Next time you won't be so lucky, pussy," Danny said over his shoulder to Dale.

J.P. pushed him up the hill to the parking lot. They could still hear Dale screaming his feral obscenities at them.

Danny lit a cigarette and unlocked his car and handed J.P. his service revolver. They leaned on the hood and smoked. J.P. was still trying to catch his breath. He puffed on his cigarette and noticed the long gold necklace that had fallen out of the top of Danny's shirt.

"You've had that since we were kids, haven't you?" he asked.

Danny looked down at the necklace and twined it around his fingers. "Yeah."

"What is it?"

"It's Saint Christopher."

"What'd he do?" J.P. asked.

"Legend has it he was crossing a river one day when a child asked to be carried across. Christopher put the child on his shoulders and found that the child was unbelievably heavy. The child, according to the legend, was Christ carrying the weight of the whole world on his back. My mom and dad gave it to me for my first communion when I was eight."

J.P. looked up at the gray clouds and let smoke out of his nostrils. "I was real sorry to hear about your dad. I don't member his funeral?"

"That's because there wasn't one. He didn't much like people." Danny thought about his father. He was a drunk, but before that, there were plenty of good memories, too. He remembered his father playing "gorilla" with him. Wearing one of his mother's old fur coats, he would hide in a tree or in some bushes until Danny appeared. Then he'd lunge out at him with a loud growl.

"When he died he asked my mom to just toss his ashes in Lake Superior," Danny went on. "He loved that fucking lake. Probably more than he loved my mom and me."

J.P. looked at him apathetically. "Not more, Danny, just different."

Danny took a deep breath. "When I was a kid, maybe nine or ten, he took me up to Two Islands. He said, 'Let's go in for a swim.' I was scared shitless, you know, this lake—it's so cold. 'Get in the water,' he said. He picks me up, tosses me in. I had to learn how to swim by trying to survive. I sunk like a stone. From then on, the old man didn't want to have too much to do with me. He called me his little girl."

J.P. lifted one shoulder in a half-shrug. "At least you knew your father." He ran his hand slowly over his face. When he spoke again, his voice was unusually quiet. "When a man's dad dies, Danny, no matter what your relationship was with him, everything changes. You become the man. And maybe then you don't have to struggle so hard tryin' to be the man *he* wanted you to be. Maybe now you can...just, be the man that you are. Another rose will always bloom." He paused and looked off into the distance. "You been by to see your mom yet?"

"Nah," Danny said. "Not yet. I was thinking about going over there tomorrow. Anyway, I don't think she's in any hurry to hear from me. We had a big fight the last time I saw her."

J.P. took out his keys and got in the prowler. "Want to go grab a beer?" he asked.

"Yeah, I could use one," Danny said. "How's my eye looking?"

J.P. stared at him. A vertical contusion was puffing up over Danny's eye like a rain cloud about to burst.

"You look sexy as ever, Rocky," J.P. said. "It's just a little bruised up. Makes you look tough. You member where the Angry Trout is at?"

"Yeah," Danny said. "I remember."

"Good. I'll meet ya there."

Chapter Eight

The Angry Trout was located at a crossroads called Moose Junction just south of town, surrounded by thick woods and nothing else. There were two signs taped to the front door. NO FAT CHICKS, read one. TERMINAL HAPPY HOUR, read the other. Danny went in and the smell of hard liquor hit him. It was one of those honky-tonk dives with a confederate flag tacked up over the bar and posters of Dale Earnhardt and scantily-clad women hanging all over the tattered walls.

It was the quiet time of night when Danny walked in. Everybody was staring down at the drink in front of them and a saloon song was playing on the jukebox. "As Good As I Once Was," or something like that.

J.P. was sitting at the long bar, his second bottle of Bud sweating in front of him. Danny signaled the bartender, ordered up a beer, and sat next to J.P. at the bar.

"Did you ever hear the story about the guy who was walkin' around Temperance River?" J.P. asked Danny, starting a favorite joke that haunted him always. "The town gets hit with an A-bomb and he's the only man left. He's walkin' around, takes four or five days, and he's finally lonely. There's nobody to talk to. So he goes to the top of the Pincushion Mountains and figures he'll end it all by jumpin' off into the lake. He takes a big step and jumps off. He's goin' down now, fast, the breeze blowin' in his face, the lake comin' up closer and closer—and that's when he hears his cell phone ringing."

It was J.P.'s favorite joke and it never really got big laughs, but it told you something about his personality.

They sat at the bar and shot the shit for a while and laughed about what Danny did to Dale on the football field. After about the fifth beer, Danny got up enough courage to ask J.P. if he thought Sadie Petersen might be interested in seeing him sometime.

"Hard to say." J.P. smiled involuntarily. "You still got those old feelin's for her after all?"

"I haven't seen her in almost fifteen years," Danny said. "I was just curious, that's all."

"She was your first love, Danny. You never forget your first love."

"Who the hell are you, Dear Abby? I was just asking; that's all."

J.P. smiled and sipped his beer. "I haven't seen Sadie much since she came back home. It's not what it was like back in high school. She pretty much keeps to herself now. I see her once in a while, maybe at the IGA or over at the library or sometimes drivin' down Main Street. She says hi to me once in a while, but that's about it. I guess she's still grievin' the loss of her husband, which she has every right to."

"Why is she working down at that dive?"

"Apache Wells?"

"Yeah."

"I don't know. Pays the bills, I guess. Tips are pretty good. There's not much else round here, Danny. It's not like down in the Cities. But you know that better than anyone." J.P. opened his mouth and sucked in the last of his beer. His eyes were red. "Where's the check? I got to get on home."

"Where is home anyway? I never asked."

J.P. looked at him and smiled. "You member that pretty little thing Emmy Bockweiler? Graduated a few years after us?"

"Yeah, we used to call her Emmy Rottweiler."

"Well, now she's Emmy Garski."

"No shit?"

"No shit. We got married a few years after she graduated."

"She still mean as a snake?"

"I'd like to see you ask her that sometime."

"Any rugmonkeys?"

J.P. got a big smile on his face. "Yep. Two of 'em. Twin girls."

"How old?"

"Six. They're as close to perfection as God allows. You know, Danny, life would be perfect if it was just kids. Now where's that check?"

"I'll get it."

"No, you won't. I'll match you."

"Have it your way," Danny said. "I'll match *you*."

They split the check and went outside and lit cigarettes.

"Sure you don't want to get a twelve-pack and go over to the lighthouse and watch some waves?" Danny asked.

"Nah," J.P. said, and he got in the prowler. He started it up and it growled like a panther. That prowler of his was about twenty years old. It had the 454 engine in it. You can't get that engine no more.

J.P. leaned out the window. "I'll call ya. What's your cell number?"

"I don't have one," Danny said.

J.P. looked at him as if he had just said he didn't have indoor plumbing. "What?"

"I don't have a cell phone."

"And I thought us poor folk up here in Temperance were backward. You must be the last person on earth who don't have a cell phone."

"Yep."

"How come you don't have a cell phone?"

"Because I prefer talking to people face to face," Danny said. "It's harder for people to lie to you when they're talking to you face to face. Have you ever thought that maybe our society's dependency on the cell phone and the lack of face-to-face communication has something to do with people's difficulty to have trustworthy relationships with one another? Is it conceivable that, when we spend a huge chunk of our lives relating to machines, we lose some of our ability to relate with people?"

"Jesus Christ," J.P. said. "You're a Goddamn Luddite."

"What the hell is a Luddite?"

"Someone who's afraid of technology. They're named after Ned Ludd, an English textile worker who broke into factories and destroyed textile machines because he was afraid of losing his job. Look it up on the internet. You know what that is, don't ya?"

"Maybe old Ned had it right," Danny said. "Maybe the machine is the enemy."

J.P. shook his head. "Machines ain't the enemy. If I was a cop back when Ludd was around, I would have tarred his ass. How do I get a hold of you if ya ain't got a cell phone?"

"You don't," Danny said. "I get a hold of you."

"Take down this number then. Two-Six-Three-Six-Nine-Four-Oh. It's my cell. Give me a jingle tomorrow mornin'."

"Can I buy off some cigarettes before you go?"

J.P. shook his head again. "You're somethin' else, Danny Pierce."

He threw Danny the pack of cigarettes and drove off.

Danny stood there and stared up at the moon and stars. Clear black sky, cold bright stars. A beautiful night. He didn't want to go back to his motel room and be all alone; staring up at the asbestos ceiling, but what else was there to do?

He threw his cigarette away, got in the Caddy, and drove over to Apache Wells.

Chapter Nine

Apache Wells was on the south side of town, up on Mount Curve Avenue; the Pincushion Mountains shining in the moonlight behind it. It was a hole in the wall that the owners tried unsuccessfully to patch up in an effort to attract the tourist trade, but the only people that went there were locals. Danny didn't know why he was going there. He just wanted to see what Sadie looked like after all these years. At least that's what he kept telling himself. Did she still have those little oil drop eyes and the little brown heart-shaped birthmark on the back of her left calf?

He felt that old spark come over him again out of nowhere, a fast rush of longing that surprised him after all these years.

He remembered kissing Sadie down in her parents' basement when they were kids. He remembered the smell of her. He could never put a finger on it, but he could never forget it either. It was fresh, not phony. Just the smell of her. Strangely, it reminded him of his Auntie Esther's homemade vanilla ice cream cones. He could still remember some of the funny things Sadie would say, and some of the clothes she wore. He remembered the little sounds of liquid desperation she would make whenever he kissed her. Things got pretty hot and heavy down there in her parents' basement, but they never went all the way. Sadie told him she was saving herself for her wedding night.

"I know how some girls feel about it," she'd say. "'Oh, it's just this one time, with this one boy. Then it'll never happen again.' But it does happen again. And before you know what happens, it's with another boy. And then another boy. And before you know it, with any boy at all. I want to get married some day, Danny. And when I do, I don't want to stand at that alter and know that somewhere some other man was laughing at my husband. Would you want to marry somebody that had been with everybody else before that?"

He found it ironic now, looking back, as close as they were then, that he had never been given that opportunity. He thought for sure they would get married. It used to frustrate him so bad, down in that dark basement with the lights turned off, kissing her and feeling her small breasts underneath her cheerleader sweater...the touch of her almost perfect skin!...those nights!...but he always respected her for it as well. It was one of the things that made him love her even more.

There was no music at the Apache Wells, just the sound of a football game playing on the old Mitsubishi television that sat on a shelf behind the bar and the loud voices of the neighborhood working men who came to complain, brag and make known the prevalence of one professional football team over another—mostly the Vikings and the Packers with a few Bears fans scattered into the mix. When Danny was a kid, he was informed by his father that no Democrats were ever allowed in the Wells.

There were about a dozen people Danny could see sitting at the long bar. Might have been others in the shadows. The tables along the far wall were scarred and the plastic covering on the booths was ripped and leaking cotton junk.

"I heard it might snow this weekend," one of the old guys at the bar said.

"It's October," his bar mate answered, "it always might snow in October. But I didn't hear anything on the news about a storm. No, the weatherman wasn't talking like that."

One guy in dirty coveralls, a John Deere cap, and ancient blue military tattoos stenciled into both arms got up from the bar, glared at Danny for a second, and then staggered over to the jukebox. He put in some change, pressed some buttons, and a few seconds later, Loretta Lynn started singing about Portland, Oregon and pitchers of sloe gin fizz.

"Waddle it be?" the bartender asked Danny.

"Bud."

The bartender reached into a metal cooler behind the bar, took out a bottle of Budweiser, twisted the cap, and slid it across the wet bar.

"Two-fifty," he said, rubbing his fingers across a stubbly chin.

Danny took out a five and put it on the bar and took out J.P.'s pack of smokes and looked up at the game on the TV behind the bar. The Patriots were beating the Eagles on Monday Night Football. The fat dude on the television was commenting on how *if you liked offense with your hot dogs, you sure had it in this one, folks.*

Danny sipped his beer and looked around the place.

Who was he kidding? Sadie wasn't here. There weren't any women in this place. He knew the kind of women who worked at places like Apache Wells—pretty decent girls, you know, but not exactly like he thought of Sadie.

He finished his beer, turned and headed for the door.

"Danny?" said a strangled voice behind him.

It was a flat voice, suspended somewhere in the noise of the bar, yet close by, like a snatch of melody from a favorite song.

He felt the flesh above his spine go cold.

That old smell hit him again; that smell of vanilla ice cream cones...

She was standing there. Right there behind him, in a button-down plaid shirt and beer-splattered blue jeans with a white towel hanging from her waist. One foot was planted flat a little way before her so that her leg curved gracefully outward to reach it. A single hoop dangled in a glint of gold from each earlobe and a gold cedar tree pendant hung loosely between her breasts.

"*Sadie?*"

She hadn't changed much. Her hair was a little darker and there were smile lines at the edges of her mouth, like crescent moons, but other than that, she looked the same as she had in high school. But there was one thing that hadn't been there before. A little slanting fissure traced downward from the inside corner of each eye, slanted like a grave accent and just as succinct as one. It couldn't have been called a wrinkle, because she was too young to have wrinkles yet. It wasn't a crease either; it wasn't deep enough for that. Looking at her, he wondered what had caused it. Tear-tracks, maybe? No, not tears alone. Tears maybe, but something else as well.

"What are you doing here, Danny?" she said through quivering lips.

"It's been a long time, Sadie."

"You didn't answer the question."

"Do you mean what am I doing back in Temperance, or what am I doing here in this bar?"

"Both."

"I'm up here working on a case."

Her eyes narrowed. "A case? What are you, a cop?"

"Something like that. I work for the Bureau of Criminal Apprehension."

The bartender called out over her shoulder. "Sadie, you working or what?"

"Give me a minute, will ya, Jake?"

"I'm not paying you to socialize, you know?"

"One minute," she said. Then she turned back to Danny. "How long have you been back in town?"

"I got in last night."

"Did you know I would be here?"

"Yeah," he said. His voice sounded to his own ears like something which had come echoing down a long valley. "J.P. told me you were working here."

"J.P. always did talk too much." She looked up at Danny and swallowed hard. "What happened to your eye?"

She started to bring her right hand up toward his face, then realized what she was doing and brought it back down instinctively.

Danny touched his eye lightly with his fingers. There was a small cut under the eyelid and the skin had turned a shade of purplish blue. "I ran into an old friend."

There was a long silence. Danny took out his cigarettes and lit one.

"You still smoking?" Sadie asked.

"Yeah. I've been trying to quit. Stopped for almost a year once. But nobody ever really quits. You just stop for a while. You want one?"

She shook her head. "I always used to tell you those cancer sticks would kill you someday."

He shrugged. "They haven't yet."

It seemed like they had been through this before, that they had played this scene a dozen times before.

She compressed her lips, drew in a deep breath, and lowered her eyes again. "Why did you come here, Danny?"

"I just wanted to see you."

"Why?" she asked, trying to control the tremor in her voice.

He came a few steps closer to her. "It's been a long time, Sadie."

"Give me a break."

"What?"

"Don't complicate my life now of all times, Danny Pierce, for God's sake, don't complicate my life now."

"Why have you changed like this?"

"I haven't changed."

"You act like you hate me."

"What'd you think, Danny? That I'd just fall into your arms the first time I saw you again? I think you better go now, I've got to get back to work."

"Wait—"

She spun on him. "What?"

He stuttered a little, feeling what little control he still had over the situation start to slip away. "I just wanted to talk. That's all. That's why I came here."

"We have nothing to talk about, Danny. What we had is long gone. That ship has already sailed. It was high school, for Christ's sake. You were my first love, Danny Pierce. Everyone has a first love, and remembers it afterward; but I don't believe in that innocent kind of love anymore. It's just not possible for me. You better just go."

"Jesus," he said. "You're so cold. When did you become so cold, Sadie?"

He knew he shouldn't have said it. He knew it before he even said it.

She glared at him. "Is that what you call it, Danny? Cold? Yeah, I guess I am cold, but that's just what people say when they can't get you to do what they want. I'm sorry if you were expecting something different. Goodbye, Danny."

She left him standing there and went to a table in back to clear away the empty beer bottles; then she made her way through the bar with the tray of empties and disappeared into a back room.

His hands were shaking and his chest felt as if it had been bound with steel bands. Bound so tight he could hardly breathe at all. He knew it had been a mistake to ever come here looking for her. What the fuck was he thinking?

He turned around and walked out the door into the cool wet night, and all he could think about was his Auntie Esther's homemade vanilla ice cream cones.

Chapter Ten

He was in his car now, with the motor off, just sitting there, staring out the window at the foggy streets. His hands were still shaking and, despite the cold, little beads of sweat were breeding on his forehead.

What had he been thinking when he came here? What did he think Sadie would do when she saw him for the first time? Throw herself into his arms...weeping...hide her face in his chest..."Oh, Danny, you're all I've got left in the world..."

Forget it, he thought. You're just feeling sorry for yourself. Don't think about it.

The fog was reaching out with translucent arms and embracing the whole town now, like some living breathing thing.

He couldn't get rid of that feeling—that mixture of anger and sorrow. He wasn't quite clear when the anger had begun to sneak up on him and he felt himself drawn with unstoppable gravity toward something hideous and familiar, its supple strains penetrating his whole being. His hands clenched convulsively and his blood was in revolt. He wanted to pull away, but the truth was, he needed it, wanted it, would do anything for it...

He reached over and opened the glove box and took out the clear sandwich bag with the white powder in it. His hands were shaking even more now and the sweat was threatening to run down the side of his cheek. It always felt that way, anticipating the first hit after an entire day without it.

He opened the bag and poured a little mound into the little crevice between his left thumb and forefinger.

He looked down at it for a moment. He knew he should quit one of these days. But isn't that what they all say: *One of these days.* You want to quit and you're scared the habit won't let you. You can't give it up and you get nightmares about going down with it. You'll lose your looks and then that's your only direction. Down.

In the end he was always able to talk himself into believing that the drugs helped him calm down and think things through more clearly, but in reality it always made him that much more wound-up and nervous. It's hard for a man to give up his pleasures, even when they don't pleasure him no more.

He brought his fist up to his nose and snorted the powder into both nostrils, immediately feeling a moment's cool rush of ice racing through the front of his skull and down his spine.

He rubbed the excess powder off the tip of his nose with his index finger and licked it. There was a burning sensation in the back of his throat and his eyes began to water.

It took awhile for it to hit, but then it came on its own way and he felt his head taking off for that other place and it felt good; it felt good.

He was almost shot out of the car seat with a jolt of energy. His heart was on fire, accelerating by the second, and he felt like he could bend iron bars with his teeth.

He pulled the car out of the parking lot, but instead of turning right on the most direct route back to the motel, he hooked a left and the veil autumnal evening led him from street to street through the neighborhood he grew up in as a kid. He knew every building, every backyard, and every fence; the iron railings that he ran along as a child banging a stick against the posts and the high brick walls. It was an odd feeling—being home again, seeing all the old houses that he knew and the yards he had played in. Those were such innocent times. Being a child is so free and easy. No one should take that away from you.

†††

It was late. The streets were empty. Nothing but the fog. It was still hanging heavy over everything. As he drove down Main Street, he glanced at the closed-up shop windows—A Daisy or Two Floral, Buck's Hardware Hank, the Dockside Fish Market, Drury Lane Books, Lake Wind General Store, Bear Track Outfitting, Devil's Track Nordic Ski Shop, Birchbark Gifts.

Fucking Temperance River. A town of one stoplight, four bars, two churches, and two dozen tourist traps, quote, 'specialty shops'. Yeah, something's never change, yet they're changing all the time...

He didn't want to go back to his motel room and sit there, staring at the ceiling and thinking about Sadie.

God, why am I here?

He drove through town, all the way to the north side of the highway. A green metal highway sign on the side of the road told him he was 23 miles from the Canadian border.

I'm in the middle of nowhere.

Out of the night a pink palsied neon sign was flashing ahead, as though self-supported in the darkness: CLASS ACT GENTLEMEN'S CLUB. Abrupt and unexplainable. The lights looked inviting, and there was the pulse-beat of music coming from inside.

He went in, bought a beer, and stood there with it.

They called it a gentleman's club, but he didn't see any gentlemen in here. A young girl was on a small stage. She was completely naked, moving snakily, with a soft undulating grind at the knees and hips, hugging a shiny brass pole that reached to the ceiling. She had caramel blonde hair, small rounded hips, and nice legs. She was so small and slight that from a distance she could have been mistaken for an adolescent girl.

There were a group of old men and a couple Mexican farmhands sitting in front of the stage, throwing dollar bills at her. Every once in a while, she would glide over, bend down, and pick the money up. She had a little purple butterfly tattooed on her left hip and it seemed to float and fly as she moved.

The music was enthusiastic and loud, and that was the mood the crowd was in. A hazy cloud hung near the ceiling, where the smoke from a thousand cigarettes wavered listlessly like tangled skeins of blue yarn, as though somebody unseen up there was busily knitting with them.

Danny ordered another beer and watched the girl. When her set was over, she bounced off the elevated stage and another girl took her place. This one was a black girl with a skinny waist, big dark breasts, and a huge ass. She got up on stage and the music switched to Charlie Daniels singing about being a long-haired country boy, and she started swinging her hips and cupping her tits, showing a complete lack of interest in her routine.

A few minutes later, the blonde girl came out from the back dressing room and started working the crowd. She was wearing a sexy dotted satin ruffle babydoll that left little to the imagination. She glided over to the bar with the same moves she used on stage and stood next to Danny.

"Hi," she said.

"Hi back."

"What's your name, honey?"

"Nope, it's Danny."

She smiled. She was young; too young. Thin; blonde hair-blue eyes, with a splatter of freckles across her pert nose. Probably some Scandinavian in her. She had nice teeth.

"I'm Shanie," she said with a child's delight.

"Like Shannon?"

"No, just Shanie."

She started peeling the label off his bottle of Bud and looked up at him.

"So—do want a private show?" she asked with forced belittling casualness.

"Truth is I'm looking for someone to fuck."

She narrowed her eyes at him, with a little moue of distaste. "I'm sorry, mister. We don't do that here."

"I'm not looking to do it here. What time do you get off work?"

"Not till two."

"Can you leave early?"

"Look here, mister—"

"Can you leave early?" he said again.

"I'm not that kind of girl, man."

"Sure you're not."

He took out his wallet and handed her two hundred dollar bills.

She stared down at the money already in her hand.

"Look, I'm not a professional. I don't sell sex. I just dance."

"I'm not asking you to sell me sex. I'm giving you that money to cover what you would have made if you hadn't left work early."

She replaced a strand of hair that wasn't out of place. Her eyes tried looking up at him, but they kept bouncing back down to the floor. "I don't know just how to put this and I don't want to make you feel funny, but—aren't I a little young for you?"

"I'm thirty-seven," Danny said, "and even my antiquated mind can't see what that has to do with anything."

"You married?"

"Nope."

Her red mouth curved faintly at the corners. Curiosity began to thaw the coldness of her eyes. She parted her lips without showing her teeth. "Where do you want to go?"

"I have a room."

She rubbed her tongue over her teeth and squinted her eyes. "Wait here for a sec."

He watched her go up to the bartender and whisper something in his ear. Then she glanced over her shoulder and went back into the dressing room. The thought crossed his mind that she could just as easily take his money and slip out the back door.

But she didn't. A few minutes later, she came back wearing tight jeans, a black leather jacket, and a blue stretch velvet top.

"Let's go."

Chapter Eleven

Sadie was exhausted, both physically and mentally. It had been a long night, and she had earned every lousy dollar in tips. She'd just finished working the five to one shift and her clothes reeked like cigarettes and stale beer, and the soles of her feet were aching. Her head was pounding. It didn't help seeing Danny again, after all these years. In the back of her mind, she kept thinking about that, but she was too tired now to give it her full attention. Besides, she didn't know if she even wanted to. Danny Pierce was almost twenty years ago. She'd lived a different life since then, a life with a husband and her children at the core. Why did Danny have to come back now of all times?

The town was sleeping. The shops were dark, the houses were dark, and the only movement on Main Street was the off-duty traffic light at the intersection of 2nd and Main. The blinker threw lonely flashes of yellow across Sadie's face. She glanced in the rear-view mirror. Her face was smooth and sullen, if a little sallow. A few small spider webs of wrinkles rimmed her eyes.

"Thirty-seven," she said aloud.

Thirty-seven years old. An age she thought she'd never be. Where had it all gone?

The streetlamps continued to blaze down on the empty, naked-looking streets. For some reason their brightness made it seem even lonelier and more barren than it was.

She wheeled her little Dodge Neon down Main and into the driveway of the little stucco house on the corner of Benjamin Street. The house was a relic of the 1900's, solidly constructed for the North Shore winters. It was a house that had no bad memories.

In the driveway she smelled wet pavement and decaying leaves, and beneath these scents was the stronger presence of the lake. She heard a loon cry and crickets chirping in the grass as she walked up the steps and put her key in the door. It was almost one-thirty and the whole house was etched in complete blackness. When she opened the door she could hear her grandmother's cuckoo clock that her parents had inherited ticking away in the dining room and the sound brought back peaceful memories of when she was a child and her and her sisters would sleep over at Nana's house. She smiled at the thought and kicked off her boots and went down the dark hallway.

The rest of the house was quiet around her, only the furnace blowing in the basement, blasting out a stream of dried air through the floor vents, sending a rush of dust bunnies across the floor.

"Sadie?" a voice whispered. "Is that you?"

She popped her head into the darkened living room.

"Dad? What are you doing up?"

Her father was sitting on the leather sofa staring out the window. Russ Petersen was a big man of Scandinavian stock, a tall spare man in pajamas, sitting in the dark waiting for his thirty-seven year old daughter to return home, as if she was back in high school sneaking in from a date.

"What's wrong, Dad?"

"Nothing, honey," her father said. "I just don't like you coming home so late in the dark. I worry about you, that's all."

"You don't have to worry, Dad. I'm a big girl now."

"I know, I know. But I still do. Come here a sec and sit with your old man."

Sadie went over to the sofa and coiled at her father's feet, resting one arm across his knees, just like when she was a little girl. She used to sit on his lap...cuddle against him...warm in his love, safe-drifting into sleep..."*Daddy's girl, aren't you?*"...

"How ya holding up, silly?" Russ Petersen asked his daughter.

"Fine, I guess. How were the kids tonight?"

"Um, well, Jeffrey had a hard time going to bed. Kim and Leah fell fast asleep though."

"Jeffrey's just going through a stage. He's nine years old, he shouldn't be doing that."

Russ Petersen took in a deep breath. "Jeffrey's dad died a year ago. I think he's doing okay, considering."

Sadie swallowed hard like she did every time the subject of Kyle came up.

Her father ran his big hand softly over her head and down her cheek. "And how are you doing? You know, you could always quit that job down at that bar?"

"And how would I support my kids, Dad?"

"Your mom and me could give you some money to tide you over for a while. We got some saved up."

"No way, Dad. That's your retirement money. You worked hard for that. We've already moved in and taken all your spare bedrooms. Heck, we're probably eating you out of house and home as it is."

They didn't say anything. They just stared into each other's eyes like they did when Sadie was little.

"I love you, silly," Russ Petersen said. "Who's my little girl?"

"I am," Sadie said, a little embarrassed.

Her father kissed her on the forehead and smiled.

"You know, I'm so proud of you, silly."

"Proud of me?"

"You betcha." Their eyes met again, and they were content with that for a while. "Sometimes it's when I see you working hard and giving your best, no matter how long or tough your day. Sometimes it's when you take a stand for what's right, and I remember how rare that is. Sometimes it's when you touch my heart with some sweet thoughtful thing you do. Sometimes it's when I watch you play with the kids or see your smile. There are so many times when I feel proud of the wonderful woman and daughter you are, lucky to be your dad, and more in love with you than ever."

"Thanks, Dad," Sadie said, standing up and kissing him on his rough cheek. "I love you. And now I'm going to take a hot bath and go to bed." She started up the stairs. "Don't stay up too late."

"I won't."

Sadie went up the stairs to the second floor and down the hall and peeked into Jeffery's room. Ever since Kyle died, Jeffrey started sleeping with a night-light again. The room was filled with shadows. Her son was tangled up in the sheets, his Denver Broncos blanket clutched to his cheek and his Golden Retriever Sam cuddled up next to him on the bed. Both were snoring soundly.

Sadie bent over the boy and brushed her lips against his forehead. She stood there, looking at him for a long time, lying there with his arms out to both sides, looking like Jesus in wrinkled pajamas. He was the oldest of her three children and the loss of his father was especially hard on him. When they moved in with Sadie's parents he had dug his old blanket out of the moving boxes. They hadn't seen that thing since he was a baby. Now he slept with it every night.

Sadie closed Jeffery's door half way and went down the hall to the room her girls were sharing. Kimmey was six and Leah was five. Sadie went into the room and just stood there, watching her daughters sleep. They were both lying on their backs on separate beds pushed up against the wall, a look of childhood peace and beauty on both their faces.

Watching them sleep made Sadie think there was still a hope deep inside her that life was worth living; that there was hope for all the beautiful things.

She brought the blankets up to their chins and kissed them both on the cheek. Then she turned, closed the door half way and went down the hall. She was grateful to her mom and dad for taking them in after Kyle died. It was only a year ago, but it seemed like an eternity already. It's strange, she thought, when it first happened it was like she was in a coma. She couldn't eat or sleep or even take care of the kids. She didn't know what she was going to do. Then after the funeral, bit by bit, she started getting a little better. Even though Kyle had been gone for only a short while, there were already days when she didn't even think of him. Not many, but a few. She still loved him, and she'd go on loving him—or the memory of him—but she knew that if she didn't get on with her life the kids would suffer. They needed her now more than ever, and despite the shitty job down at the Wells and the lack of money, she finally felt okay. And she owed a lot of that to her parents.

Sadie's bedroom was at the rear of the house, with a single window facing the lake. She tiptoed down the dark hallway and heard the sound of the toilet flushing in the bathroom. Her mother came out, her form backlit in the dull yellow light in the hall, catching her gaunt cheekbones, the black hair which was severely pulled back and showing just the first traces of white.

"Oh, Sadie, you're home," her mother whispered.

"Yeah. How were the kids tonight?"

"Fine. Fine. How was work?"

Sadie shrugged. "You know. It's work."

Her mother yawned heavily. "Well, you go to bed now. It's late."

"I think I'm going to take a bath first. Wash some of this bar smell off me."

"Okay, honey." Faith Petersen reached out and kissed her daughter on the cheek.

"I love you, Mom," Sadie said.

"I love you, too, sweetie."

Sadie watched her mother disappear down the shadows of the dark hallway. Then she went into her old bedroom—the same bedroom she had when she was a kid—and flicked the light on. It was a very simple, lovely room, hauntingly chaste, almost needlessly ascetic.

Sadie went over to the window and looked out at the lake, shivering in the distance. The fog was lying over the still water like a heavy wool sweater. She loved the lake. Ever since she was a little girl she's thought that Lake Superior must be the most beautiful thing in the world.

She drew herself away from the window and went into the attached bathroom, stripping off her beer-splattered jeans and her cigarette-smelly blouse and throwing them in the hamper. Then she turned on the water for the tub, tied up her hair, took off her bra and underwear, and climbed in, with the hot water pouring in and the drain open to let it out again.

She lay back with her head on the rim of the tub and flipped the lever to stop the drain and eventually turned the water off with her big toe, then just laid there and soaked, letting her mind just drift off, not thinking of anything. She became so relaxed she almost fell asleep.

Twenty minutes later she sat up and let the plug out of the drain and watched the water disappear. Her skin was wrinkly. She climbed out of the tub and toweled off, rubbing her skin back to life. Then the thought of Danny Pierce suddenly overtook her again, like a drug. She remembered how she loved him so much back in high school. From the very first instant she had seen him, in his blue and gold football uniform, she was hooked. She used to love to watch the football games when he was playing, how proud she was and yelling and cheering every time she would see the #21 running by. She remembered the way he used to laugh, throwing his head back, and how he gave the best hugs, his arms tight around her back, and she thought of what that would feel like now. When she was a kid she'd always believed that there was one person out there in this great big universe that was meant for you and you had to fight with everything you had inside to find that person and keep that person.

She went back to the bedroom, sat down on the narrow bed, and stared at the bare walls, the plush white carpet, the child's dresser in the corner of the room and the small closet door shut tightly. When she was a little girl, she had always been afraid the bogeyman was in that closet, and whenever she called out to her parents to tell them how scared she was of the man in the closet, her father would go to the door and pull it wide open while she cowered in the small bed, clutching the faded checkered quilt Nana had made for her around her head. And of course the bogeyman was never in the closet.

She sank down into the bed; the cotton towel pulled tightly around her, and stared out the window. To the north reared the spires of St. Charles Cathedral, so high that the neon cross seemed to swim among the stars. The bed was covered with all her old stuffed animals from when she was a kid, and she grabbed an armful of them and hugged them to her.

Why couldn't she get Danny out of her head?

Seeing him again, after all these years, was like traveling back in time. She knew it was only an attack of nostalgia. It was autumn when she first met Danny and it was autumn now, and autumn is the only season when nostalgia never seems to turn bitter. Danny Pierce had been her "Homecoming King" and she was his "Queen" in their senior year of high school. She still had the crown tucked away somewhere in a box, some of the fake diamonds missing now.

Those days seemed like a paradise, and at the time it was just normal, regular everyday life, no better or worse than anyone else's. Now she wished she could go back and enjoy it for what it really was.

Why couldn't she stop thinking of Danny after all these years? Or had she always thought of him? Even when she was married to Kyle?

Kyle.

Had she ever really loved him?

Yes, of course she did.

But was it a different kind of love? A convenient love?

She fought herself: "No, it was true love. The love of a faithful and doting husband. The father of my children."

She curled up on the bed and ached for one more hug from Kyle. Just one more hug.

Just one more kiss.

But it was not to be.

It was never to be again.

Her Kyle. Enough time had passed that he was still a dull ache in her soul, but not the sharp wound the memory of him once was. Should she feel guilty? Shouldn't she feel more pain?

Sadie closed her eyes and felt the tears rolling out of the outside corners, along her temples, into her ears.

She looked beseechingly toward the ceiling again, but none of the answers were there.

She crushed her eyes closed hard this time and shuddered all over as though she felt cold and as though she felt old and as though she felt lonely.

She *was* so lonely. She was so, so lonely.

Chapter Twelve

On the way to the motel, they stopped at the Seawall Liquor Store and Bait Shop, picked up a twelve-pack of Budweiser, a bottle of Glenn's Creek whiskey, and a hard pack of Marlboro Lights. It was about one when they pulled into the parking lot of the Aurora Bora Palace. The girl, Shanie, was giggling now and Danny was trying to keep her quiet. He didn't want Millie to come out. He had a feeling that Millie Hjermstad wasn't exactly the most reserved individual when it came to town gossip and he sure as hell didn't want it spread throughout the annals of the Temperance River Old Ladies Club that he had brought a stripper—barely of legal age—back to his motel room.

But they got into Danny's room without being seen by anyone. Shanie went to the portable CD player on the dresser and glanced through Danny's collection of discs—Bruce Springsteen (his old stuff), Bob Dylan, the Stones, ZZ Top—artists who had been putting out albums two decades before she was even born.

"Geez, have anything from this century?" Shanie asked; the CDs dismissed and restacked in a sliding topple.

Danny handed her a beer. "There hasn't been any good music made in the last twenty years."

She settled on a Ray Charles CD and sat on the bed with her skinny legs crossed.

Danny sat in a chair next to the bed, sitting close so he could feel how warm she was and how soft.

"You're not afraid of me, are you?" he said at one point. He indicated the four sides of the room by swinging his thumb around them in a twirl. "Of this, and me, and tonight?"

"No," she said, looking at him intently, there in the dim light from the floor lamp at the end of the bed.

They drank their beers and passed around the bottle of whiskey and talked a little about themselves, and before they knew it they finished off the twelve-pack and half the bottle.

"Got any weed?" she asked.

"I'm a cop. You know that, right?"

"So. I've known plenty of cops that toke." Her bluish pupils looked like match heads in her narrow eyes. "So, do you have any?"

"Nope."

He looked at her and sipped the last of his beer. She was so cute and he was starting to feel relaxed, a little drowsy. He knew she was feeling pretty good, too. God, she was so young.

Against his better judgment, he took the sandwich bag out of his jacket and laid it on the bed next to her feet. Her toes were long and pretty and painted neon green. He wanted to grab them and pull on them.

"What's in the bag?" she asked.

"You know what it is. Have you ever done it?"

She shook her head.

"Want to?"

"I guess."

He opened the bag and poured a little into his left hand. "Watch how I do it," he told her.

He lowered his head and snorted it in both nostrils and almost sneezed but held it in. For a moment he held still, feeling something like pain behind his eyes. Then he took her hand and poured some of the powder in the crevice between her thumb and forefinger.

She put a little "V" between her eyebrows.

"I'm scared," she said.

"You don't have to do it if you don't want to."

"No, no. I want to. Just go easy on me if I fly the coup, okay?"

He brought her hand up to her nose and she snorted half of the white powder in one nostril and threw her head back.

"Shit!" Her voice was wet and hoarse.

She brought her nose down and inhaled the rest of the coke. Danny grabbed the bottle of whiskey off the table, took a sip, and handed it to her. She took a long gulp.

"It tastes good with whiskey," she said, glassy-eyed, her speech slowing as she tried to blink away the wet eyes and twitchy nose.

He put the sandwich bag back in his coat pocket. There was no feeling in his whole body except in the hot ends of his fingertips and inside his skull. His lungs felt cold.

The CD stopped. Danny got up and put in the Rolling Stones' *Metamorphosis.*

Shanie's eyes were little half-moons now and she had a come-hither look on her face. She motioned for him to join her on the bed.

"Take your shirt off."

He pulled his shirt over his head and dropped it on the floor like dead skin. She leaned into him and rubbed her hand over his chest. She took the gold pendant in her fingers and looked at it.

"What's this?" she asked.

"Saint Christopher."

"The guy who helped baby Jesus cross the river?"

"You know about that?"

"Yep. I'm a good girl. I went to Sunday School." She laughed, and said, "I'm making a point of all this so you'll realize what an unblemished girl I really am."

He leaned down and kissed her. Her breath had the airy scent of booze and cigarettes and Juicy Fruit gum. He lifted the blue velvet blouse over her head and threw it on the floor next to his own shirt. She was wearing a white silky bra and her breasts were like two small apples ready to be plucked. She reached around her back and undid the clasp and cupped the bra off her breasts. He brought his tongue over them lightly. She let out a liquid gasp and ran her fingers through his hair.

"Take off your jeans," she moaned.

He stood up and undid the belt and let them fall to the floor. She smiled and rubbed his thigh.

"Now the underwear."

He took off his boxers and stood there.

"Ummm."

She crawled toward him on the bed and pulled back her long blonde hair.

Danny's eyes drifted out the window, at the harbor and the highway. He heard the drone of a semi go by. The fog had moved out and lights winked in the distance across the marina. The full moon showed itself, watery and incandescent, stunning in its sadness.

She slipped him out of her mouth and smiled a captivatingly crooked smile. "You're ready to fuck now."

She looked away for a moment, almost guiltily; then met his eyes again.

He twirled his fingers into her hair and kissed her, long and hard, so hungry for her that he wanted to swallow her whole.

She let out a mousy little laugh and lay flat on her back.

He unbuttoned her jeans and slipped them over her boney hips and down off her feet. She had a tattoo of a rose on the top of her foot and he thought that it must have hurt getting a tattoo there.

She was wearing tiny white thongs and they were so beautiful he almost hated to take them off. He ran his hands up over her thighs and hooked his thumbs into the waistband and slipped them off. Her pubic area was completely smooth and the purple butterfly fluttered before his eyes. He stuck a finger in her and she jerked her hips forward. He bent his head down and ran his mouth and tongue over her in an alphabetical motion. She was almost convulsed now and she was wet and smelled nice, not like a lot girls he had been with before.

She was digging her fingers in his hair and telling him not to stop. He thought she was going to come, so he grabbed himself and entered her. Her mouth twisted and she gave a skittering cry. She didn't moan. She was too far in ecstasy for any of that fake shit. She came a few minutes later and told him to come; oh, baby, please come. He came and then collapsed next to her on the bed. They were both wet with sweat. She turned on her side and wrapped her skinny brown arms around his chest.

He could smell the fruity aroma of her shampoo and her good perfume, but something inside him had gone a long way away. After a few minutes she fell asleep and started making little noises with her mouth and nose. It irritated him a little. He took a deep breath, smelled the lake through the open window, and slowly fell asleep with the sounds of Mick Jagger singing about Downtown Suzie walking through a sleepy unknown city.

Chapter Thirteen

The first thing Dale did when he got home that night was head to the refrigerator in the shitty Airstream and grab a beer. He cracked it open, took a long gulp, and then brought the cold can up to his sore nose and held it there.

Fucking pig. That fucking cocksucker broke his fucking nose and it hurt like a bitch.

"Dale?"

God, he almost jumped out of his socks. Why was that fucking twat always doing that, sneaking up on him like that?

"What do you want, Michelle?"

There was a vast bib of dried blood on the front of Dale's shirt and more blood was crusted beneath his nose, on his lips and chin.

"Oh my god, what happened to your face?" Michelle cried. "Did that policeman do that to you?"

Dale inclined his head, closed his eyes; and licking his lips profusely, he began to mock her in her own voice, *"Did that policeman do that to you?"* His eyes narrowed on her. "Fucking cop cheapshotted me, that's what he done!" He glared at her. "How do you know about that cop anyway?"

He was scaring her. With his tone, his eyes, his presence altogether, he was scaring her. He got that way when he was drunk. His nose was puffy and shiny and comical and yet not at all funny.

"He came here," Michelle mumbled evasively.

"That cop came here? When?"

"This afternoon."

Dale's eyebrows bunched. "What did you tell him, Michelle?"

"Nothing, Dale. I swear."

He took another sip of beer and rubbed his ruined nose gently with his fingers. "I'm going to pay him back." His voice was thick and funny-sounding because of his swollen nose. "Oh sonofabitch, ain't he gonna get a payback. And you can take that to the everfucking bank."

"Don't go getting' into trouble," Michelle said. "God knows we don't need that right now."

"Mind your own fucking business," Dale said, and took his beer into the TV room. "Goddamn it, girl, don'tcha ever clean up around here?"

He threw an empty Diet Coke can off the table he was planning on using for a footstool and turned on the television.

Michelle came into the room and sat down in the chair next to him. "Whatcha watching?"

He didn't say anything and she just sat there looking at him.

Finally, he said, "What the fuck are you looking at?"

"I ain't looking at nothing," she whined.

He dragged his eyes off the TV, looked at her slowly without changing his expression. "The hell you ain't. Why don'tcha make yourself useful and get me another beer."

She stood up and pierced him with her eyes. "Why don'tcha get it yourself!"

"I said get me another beer, bitch!"

"Fuck you," she said, and stormed off into the bedroom.

Dale got up and went into the kitchen. It was a fucking sty. He threw his empty beer can in the sink and went into the fridge to get himself another. He thought about going back into the bedroom and teaching Michelle a lesson or two about how to speak to a man. Goddamn women these days didn't know their place. His mom would have never talked like that to *his* old man, and if she ever did, she'd get a mouth full of knuckles and a foot up the ass for her bother.

He took his beer back to the TV. He stood there for a moment and looked down the hall of the trailer again.

The whirlwind of the last couple days was blowing through his mind. He'd been drinking too much lately. He knew that. Time had gone missing for him. Hours and days turning to cinders in his mind, so that he wasn't sure what he'd done. He wasn't certain anymore that he could arrange events in his head correctly anymore. Some things he could remember clearly. Other things he could remember only as shadows, or not at all. Something had gone wrong, terribly wrong, but he wasn't quite sure what. Something happened beyond what happened. Sometimes you get caught up in moments, in the whirlwind of things.

The image of Rose appeared before him and a flood of guilt rushed forth from his heart. No; not guilt. He didn't feel guilty. That is, he didn't feel like he was guilty. But he sure as hell felt remorse and sadness. He was sorry. And he felt sick. He was so sorry. A right sorry son-of-a-bitch.

He could almost see her sometimes, late at night or in the long clean drench of morning after too much booze. *She stands in the hallway, just outside the doorway smiling.*

His nose hurt, real steady, not bad, but steady, like a toothache.

He sat down on the couch and flipped through the hundred channels of nothing on the TV. Goddamn, why did he pay fifty bucks a month for this shit? He finally settled on an old rerun of the *Addam's Family* on TV Land and smoked a few more cigarettes and drank a few more beers and then mercifully fell asleep in the chair. He knew he'd be late for work in the morning, but who the fuck cared?

Chapter Fourteen

The first thing Danny saw when he woke up the next morning in the cold box of the motel room was the asbestos ceiling. The second thing he saw was the girl lying naked next to him on the bed and both their clothes lying lifeless and deflated on the floor.

The memory of last night suddenly hit him like a Louisville Slugger. He remembered the girl, the booze, the coke, the sex. A crazy waste of time and brain cells. He felt cheap and foolish. Sometimes so many things get in the way when you're trying to do something good, that every moment of existence seems like some dirty rotten trick.

There was a painful cramp in his right calf and his throat was dry. The room smelled liked stale booze, stale cigarettes, and even staler sex. Suddenly the girl lying next to him seemed younger and younger. She rolled over and smiled her big, sleepy blue eyes up at him.

"Hi."

"Hey."

"I had fun last night."

"Yeah, me too."

"When can I see you again?" she asked.

"Huh?"

"I'd like to see you again. Is that alright?"

"Look, I'm not looking for a commitment right now."

"I'm not asking for a commitment," she said. "It's not like I'm asking you to marry me. I just thought it would be nice to see each other again sometime."

Danny closed his eyes hard and then opened them again. What the fuck was this all about?

The girl got off the bed and stood there naked, looking down at him. He didn't say anything. She gave him a sharp, dry look.

Silently, she slipped into her underwear and jeans and pulled the blue velvet top over her head. She picked up her bra and purse and jacket and went toward the door.

Halfway across the room she stopped and turned to him again. A shaft of morning sunlight caught her blonde hair and turned it into a halo.

She closed her mouth and her chin dimpled. After a moment she said, "You know, you're a real asshole."

She threw the door open and disappeared into the dark hallway. The door closing behind her was like a gunshot and he was alone again. A wave of self-hatred washed over him.

Ah, hell, she was just a stripper. What did he care about a stripper?

Still, she was someone's daughter, someone's granddaughter, someone's sister.

He felt old. He stared at the asbestos ceiling for a little while; then got out of the bed. He had to crack his spine and roll his shoulders and his knee was on fire. The cramp in his right calf tightened and if felt like he had been shot there. He rubbed it, but that did no good. After coughing up last night's cigarettes, he stumbled into the bathroom. The harsh one-hundred watt light hurt his eyes and he saw his pale face staring back at him from the mirror above the sink. There were purple pouches under his eyes that had never been there before, and the wrinkles in his forehead seemed deeper. He stripped off his clothes and got under the hottest shower he could stand, trying to wash away the night. This damn case, and just being home again, after all these years, was making him feel dirty somehow. He'd never had that happen before.

He spent a long time under the shower tap and when he got out again the little musty bathroom was filled with steam. He went to the sink, shaved close and clean, and put on a fresh pair of clothes. After a while his head felt a little better and he sucked down a couple handfuls of water so his throat wasn't so sour and withered. He went over to the beat-up dresser, strapped on his Sig Sauer, threw on his trench coat and locked up the room.

The hallway was dark and empty, and smelled faintly like mold and bleach and loneliness. He put on his sunglasses and walked through the front door into the morning coolness. The sky was that early-morning mixture of pink and blue, and the fog that usually hung off the lake was conspicuous by its absence. That happened sometimes up here, he remembered, it'd be gray and rainy and below freezing, and then one day you'd get one where the sun shone like it did in August.

He got in the Caddy and aimed it toward downtown. Twenty minutes later, the day dawned clear and bright, and slowly the cars came rolling to a stop along Main Street and the tourists came out of the woodwork like beetles. The very streets that Danny had known so well, had remembered through the years in their familiar semblance of early-morning emptiness and drowsy impassivity, were now foaming with life, crowded with expensive traffic, filled with new faces he had never seen before. Occasionally he saw someone from the past that he knew and in the strangeness of it all they seemed to him like characters in a book or faces he'd seen in a magazine. Sometimes he felt that memories were a lot like booze or drugs. An addiction that seems to bring meaning to your life, but just wears you down and consumes you in the end. He had to consciously prepare himself to see his mother, as if he had only this one shot left to him. How many years has it been?

He felt a surge of panic and instantly hated himself for being afraid.

Why was he so terrified?

Great, I'm thirty-seven years old and I just discovered that I'm a coward.

He turned right onto East 24th Street and drove the few blocks to his childhood home across the leafy street from where Old Prescott School had stood. He knew this street well. He used to play touch football and whiffle ball and games of sixty and kick the can on this street when he was a kid.

It was a narrow lane, shadowed by big oak trees that had recently spilled most of their leaves into messy piles. He didn't see any kids playing on the street though. It was a sign of the times. Parents these days hardly let their kids out of their sight even for a minute. Especially with the recent disappearance of Rose Violette. That really touched close to home for most people living in Temperance. That sort of thing wasn't supposed to happen in a small hillside community. But it did.

And now a collective queasy feeling had settled over the whole damn town. Danny knew the fear was irrational. He knew the statistics and knew that most children reported missing were either runaways or were taken by non-custodial parents. Only a small number were victims of "classic kidnappings." According to research conducted by the National Center for Missing and Exploited Children, in cases of long-term kidnapping in which the child was found alive, 85 percent of the victims did not consider the kidnapper to be a stranger. In at least 75 percent of the cases in which a child was found dead and the perpetrator identified, it was clear that the child would not have considered the person a stranger. Kids were just as safe at the parks and playgrounds now as they had ever been, and despite the frenzy of the radical media there weren't bogeymen lurking everywhere, waiting to snatch up every child that came strolling down the sidewalk with their lunchboxes swinging in the air.

But the statistics wouldn't bring Rose Violette home, and he knew that she was probably dead.

Danny wheeled the Caddy in a U turn and pulled it up in front of a dull frame house; the house he had grown up in, the house that still held all his secrets. He had grown to adulthood here. He'd snuck cigarettes from his father's stash and smoked them under the big elm tree in the backyard, and lost his virginity to Kristy Lundmark in his upstairs bedroom one afternoon when his parents were at work.

The house had been white at one time, but years of bad weather and little upkeep had turned it gray, stained by the storms of generations and the slow yet mighty pressures of time. The yard around it had been overrun by timothy and thistle. Its windows were nebulous with reflected clouds and shadows cast by the oak trees growing close to its spires. Clean laundry was hanging outside with the wind blowing it back and forth, waving like forgotten friends.

There was a careworn bay-window to the right of the porch, window curtains of starched cheap lace revealing a small wooden kitchen table inside with a conch shell and a family Bible. Danny believed houses had their own life that they took from the people who lived in them. He really believed that. As a kid his mother was a hostile, domineering, and frantically religious woman who railed incessantly against the sinfulness of young girls. She would berate him with guilt and visions of purgatory whenever she found out he had a new girlfriend. His emasculated father was no help. He either alternated between periods of sullen passivity and alcoholic rage.

Danny climbed the second and third porch steps and saw her there. His mother. She was planted on the porch in a bright slant of unseasonably warm autumn sun. It ran across her face in a bright, hard stripe, and his first thought was that she had lost at least a hundred pounds since he had last seen her. The skin on her face was thin, translucent, like porcelain held up to a light.

"Hi, Ma."

She looked up at him, the son she hadn't seen for almost twenty years and he was shocked by the bright hate on her face when she raised her head.

He sat down on the steps of the porch and looked up at the empty street, full of trees and warm sunlight. And dry grass and dead flowers now that autumn was here. There was a steady rain of dried leaves floating in the air.

"How you been, Ma?"

Her gaze made him acutely uncomfortable.

He took out his pack of cigarettes and lit one. She made a small sound in her throat.

"You're still smoking those things, huh?"

"Yep."

"They'll kill you one day."

He flicked the ash off his cigarette. "At least I'll die happy."

"Will you?" she said, her gray eyes boring holes in him.

There was a tense silence, pregnant with unspoken thoughts.

"You look old," she finally said.

"Thanks, Ma."

"What's wrong with your eyes?"

"What do you mean?"

"They're all red."

"I'm just tired, that's all." He stabbed out his half-smoked cigarette and lit another.

"You're not taking drugs, are you?"

She always had that ability, to see through him like a piece of old tattered cheesecloth. Back when he was in high school and he would come home late on Saturday nights from partying down at the bluffs, she would immediately know that he'd been drinking, even if she had been in bed for hours. She used to accuse him of being just like his good-for-nothing father. In some ways, he blamed her for his father's drinking. By the time she was done with him she had worn him down to nothing more than a small nub.

"I didn't come here to fight, Mom."

"Why *did* you come here?"

"To see you. Jesus Christ, I'm still your son."

She looked at him for a long moment, longer than she'd ever looked at him before. It was like she was seeing someone else's son, not seeing anybody that had anything to do with her.

"My son left me twenty years ago." Then, staring at him with dead, old eyes, she said, "You'll never change. You're just like your father. May God take pity on his soul."

"That's why you finally walked out on him, isn't it?" he said. "I remember the last fight you had with him. I was there, remember? I was on your side—you made me choose sides—even though he was still my father, because I loved you so much. I remember you putting on your poor-woman stuff, saying you were a slave to his infidelities and telling him that he treated you as nothing more than a piece of property he owned. I remember that you got mad and you told him, 'I don't like living with a no-good cheater and a drunk.'" Danny paused and looked up at the sun and the white clouds and the drifting leaves. "I think that's why he still respected you, even to his grave, because it was you who left. You beat him to it. He couldn't leave you, because he still loved you. You got sick of the others before they got sick of him. And he was scared—scared to be alone, without real love, the love he still had for you. I don't think he ever really cared much about the others, anyway. He just had to keep on having them to prove to himself that he was still a man. It made home a lousy place. I felt like you did about it. But I'm nothing like him, Ma. I'm still your son. You got to stop treating me like I was him."

"Is this where you storm off in a rage?" she asked. Then, after a long, agonizing pause, "Well, let me save you the trouble."

She stood up, glanced down at him once, and went inside the house, slamming the screen door after her.

Danny sat there for a moment longer. He looked around the porch and remembered sitting with his father out here on warm summer nights, when the evenings seemed to stretch into forever, his father drinking his Fitger's beer and smoking his Winstons, listening to the Minnesota Twins on WCCO radio out of the Twin Cities. It was one of only a few pleasant memories he had left of his father. He wasn't going to let her take that away from him.

After picking over those old bones for a while, he put them aside and got up, looked back at the old house one last time, and then crossed the sidewalk to his car.

Chapter Fifteen

The town of Croftville is a one-industry town in the region of the state known as "The Iron Range" or better known simply as "Da Range." It's a taconite town. Unlike Temperance River and the rest of the towns on the scenic north shore, Croftville is dank and dark all year round. Even on one of the few clear days like today, it reminded you of an old town in a Nineteenth-century English novel. The reason for this dankness is the taconite factories belching their smoke out into the air, turning the whole world into a sooty charcoal line drawing, all black and gray.

Danny parked the Caddy in the full lot of the Reserve Mining taconite plant and had to walk a couple hundred yards to the front entrance. It was breezy up here and he could hear the wind in the flags out front. He went inside and was greeted by a rather fat secretary with a lazy eye and a sour disposition.

When Danny asked to see Dale's manager the fat secretary didn't respond, and when he flashed his badge she looked at him doubtfully. Finally she picked up a phone and punched in some numbers. A few minutes later an attractive woman appeared out of nowhere wearing an expensive beige suit and a public relations smile, looking very smart and businesslike. She looked about as out of place here as a recliner on a battlefield. She was tall and thin and she fiddled with a pen as she spoke.

"Hello, Mr. Pierce." Her voice was firm and somewhat husky. "I'm Laurie Jackson. What can I do for you?"

"I'd like to speak to one of your employees," Danny said, his voice matching her firmness. "Dale Jacob."

"May I ask what this is concerning?"

"His daughter is missing."

"Yes, I'm aware of that," Laurie Jackson said, a bit defensively.

"I'm with the BCA—the Bureau of Criminal Apprehension. I'm investigating Rose Violette's disappearance. I need to ask Dale a few questions."

He thought she was going to play tough, but after a moment she was more than willing to accommodate his demands. She smiled her practiced smile and then, without another word, led him to a room on the second floor. It was a large meeting room, reserved for upper management, and Danny suspected Dale had never been in here before. There was a long mahogany boardroom table in the center of the room and several chairs surrounding it, but the rattle of machinery still stirred the crimson air, even way up here in the executive meeting nest.

Danny took a chair next to the end of the table and laid out the manila file in front of him. He waited several minutes and started wondering if Mrs. Public Relations had forgotten about him.

Then Dale walked in alone. He was wearing a white mid-length lab coat, tattered jeans, and a cheesy-looking Western-style shirt. A white hard hat was perched on his head, with tufts of greasy brown hair sticking out of the sides like wings. Printed on the hard hat was "D.JACOB."

When he saw Danny, shock filled Dale's eyes, replaced in an instant by cold hatred and contempt.

"What the fuck you doing here, man?" he said in a voice that held the faintest hint of a quiver.

Danny immediately noticed that Dale's eyes were tired—more tired than his own felt. And in his face there was a trace of that wild fierceness which belongs to something lawless in nature, at once course and murderous, tender and savagely glowing.

"Sit down, Dale,"

"You didn't answer my question, pig. What the fuck are you doing here?"

Danny's eyes didn't feel worn any longer. Rage escaped him like melted snow water pouring out of a gutter. "Sit down, Dale, or do I have to drag you out of here in cuffs? I didn't want to come here, but last night when I wanted to talk, you wanted to play the tough guy routine. Now sit down."

Dale stared at him for a moment. Then, reluctantly, he took a deep breath and sat in the chair Danny had pulled out for him.

"Can I smoke?" he asked, his teeth meeting in frustration.

"Suit yourself."

Dale shook a cigarette from his battered pack, lit it, and blew the smoke out of the side of his mouth.

Danny watched the smoke corkscrew up from Dale's cigarette. It almost made him retch. He loved cigarettes, but watching Dale smoke was enough to make him quit forever. He didn't want to have anything in common with this animal.

"So; what do you want?" Dale said. "I got to get back to work. I don't have some cush job like you."

"Is that what you call what I do, Dale? *Cush?*"

Dale smiled, his upper row of large teeth showing intermittent black spaces. "Yeah, I do."

"I need to ask you a few questions about Rose."

"Why? I already told your buddy Barney Fife everything I know."

"That's funny, Michelle said the same thing."

"Michelle's a dumb cunt. She don't know shit about shit. Sometimes I think she's half-retarded."

"You know, Dale, most parents when their child is missing want to cooperate with the police. They'll do anything to get their kid back. Don't you think it draws a bunch of red flags when you and Michelle don't even check up on how the search is going?"

Dale stared at him and Danny could see the murder come on his face again. "Search? Is that what you call it? This ain't no search. This is fucking harassment, man. I know my rights."

"You don't know anything, Dale."

Dale leaned forward and peered at Danny closely. "I know I don't need to say anything without a lawyer present. I know that much."

"Why do you need a lawyer, Dale? Did you do something wrong?"

"Don't pull your *Law & Order* shit with me, cop."

"You watch too much television, Dale. I'm just trying to find Rose, that's all."

"Like hell you are."

"What happened, Dale? What happened to Rose?"

Dale took another drag off his cigarette. "I don't know. I wasn't there. I already left for work."

"Why did it take you forty-five minutes to get to work that day, Dale? A trip that should have taken twenty-six minutes at most? Why did they find Rose's pajamas in your car? There's a shitload of unanswered questions and inconsistencies that all lead back to you and Michelle."

"You don't believe me?" The crack in Dale's voice was small, but it was there. "You calling me a liar?"

Danny glanced at him, and for a brief moment he was stirred to sardonic pity. "You put it that way, I guess I am," he said. "I think you're scared, Dale."

"I've never been scared of anything my whole life," Dale replied, in a callous, brutal tone. "Much less you, Mr. Star Quarterback, or that jerk-off J.P. Garski, for that matter."

There was a pause while their glances threshed.

"I'll tell you what I think," Danny said. "I think you killed Rose that morning and dumped her body somewhere on your way to work. Then you and Michelle made up some bullshit story. But I promise you this, Dale, I'm going to find her, and when I do, your ass is mine."

"I don't care what you think." The pitch of Dale's voice rose unevenly. "That's all just speculation on your part. Where's your proof?"

"I'm not particularly interested in proof at the moment, Dale. But when I find it, I'm going to bring you down. It's too bad this state doesn't have the death penalty."

"Is that a threat, cop?"

"Call it any name you like."

This got a laugh out of Dale, or something like a laugh. It was a nasty sound. "You don't have shit. If you did, you wouldn't be here. Instead of trying to find Rose, you're here harassing me, man. Like some big shot fucking city pig." His voice dropped to a hoarse whisper. "You always did think you were hot-shit. Mr. Star Quarterback of the Temperance High Tommies. Mr. Typical Tommy. Isn't that what you and that nose-in-the-air Sadie Petersen were back in high school? Oh, I remember her all right. I remember how cute everybody thought you two were together. But you ain't in high school anymore, Mr. Star Quarterback. Mr. Typical Tommy."

"I'm going to bring you down, Dale. I'm going to find something that will put you away for life. You and that fat pig you call a girlfriend. For life, Dale. No more partying, no more booze, no more TV, no more anything. I'm going to keep looking until I find something. Somewhere along the line, you fucked up. I may not know where or how yet, but you can bet your ass I'm going to find it."

Dale gave another humorless laugh and stubbed out his cigarette. "You could never seal the deal, could you, Mr. Star Quarterback? Everybody thought you were going to bring a state championship to Temperance River, but you got hurt. I'll bet you never even got in the pants of that little hottie Sadie Petersen, did ya? The star quarterback and the cheerleader. What a joke. You're nothing and you've got nothing on me."

Danny suddenly pushed himself out of the chair and leaned over the table, with both hands gripping the edge. He towered over Dale Jacob, and he wanted Dale to feel every inch of his presence.

"Where the fuck is she, Dale! Don't make me get a warrant for your arrest."

Dale didn't even blink. He met Danny's eyes and glared back at him. "Go ahead, pig. You can't arrest me on speculation, and you can't make me tell you what I don't know. I told you and I've told that buddy of yours Andy Griffith. I don't know where Rose is. I don't know what happened to her. And if we're done here, I got to get back to work." A smile of savage triumph carved itself across Dale's lean face. "Go peddle your papers, Mr. Star Quarterback. Some of us have real jobs to do."

"You're poison, Dale. Everything you touch is poison. Don't you even care if Rose is dead? Don't you even care if we find her? You're her father, for Christ's sake. Your blood is running in her veins."

Dale didn't answer him. He just sat there, glaring back at him. Then he pushed back his chair, real slow, went to the door, and walked out.

Chapter Sixteen

Danny was back on Highway 61, going south to Temperance. It was unseasonably warm and he had the top of the Caddy down. Despite the sun shining brightly and the orange brilliance of the trees around him, he felt bad. He was getting tired of his job, dealing with people like Dale Jacob every day. It was a living, but not like being a locksmith or fixing shoes. It was more like being a hooker, he imagined. Even if you were lucky enough to survive, you ended up feeling dirty at the end of the day.

That's it. The whole thing made him feel *dirty*.

So why did he do it?

He didn't know how to do anything else, that's why. But there was another side to it as well. He did it because somebody had to. He didn't ask for any of this, but if you've got to do it, you've got to do it. He'd abandoned anger a long time ago. Hatred and self-esteem were luxuries now, and he was figuring all the time, trying to find out what happened to little Rose on that fateful morning when she disappeared.

TEMPERANCE RIVER

He had handled hundreds of cases in his time with the BCA, and he knew that they almost always fell into a distinct facet. He would come into contact with people he hadn't seen in years or never at all, into a little world in which some terrible event had shaken it to its core. He would enter this world as a stranger, an outsider; the people he encountered would be unfriendly, insidious, giving nothing away. He would sniff around for clues—observe people's reactions—any one of them could be guilty, or complicit in the crime.

I've got to think right all the time, he was thinking. I can't make a mistake. Not a mistake. Not once. Well, I got something to think about now all right.

Danny took out his pack of cigarettes. He stared at them for a minute; then threw them out the window onto the side of the highway. It was getting to be an expensive habit. He'd buy a new pack, smoke six or seven cigarettes, then get displeased with himself for his lack of self-control and throw away the rest. A day or two later, he would feel the craving again and buy another pack, or worse, he'd dig around in the trash can through the coffee grinds and half-eaten fruit, the banana peels, canned spaghetti, milk and cereal until he found the pack. A fire at one end and a fool at the other.

He reached over and opened the glove compartment and took out the bag of cocaine and looked at it disgustedly. He was thirty-seven years old and still messing around with this poison. What the fuck was he doing? He stuck the bag in his coat pocket and looked for a place to pull off the highway. There was a scenic overlook on the left side of the road at Palisade Head. There were two parking lots for the overlook; the first lot was for the picnic shelter and the restroom blockhouse. The second lot was a hundred yards up the highway and hidden by a thick stand of pine. Danny slowed down and swerved the Caddy across the highway and into the second parking lot. There were no other cars or people around.

He got out of the car and walked down the path to the edge of the overlook. The cliff of Palisade Head rose three-hundred feet from Lake Superior's crashing shore. Far below, the water loomed large; rolling waves crashing on a confusion of bone-white jagged rocks, the cerulean water sucking in and out of the caves that time had worn in the base of the hill.

As if in response to his mood, a dark cloud had suddenly formed over the lake and the wind was blowing, just like the wind that blew at Pentecost. Looking out there at the lake, along a craggy arm of rock, he could almost see the curve of the world.

Slowly, he took the plastic bag out of his coat pocket and studied the cocaine.

How many years had he been its slave?

It was as though he had been trying to cover up from something, or cover up something, or both. It was a bad thing to corrupt yourself like this. You destroy the *you* that was meant to be, far more integrally than the world around you ever could. It was a form of suicide, and he was committing it every day. He thought of Sadie for some reason, how she used to cringe at the thought of drugs. What would she say if she could see him now?

He opened the bag and poured the powder over the edge of the cliff. It caught on the wind like snowflakes, white and lovely crystal lace. Then it simply disappeared in the breeze.

He stood there for a moment and he felt like the last person on earth. In a dreamlike sort of way, he realized that he was undergoing a transmutation. He felt himself to be abruptly changing into someone else, or someone else was abruptly changing into him. His own personality was disappearing and he found another and more omnipotent personality had been transposed into, or had overcome his own. He felt the burden of the case—as terrible as it was—to be strangely exciting, as though espoused by the burning vivification which boiled and bubbled and trembled inside him.

He was going to burn Dale Jacob. That was the only thing remaining of his faith in this fucked-up world—bringing Dale Jacob to his judgment. That was the only thing that mattered anymore. He felt that his destiny was set in the playing field laid out before him, as though his life, his soul—his all—hung in the balance of the biggest game he was ever going to play.

Chapter Seventeen

He got back into Temperance around sundown. The calm of evening was on the world, lit by the warm glow of the blue-tinted twilight. The lights from the windows of the big newer homes on the far bank of the lake glimmered in the dusk.

Temperance was winding down. The tourists had all but disappeared and the stores that lined Main Street were closing up for the evening, the idle storefronts decorated and decked-out in blue-and-gold poster board for the upcoming high school football game. The sun was setting earlier and earlier these days. Seven o'clock and the sky was dark blue going black.

Danny looked out across the lake at the setting sun, something he missed all these years living down in the big city. He always felt sunsets were a little sad, they always seemed so final. It's only a very little sun and the lake was such a big lake. Every time the sun set in the lake he expected to see steam coming up. He didn't know why.

Danny pulled the big Caddy up in front of the Public Safety Building.

"Back again?" the pink-faced dispatcher said when he walked in.

Danny indicated with his head. "He still here?"

"Uh-huh. Working late, as usual. You want me to ring him?"

"Don't bother."

Danny walked down the hall to J.P.'s office. He peered in and saw J.P. sitting behind his desk smoking and shuffling around a mountain of papers. There seemed to be far too many papers in the In basket and nowhere near enough in the Out basket. He looked like ol' Bob Cratchit from Dickens' *A Christmas Carol.*

"Hey, Sherriff," Danny said.

J.P. jumped, dropping the cigarette from his mouth into his lap. "For Pete's sake, Danny! You scared me outta a year's growth, sneakin' in like that. Don'tcha knock?"

"Nope," Danny said, trying not to let out a full-fledged laugh.

J.P. flicked his cigarette into an empty Starbuck's cup that was perched precariously on the edge of the desk. "I just had to arrest the son of my mother's best friend," he said, but in a lower voice this time, as if he was not sure of what he was saying, or what it meant. "Sixteen years old. Kid was pushing meth behind the high school. It's not like when we were in school, Danny. A little joint now and then. Things have changed so much. I don't know what's happening these days. Sometimes I think God musta pitched a bitch on the day he created the world." He shook his head to give this last statement some emphasis. "This fuckin' town. You'd think I'd be used to it by now."

"Take it easy," Danny said.

"You know why we couldn't have a nativity scene in Temperance River last Christmas?"

"No, why?"

"Because they couldn't find three wise men and a virgin."

Danny smiled, showing the tips of his teeth.

"Want a smoke?" J.P. asked him.

Danny winced. "I quit."

"Me, too," J.P. said. "I'm the amazing Quitting Man. Do it at least once a week. I'm getting real good at it." He pulled out the Marlboro Lights, got one lit, dragged madly as if he could inhale the rage. "What'd you do today?"

"I went to see Dale Jacob at work. Up in Croftville."

"Yeah?"

"Yeah."

"And—"

"And—I think he's guilty as shit. I hate to say that. Not that I like Dale. I hate him. But I'm sure he did it. That means Rose is most likely dead. I almost wish some perv took her, or some religious cult. At least then we might have a shot at bringing her back."

"Not much you can do after five days," J.P. said. "It's getting late in the ball game, man."

"Yeah, but that's what I get paid to do, J.P. Bring them back. I'm telling you, that fucking Dale Jacob; he sure is a cold fish, you know? He had no feelings. It was as though he completely lacked what Twain called the Moral Sense, the faculty which enables us to distinguish good from evil. He showed nothing about his daughter. I've never been a parent, but how can you have no feelings about your own kid?"

J.P. looked at him and said gently, "You regret never being a father, Danny?"

"I regret everything," Danny replied more harshly than he had intended.

"How profoundly Minnesotan of you."

Danny chewed a stick of Big Red contemplatively. "Does Dale have any priors for child abuse?"

"Nope, not with us." J.P. rubbed the gray hair on his temple. "Want me to bring Dale and Michelle in for questioning yet?"

"You couldn't hold them. We need a body. We need to find out what they did with Rose and where they put her."

J.P. looked at him sullenly for a moment longer and then said, "No, you're right, we couldn't hold them. Not yet, anyway. I just can't help holdin' out hope that we'll still find her. I'm just tryin' to keep the idea of Rose turnin' up on the respirator."

"Let Dale and Michelle hang themselves," Danny said. "But give them plenty of rope. If they did it, they'll screw up eventually. They ain't going anywhere. Dale's not the smartest bulb on the Christmas tree, if you haven't noticed. In the meantime, all we can do is keep searching. His luck can't last."

"Dale's actions so far indicate somethin' more than just luck," J.P. said. "Even dumb luck."

"No argument," agreed Danny. "But nobody's plan ever works perfectly. Just when you think you've taken care of everything, something or somebody pops up to block the deal. It's human nature, J.P. Eventually, something that Dale hasn't planned for will drop him right in our laps."

"And I can't wait to be there when it happens. If he did anything to that girl, I'm gonna put him away for a long time. Forever, I hope."

"All we can do is keep pushing him and wait. Let X equal the unknown. Hemingway once wrote that a good writer had to work from the inside out, not from the outside in. It's the same for cops. We have to try and stir up that unknown factor. You told me once about bits and pieces put together to form a semblance of a whole. Well, the pieces never fit together right away. The conclusion smart cops make is that we're not so smart as we are just lucky."

"Well, my luck has been about as faithful as a Bangkok hooker lately," J.P. said, pressing his cigarette out into the full ashtray. "Wanna go grab a beer?"

"Nah. I think I'll call it an early night. You should, too. You look like you need it."

"Yah, been puttin' in a lot of hours. Got my deputies workin' double overtime. The City Council is gonna shit a solid gold brick when I submit my next budget proposal." J.P. paused and his eyes ran over Danny's face. "We're gonna find her, ain't we, bud?"

"I don't know."

"You holding up okay? You seem a little—I don't know."

Danny looked hard into his old friend's eyes. "My head's a little fucked-up the last few days, that's all."

"Ever been to a shrink?"

Danny laughed. "Are you kidding me?"

"It could help. There's one down in Silver Bay that the county provides to its public employees. Part of our benefits package. I could see if I could sneak you in."

"Don't tell me you—"

"Yah, I went to see her couple of times. It's not like what you think, Danny."

"Next thing you'll tell me is that you do yoga, too. That's what's wrong with society today. We're turning our male population into pussies, sending them to shrinks and making them cook and clean around the house. I ain't going to no fucking shrink."

"All I'm saying—"

"Go home, J.P. Get some rest. Kiss your kids, have a beer, make love to your wife. Thanks for the advice, but I'll get through this without yoga or tantrism."

†††

It was a beautiful night, unseasonably warm and dry. He hated to waste it. He knew there were only a few of them left before the real cold came and the snow started flying. It usually happened right after Halloween. That was the thing about the weather up here in Temperance. It could—and usually did—turn on a dime.

Danny parked the Caddy in the deserted lot of the Aurora Bora Palace and took a walk down to the harbor. There was a full moon and he could see a slight outline of the Pincushion Mountains in the distance. He looked up at the low hanging sky, the stars almost appearing as if within his reach, like that story of the cowboy lassoing them.

He stood on the shore and watched what was left of the town lights rippling across the bay like sprays of colored water.

Waves staggered in, dawdling onto the shore. The clear water lapped at the rocks on which he stood. He went to the edge of the wet rocks where the inward waves slithered almost to his feet. He looked down into the water where a silver reflection of himself wavered back. He looked out across the water; cold and shimmering through the dark with the wind blowing with the tide, black-blue in the evening moonlight. There were white gulls flying over the rocky beach and a grunt fishing boat painted dark green passed him out in the harbor by the lighthouse. To his left he saw a family walking on the beach. The father had a girl of about four or five on his shoulders and the attractive mother was showing a boy of about nine how to skip rocks into the lake.

Seeing them—this happy family—deepened the cracks in Danny's soul. He envied them.

That was it.

He wanted what they had.

But he knew he was too old now; too bitter and too old to have what they had.

He walked slowly back to the motel, kicking pebbles along the beach as he went, and drifted quietly into his room. It was cold and lifeless, just like all the other hotel rooms he's stayed in while on the job. A motel room is a motel room, whether the place outside your window is called Temperance River, Minneapolis, Duluth, Silver Bay, or Thief River Falls; they all look the same. That's all there is, our images of things. There are no actualities. There are only the hundred different approximations of actualities that are our images of it, no two the same, from man to man, from case to case, from place to place.

Danny kicked his shoes off and lay down on the bed in his clothes, looking up at the ceiling and missing smoking again. He was unaccustomed to passing the time without a cigarette. He had nothing to read, nothing to do while the clock ticked by slowly.

The day was over, but the feeling that he had forgotten something nagged at him.

There was rain in the window, a storm was moving in and he fell asleep to the pleasant patter of rain upon the window panes and the dull growling of distant thunder...

and then he dreamed...

†††

He was back at Palisade Head.

The drop was as sheer as he had remembered it and he got a queasy feeling as he looked down.

Mists hung over the waters.

He spread his arms and plunged off the ragged cliff and fell three hundred feet into the surf that boiled among the rock clusters and chewed at the cliffs with their thundering rage.

First was the shock of the cold; the freezing water in his ears and in his eyes and his nose. The taste of algae in his mouth. Then a swelling sheet of water coiled over him, fell down upon him, blinded him, strangled him, and he kept going down, down into the black abyss.

He couldn't see anything. He didn't know if his eyes were open or shut. His lungs swelled and burned.

He clawed the water above of him. He could feel his face twisting in pain, his ears were roaring, and all was cold.

He opened his eyes and saw nothing.

Lonely.

A fish slid along beneath his eyes and he heard the rush of his own body parting the water. Then a dim shape emerged, shimmering through the dark; a person, swimming along the murk, as if searching for something or someone. Danny swam toward the image and realized it was a young girl. She was wearing pink pajamas. Her back was to him and her long blonde hair floated in the black water like seaweed.

When he got close enough, he reached out a hand and touched the girl on the shoulder.

She spun around and he tumbled back in shock and cold fear—her hair was in tangles about her face and her skin was bloated and blue. Her left eye was missing.

Rose! It was Rose!

She opened her little pink lips and her mouth formed a hollow, toothless scream:

"Help meeeee! PLEEEEEEEASE..."

He tried to reach her, to take her in his arms, to protect her, but he was ripped away from her, suddenly cartwheeling head over feet and floating in water that felt rough and clear and freezing, and Rose was slipping farther and farther away...

Help meeeee! PLEEEEEEEASE...

†††

Danny opened his eyes, his body drenched with perspiration. For a moment he had the strange feeling that some small bluish animal had just rushed out of the room. He sat up quickly on the bed and reached for the pack of cigarettes that wasn't there. His mouth was so dry and the sweat on his body made him shiver. The room was dark and barren and lonely.

Dark, barren, and lonely.

†††

Dale Jacob went to the Apache Wells after work that night. He wanted to get drunk. Plain and simple; swift and sloppy. His head felt like it had been put in a vice and that damn cop Danny Pierce was putting the screws to it.

The fucking pig had the balls to come to his work?

That was fucking harassment.

He knew his rights. And that cop had overstepped his bounds.

First he breaks his damn nose; then he comes to his work?

Goddamn.

When Dale was walking out of the plant today, he could tell people were talking about him behind his back. And that fucking boss of his. What did she think of the whole thing? A cop coming up there to talk to one of her employees? It just didn't sit well, that's all there was to it. He was a hard worker, but that didn't seem to matter anymore. You had to kiss ass to get anywhere in the world nowadays.

Yeah, he wanted to get drunk all right.

He was sitting at the bar behind a half-empty pitcher of Pabst Blue Ribbon. Stevie McIntire was sitting there next to him, bitching about getting laid off at the textile mill or something or other. Dale wasn't paying much attention to Stevie though. He never did. He had his own problems to worry about. Much bigger problems.

Stevie was as stupid as a stuck pig, but he was an alright gee to drink with now and then. He was one of those guys who everyone likes, a softhearted nit, without malice. He had known Stevie a long time; they grew up together and graduated high school together, and that should count for something.

"I was afraid to go home tonight," Stevie was saying. "My old lady gave me hell this noon like it was my fault I got laid off."

"What's a matter with your old lady?" Dale asked. "Why don'tcha smack her?"

"You smack her," Stevie said. "I'd like to see what she does. She's some old lady to talk. She hasn't had a job in six months."

Dale lit a cigarette and blew smoke up to the ceiling lights.

"You got to smack them around once in a while," he told Stevie. "Keep 'em humble."

Stevie laughed and drank his beer and bummed a smoke off Dale.

†††

Sadie saw Dale Jacob sitting down there at the end of the bar; smoking and drinking like some college kid at a frat party. She stared at his face, the firm mongrel cheekbones, the narrow eyes, the nose broken at the bridge, the wide mouth, the round jaw. He was almost handsome in an odd sort of way. Like a villain in an old Clint Eastwood movie.

She was glad he was at that end of the bar and not sitting at one of her tables, that way she didn't have to wait on him. She didn't like Dale Jacob and she was trying not to go anywhere near him. He was a mean drunk and the whole town was talking, whispering accusations about how he killed his little girl. Sadie knew that people reacted to personal tragedies in their own personal ways. She understood firsthand from losing her husband that grief comes down on someone in swells. The truth of what happened becomes more painful as the horror of the loss sets in, and the mind slowly emerges from the shock that has enveloped it. But God, just look at him. Sitting there like he didn't have to put on his pants one leg at a time like the rest of us, while his little girl is still missing, as if he had nothing at all to be concerned about.

She'd heard how Dale and his girlfriend hadn't participated in any of the searches for little Rose. She studied him with wondering eyes. How could a person be like that?

Her thoughts were broken by someone at one of the tables in back calling for another beer.

Sadie went back to the table, the guys scoping her out as she came up. It was a feeling she didn't know what to do with. Some nights she didn't think she could go on. God, why did she have to put up with it? This stinking job with its stinking smoke and stale beer and the leers of all the dirty old men? And then there were the drunks who wanted to be her friend. Though it had only been six months since she started waitressing down at the Wells, she felt like she had been doing it for an eternity.

It was just a job, she told herself. She didn't have to love it. She tried to remind herself that it was only temporary. She was saving up to buy the kids Christmas presents. Jeffrey wanted the Star Wars Trilogy DVD set, Kimmey's list included a My Barbie Digital Camera, and Leah asked for a kids Rapala fishing pole and tackle box.

Maybe she could quit after the holidays and get a job at the J.C. Penny down in Two Harbors, but she dreaded the hour commute. There just wasn't a lot of jobs in Temperance. She'd never had to worry about money when Kyle was alive.

Why did he have to die, why did he have to leave her with three kids to raise by herself? It wasn't fair. There must be no one in the whole world feels as desperate and alone as a woman on her own with kids depending on her.

She went to the other side of the long bar and told Jake to pour another pitcher of draft for the boys at the table in back.

"Give me a sec, will ya, Sadie," Jake said.

He was flushing the leads to the taps, taking forever to draw beer through the sputtering pipes.

While she was waiting, Sadie glanced at Dale Jacob's reflection in the mirror behind the bar.

Then the bastard caught her looking at him and he slowly turned his head toward her and grinned his wolf's grin.

She braced herself, twisting the wedding ring she still wore around her finger, willing Jake to finish with the taps.

Jake finally finished pouring the beer and slid the full pitcher down the bar to her. She took it and brought it to the table in back. When she turned around again she almost ran into Dale. He'd gotten off his bar stool and walked over to the jukebox at the end of the bar. He smiled at her again and she felt literally sick to her stomach.

He put his quarters into the jukebox, his head turned toward her, watching her. A few seconds later Johnny Cash started singing about murder and Dale was smiling his wolf's grin and swinging his thin hips around like he was screwing something. Sadie went and stood at the bar again with her back to him. Then she felt his presence beside her, close enough for his scent to reach her—dirt and oil and Pabst Blue Ribbon and whatever chemicals he had injected or snorted into his body earlier in the evening.

"Hey, Sadie," he said with a bleary, cocky smile. "Howya doing?"

"Do you want something, Dale?"

"Yeah, I want something," he said, his eyes looking her over, from head to foot. "You don't remember me, do you, Sadie?"

"I remember you," she said, trying not to stare at the dark tattoos on his forearms. "It'd be pretty damn hard not to remember you after the last couple of days."

Dale's lips stretched into a thin, cold line.

"You think I killed my kid?"

"I didn't say that."

"You didn't have to." He moved his skinny finger and touched her forehead between the eyes. "I can see it in your eyes. You're afraid of me."

"I'm not afraid of you," she said in a voice as strong and supple as a dancer. "I just don't like you, Dale. Do you want something to drink or not?"

Dale held up his glass of beer. "I already have something to drink."

She turned to go, but Dale grabbed her by the elbow.

"Let go of me, Dale!"

Dale stared hard into her eyes and for a moment she thought she saw actual fire in his pupils.

"I ran into that boyfriend of yours," he whispered. "He did this to my nose. But I plan on paying him back. Oh, man, do I plan on paying him back."

"You're hurting my arm," Sadie said. "Let go of me."

"Okay, Dale, that's it," she heard Jake holler from behind the bar. "Get outta here."

Dale smiled at Sadie again with a stoned, loose-lipped smile, and then with wicked calm he let go of her elbow and turned his attention to Jake.

"Fuck you, fatso."

Jake reached below the bar and came up holding a wood baseball bat in one of his ham hock fists. That old bat looked like it had been used before.

Dale uttered a hollow chuckle. "What are you going to do with that? Stick it up your fat ass?"

"Time to go, Dale."

"Fuck you!"

Jake swung the bat over the bar and it struck Dale under the left shoulder, in the meat of the triceps.

Dale let out a little yelp, like a dog that has been ground under the tires of a semi. "What the fuck you do that for?"

"I said it's time to go, Dale."

Dale held his arm and stumbled away from the bar. "You'll fucking pay for that, fatso! You'll fucking pay. I ain't through with you yet. I ain't through with any of you."

"You're not making yourself any friends around here, Dale," Jake said. "You'll be in a long box with a silk pillow under your head before I let you back in my bar. Now get the hell outta here, ya hooch hound."

Chapter Eighteen

That fucking fatso! Who the fuck did he think he was anyway? Hitting him with a fucking baseball bat! He had a mind to go back there and burn the whole shithouse of a bar down to the ground. Fucking fatso! And that nose-in-the-air skank waitress of his, with her pretty brown eyes and her tight ass? He'd like to rip himself off a piece of that shit and show her how a real man was in the sack. He wondered if that sonofawhore cop Danny Pierce was getting any again, now that he was back in town.

Out in the parking lot Dale started his pickup and put it in drive. It sounded as though it were shaking to pieces, then it recovered and rattled away, farting down the length of the exhaust pipe that was unencumbered by anything so trivial as a muffler. A sticker on the left rear bumper read: MY OTHER CAR IS A PAIR OF BOOTS.

Dale drove slowly through town. The last thing he needed now was another DUI.

The streets were dead. He thought about going over to the C&M Tap, but shit, why go spend his hard-earned money when he could just as well drink his own beer back at his place? *His place.* What a joke that was. That fucking shittrap trailer with that whale of a woman. Good for nothing whale of a woman that she was. What the fuck had happened to her anyway? She used to be so good looking and good in bed. Now all she wanted to do was mope around eating Cheetos all day. Jesus Christ.

He turned into the Big Timber Trailer Court and almost hit a stray dog eating garbage out of a trash can in one of the alleys. He should have run the mangy mutt over, put it out of its misery. Instead he almost hit the mailbox as he parked the grumbling truck in the dirt of what passed for their driveway. The truck backfired, not wanting to turn off. It was parked half on the drive and half on the grass. Ah, hell, the grass was brown and half-dead anyway. Pretty soon it would snow and nobody would know the difference.

Dale got out of the truck, side-stepped some crumpled McDonald's bags and empty beer and soda cans littering the yard, and staggered up to the door. The light in the kitchen was on, but the rest of the trailer was in darkness. He could hear Michelle snoring in the back bedroom and he thought of something he had been forced to read back in high school. It was one of the few things he remembered:

Nay, but to live
In the rank sweat of an enseamed bed,
Stew'd in corruption, honeying and making
love over the nasty sty...

He didn't even know what the fuck it meant. All he knew is that it was written by that English cock-sucker that everybody loved, William Shakespeare. William fucking Shakespeare. Now why in the hell would he remember that? But those strange words gave him a reason for hating Michelle even more, and they made his hatred more real; they even made Michelle, snoring away in the back bedroom, more real.

Fucking whale. Even the sound of her snoring made him sick.

He went to the fridge and grabbed a cold beer. He swallowed it in two gulps, threw the empty can in the sink, and opened another one. He knew he was going to have one mean hangover at work in the morning, but what the fuck, he didn't care anymore. That fucking cunt of a boss could kiss his ass.

Maybe he'd call in sick tomorrow. He only had a few sick days left, but who the fuck cared? Let them fire him. He was probably getting cancer from all the taconite emissions anyway. Fucking factory job. Fifty hours a week, nine hours a day, just wasting his time chasing nickels and dimes. Some job. Some way to make a living. It drove him crazy, that job and this fucking town; to stay in one place your whole life, just working, working. Life shouldn't be like that. It was a form of slavery. People should go out and see the world and get their fill of wanderin'. Maybe he'd join the fucking Peace Corps or something and move to Bulgaria to teach little Bulgarian kids how to speak English. Probably paid more than what he was making down at the taconite factory.

Dale glanced drunkenly around the small dirty trailer and thought, I work fifty hours a week to be this fucking poor?

He sat down and tried to find the clicker to the TV—the whale was always moving it on him. He finally found it hiding in the cushions of the LazyBoy. When he turned on the TV some fag on HGTV was talking about home makeovers. God, why did Michelle watch this shit? It was like she was dreaming of having a real home someday. Fat chance in hell of that ever happening. Some trailer. Some fucking trailer.

He flipped through the channels until he came to ESPN. The pompous asshole on SportsCenter was talking about this weekend's NFL games. Dale let loose with a wave of obscenities when the pompous asshole told him that the running back on his fantasy football team wasn't going to play this Sunday because of back spasms. Fucking pussy. These pansies got paid two million a year to sit on the bench while he slaved away in some sweatbox taconite factory?

He was sick of watching sports, his fantasy team sucked anyway. He flipped the clicker to E! and caught the last of a *Girls Gone Wild* commercial. Young college girls flashing the screen with their titties blurred out by a black line across their chest, but it still left a lot in to get his fuzzy brain hopping. He started getting real horny. He remembered all the times back in high school, getting drunk and stoned, listening to Van Halen in his hand-me-down Monte Carlo (whatever happened to that old car?), in the backseat, slipping his dick into the freshman girls who were too dumb or too drunk to know any better. He remembered the first time he got laid. He was thirteen. Her name was Trisha. She was sixteen. He brought his friends to see her because they didn't believe him. Stevie, Peter, and Beaver waiting outside her bedroom window in the alley. She took out a Hustler magazine to show him how it's done; cunts and cocks, tits and ass. It looked like open-heart surgery. The sad, sad bedroom, television blasting away, a little sister somewhere in the living room, dirty dishes piled high in the sink, mother at work, bloated Irish father out on another binge. It didn't last long, fifteen seconds or so. He was embarrassed and ashamed. His friends laughed at him. It was the last time he ever saw Trisha.

He thought about Sadie Petersen down at the Apache Wells tonight. Yeah, he sure would like to rip himself off a little of that.

He stood up unsteadily, went into the fridge to get a fresh beer, and staggered through the blue-black darkness of the tiny trailer to the back bedroom. For a second, as he passed Rose's empty room, a wave of sorrow seeped into his sodden mind, but it passed just as quickly and he stumbled into the musty bedroom.

The room was a mess, dirty clothes tossed everywhere. He stood in the doorway and looked disgustedly at Michelle lying on her stomach, snoring, the dirty sheets tangled around her meaty thighs, with an empty carton of *Ben and Jerry's Chunky Monkey* ice cream on the floor beside the bed.

When he is drunk asleep, or in his rage
Or in the incestuous pleasure of his bed...

Dale sipped his beer and went over to the bed and pulled back the sheets. Michelle's polka-dot panties were hanging askance on her big white butt.

He sipped his beer again, finishing it and crumpling the can, tossing it on the floor.

He undid his belt buckle and unzipped the fly of his dirty Levi's.

Michelle made a little noise in her mouth and turned her head on the pillow. It had been a while since they last fucked, and it hadn't been very good. Dale had been stone drunk and flying on

Vicodin and Michelle just laid there waiting for it to be over. Goddamn women didn't know how to fuck these days. It was all that shit they read in *Cosmopolitan*, filling their little brains with all that horseshit.

Dale pulled the panties off Michelle's wide hips and she brought one of her thighs up in the bed. Good, he thought, easy access.

He bent down and drew his hand between her legs, felt the steel wool hair there, and spread the lips.

Jesus Christ, when was the last time she took a shower?

Michelle moaned a little and tried to turn over, but he put his hand on her back and put his cock into her. She opened her eyes and looked over her shoulder at him.

"Dale?"

"Sssh."

He pumped her from behind and took a wad of her dirty blonde hair in his left hand. He was riding her hard and her head was slapping against the headboard. He closed his eyes and thought about Sadie Petersen in her tight jeans with that little ass and those two little titties. He thought about the college girls on the *Girls Gone Wild* commercial, smiling through the TV at him, rubbing their skinny little bodies and licking their sweet, juicy young lips. He thought about that bossy twat Laurie Jackson. When he was about to come, he pulled out and spurted himself all over Michelle's back.

Michelle rolled over in the bed and stared up at him. Just like the whale in that Hemingway book. That's what she was, a fucking whale.

"That felt good, Dale," Michelle said in a sleepy voice. Her breath smelled like sleep and stale

Cheetos and Chunky Monkey. "That felt real good. Did it feel good for you?"

"Yeah," he said, zipping up his fly and buckling his belt again.

"Where you going?"

"To get another beer."

"Do you have to?"

He looked at her disgustedly. "Yeah, I have to. Look at yourself. You're getting fatter and fatter every day. Why don'tcha try a salad once in a while, you big disgusting mountain of blubber. Fucking you is like getting on top of a hay mow. And when was the last time you took a shower? Now my dick is all dirty from your smelly beaver." His eyes were like dull coins. "There's other girls out there, you know, Michelle. Other girls in this town that would love to fuck me."

Michelle sat up on her elbows. "You're a fucking asshole, you know that, Dale?"

"Fuck off."

"You ain't so hot, Dale. Look at you. You come home drunk every night. You reek of alcohol. What good are you to any woman?"

"What do you reek of, you slut."

"Don'tcha call me that, I'll leave you."

"You slut."

"Alright," Michelle said, "it's over. If you weren't so conceited you woulda seen it was over a long time ago. You're not a man. Not a real man. You're just a crown of thorns I wear around my head. You're worse, because a crown of thorns don't get drunk and then come home smelling of stale beer and wanting to throw a fuck in you at two in the mornin'."

"You slut."

"Well," she said, "I'm not a slut. I've tried to be a good woman, Dale, but you're a selfish and conceited little child. Always crying, poor me, poor Dale Jacob. I never met a man as good at the poor-me's as you are. Well, I'm sick of you. I'm through with you."

"No, you're not," Dale said threateningly.

"I won't say it again, Dale."

"What are you going to do, move back in with that alcoholic mother of yours? She doesn't want you. Nobody wants you anymore, you little Irish slut."

"Don't call me names; I know the word for you. Oh, that's right, Dale. Do you want me to tell everybody what you are?"

He reached over and slapped her. Hard. The back of her head bounced off the headboard.

"Keep your mouth shut," he screamed at her. "You're going to keep that fat mouth shut!"

He clenched his hand into a fist and hit her. She tried to sink down into the bed, but he hit her again.

"You'll keep that mick mouth of yours shut! Do you hear me; you'll keep that mouth shut!"

Chapter Nineteen

J.P. got home late that night. Emmy and the girls had already eaten and there was a plate of meatloaf and potatoes waiting for him in the oven. The girls were in the living room watching *Hannah Montana* and Emmy was sitting at the kitchen table reading a Midwest Living magazine.

"How come you didn't wait for me to eat?" J.P. asked.

"I didn't know what time you'd be home," Emmy said, without looking up from her magazine. "I never do anymore."

When he had been elected sheriff, J.P. had promised himself and Emmy that, as much as possible, the job wouldn't get in the way of his family, especially the kids. But deep down he knew it was a delusory promise. As sheriff of a small town with only a few deputies and one full-time dispatcher, you're on call twenty-four hours a day.

"It's this fucking case," he said in a long, shaky sigh.

He went to the fridge and got himself a beer.

"Don't swear," Emmy said. Her voice was exasperated, like she was talking to a child who has just spilled its second glass of milk at the dinner table.

"The girl's can't hear me," J.P. said. "They got that damn TV cranked to the highest level. How come you always let them watch that thing? Don't they have homework or somethin'?"

Now she looked up at him. "Yeah, they have homework. And they just started watching it."

"How come every time I come home they're sittin' in front of that TV?"

"Don't judge me as a mother, J.P."

"I'm not."

"Good."

"Let's not do this right now, okay? It's late and we're both tired and this isn't how I wanted to start things out. Can I have some dinner?"

"You know where it is," Emmy said.

He let out another tired sigh, went to the oven, and took out the plate of food.

"Ain'tcha even gonna ask me how the case is goin'?" he said between bites of meatloaf.

"No."

"Don'tcha care?"

"No."

"Jesus, Emmy. What's wrong with you?"

"I'm sick of never seeing you, J.P. I'm sick of eating alone with the twins, sick of putting them to bed by myself at night."

"Hey, I'll quit if you want me to. Just give me the word and I'll quit. *You* can get a job."

"Don't give me that shit."

"Don't swear, Emmy."

She threw the magazine down on the table. "We can't talk, J.P. We can't even hear each other."

†††

When he finished eating, J.P. put the dirty dishes in the sink and went upstairs. The girls were in the bath, the clawfoot tub full of bubbles and toys for them to splash. He scooped a handful of soapy bubbles and made a Santa beard on his chin and the girls laughed and called him Silly Daddy.

"Are you going to read bedtime stories to us tonight, Daddy?" Jenny asked.

J.P. smiled and let the drain out of the tub.

"Come on, Little Butt," he said, referring to his pet name for Jenny. "Out of the tub."

"Okay, Big Butt."

He grabbed two towels and took Jenny and Kasey out, rubbing pink back into their porcelain skin so they didn't get the shivers.

"I want to read 'May I Bring A Friend' tonight," Kasey said.

J.P. rubbed the top of her little wet head.

"Go potty and brush your teeth, girls. I'll meet you in your room."

He went into the girls' room and picked out pajamas for each of them. When they came in, wrapped in their big towels, he put them into their pajamas and sat down on the floor next to Jenny's bed. The girls sat down beside him on each side.

He started reading: "The King and Queen invited me to come to their house on Sunday for tea..."

When he finished with the story he set the book down on the floor and tucked the girls in bed.

"Will you lay with us for a little bit, Daddy?" Jenny asked.

"Sure. After you say your prayers."

The girls folded their tiny hands simultaneously. "Angel of God my guardian dear," they pronounced slowly and in unison, "to whom his love commits me here. Forever this day be at my side, to light and guard, to rule and guide. God bless Mommy and Daddy and Jenny and Kasey and grandmas and grandpas and aunties and uncles and cousins and friends and Nala our cat and our fish and Buddy our dog and everything in the world, Amen."

Their little voices filled him like warm milk. He sunk down next to Jenny in her bed. She wrapped her tiny arms around his neck, her damp hair against his cheek, and kissed him on the chin, where his whiskers were the softest.

"I love you, Daddy," she said.

"I love you too, pumpkin."

Jenny snuggled tighter against him and soon he felt her breathing grow heavy and he knew she was sleeping.

He got up and crept across the room, real slow and easy, so as not to wake her up, and went over to Kasey's bed where he wrapped his arms around her.

"Goodnight, Daddy," Kasey whispered.

"Goodnight, angel," he said, pressing her nose like a button. "I love you."

He lay with her a while, and when Kasey finally fell asleep he turned on the nightlight and went out of the room, pausing once to look back at them.

He loved them so much it almost hurt. He hadn't realized you could love something so much. He thought back to the warm autumn day they were born. The doctor asked him if he wanted to assist in the delivery. Reluctantly, and scared out of his socks, he agreed. After donning rubber gloves and a yellow smock, he helped pull Jenny out of Emmy. She was so small and tiny. Kasey came next, diffidently, and when she finally came out he heard a distinctive "pop" and he immediately thought he had killed her, but the doctor reassured him that everything was fine, she had merely broke her collarbone coming out of the canal. Simple. And just like that they were a family—J.P., Emmy, and the twins. The doctor plopped the girls into Emmy's arms, their skin pink and still wet. Kasey was crying and J.P. cooed her, and she opened her eyes and smiled at him. The doctor and even Emmy told him it wasn't a smile, that babies couldn't smile; but deep down, he knew better.

J.P. walked down the dark hall and into his bedroom. Emmy was already in bed, reading some trashy novel by Nora Roberts. He fell into the bed next to her and moved his hand across her breasts. She was wearing a tight T-shirt and her nipples were poking through the thin fabric.

"The girls are sleeping," he whispered into her hair.

She cocked one sleepy eye at him, irritably, and set the book down across her chest.

"You expect me to just make love to you now?" she said, her voice still quavering.

"That's what I was thinking," he said, kissing her on the cheek.

"You questioned my ability as a mother tonight, J.P.," she railed at him accusingly. "You know we're supposed to be in this thing as a team. Sometimes I think you forget that."

"What's gotten into you, Emmy?"

She glared at him. "Maybe it's you that's gotten into me. Did you ever think of that?"

"Oh geez, you're not gettin' your period again, are you?"

"That's fucking great, J.P. God!"

"What do you want me to do, Emmy? Quit my job?"

"I never said that. It's just that I don't feel appreciated around here sometimes. You just come home and demand everything and never ask me how my day was. You never do that anymore."

"I swear, Emmy, sometimes I think you like to fight more than you like to fuck."

He knew he shouldn't have said it the minute it came out of his mouth.

"Oh, that's real classy, J.P.," Emmy almost shouted.

He got up and walked out of the room.

Downstairs it was dark and quiet. He went to the fridge and grabbed a beer and listlessly went into the living room.

He didn't understand why Emmy was jumping on him every chance she got...as if everything he did disgusted her. It wasn't like he didn't have other shit to worry about. He had a missing little girl who he believed was dead, who he prayed and prayed he'd find, and all Emmy could do was whine about how he wasn't there for her. She had developed into a world-class nag when it came to his job.

His job. His fucking job. And this fucking case. Five days had gone by now and nothing had turned up. Most of what he did everyday was make phone calls and answer the phone. The case was going nowhere and Mayor Dickhead was breathing down his neck to turn something up...fast. Five days Rose has been missing. Simply lost. Among the missing. It was mind numbing trying to figure out what happened to her. You go into the office everyday and sit at your desk, waiting for something to happen. And nothing ever happens. So you wait and go over the facts again and again. It's all a question of method. He knew that the key to good police work was a close observation of the facts—just the facts, but after struggling with the facts, he felt no closer to finding Rose Violette now than when he had first started. He felt trapped by the whole thing, trapped into a feeling of doing nothing, into being so inactive as to reduce the whole thing to almost nothing at all. He was a man condemned; condemned into trying to figure out a puzzle without having all the pieces, like Henty in Waugh's *The Man Who Liked* Dickens.

He had followed every lead, every fucking theory, and had cleared them all, and at this point, there didn't seem to be anyplace left to go. He was becoming disillusioned, for no matter how often he turned the case over inside himself, he got no closer to solving it. He knew in his heart that Dale killed Rose. But how could he prove it? The truth was, he couldn't prove it, and that's the worst fear of any cop. There were times when he just wanted to say Fuck it! and throw everything to the wind. Just walk away, lose himself in the woods or disappear somewhere down in Mexico like that writer Ambrose Bierce.

He took his beer and sat down in his favorite leather chair and flicked on the television. What was that Bruce Springsteen song? 57 channels and nothing on. He surfed his way through 56 of them and finally settled on AMC which was showing *Halloween 5*. It was mindless trash, but he needed that now. For the first time today, he was totally alone, among the shadows of dead thoughts and haunting repressions. He finished his beer and went and got another, searching through the cupboards for the ashtray that had the flowers printed on it. Emmy had bought it for him at a garage sale up in Hovland a couple years ago. She didn't like it when he smoked in the house now, but he needed one badly.

He sat in the blue glow of the television set and drank a few more beers and smoked a half dozen cigarettes until he started feeling a little better.

He was tired, haunted with the idea of sleep, but he knew he would never be able to fall asleep, not with all the shit that was throwing down inside his head. Not with the thought of little Rose Violette out there somewhere, or worse, dead.

He wished for one good night's sleep, the way we all slept when we were kids. He supposed that was the thing about growing up and marrying and having kids of your own, and then drinking too much and smoking too much and doing all the things you shouldn't. If you could sleep well at night, just one night out of seven, he didn't think any of it would be bad for you, except drinking too much, he supposed.

He thought about Danny and Sadie, remembering the good times they had that last summer after high school, so long ago; the summer before college and jobs and reality. Lots of things. Lots of good things. He remembered them sitting on the big rocks out on Artist's Point, looking across the bay at Spirit Island, talking about legends; the island was riddled with caves and the caves were rumored to be full of pirate treasure. He remembered the Friday and Saturday nights grabbing an Uff-da-Za down at Sven & Ole's Pizza Emporium or drinking beer down at the Bluffs or over at Indian Hill, wherever they could go without their parents finding out. The three of them had been practically inseparable back then.

It was good to have Danny back in Temperance again, he thought, with a feeling almost like deification. It was this feeling that had first brought them together when they were just kids. Danny had always had that athletic competency and the rough-and-readiness of character that J.P. would have given almost anything to have had himself. And he had always had a crush on Sadie. One day in school she'd snuck up behind him and put her hands over his eyes and whispered, "Guess who?" Her hands were long and white and thin. Smooth and white like ivory, only soft. And then, all of a sudden, she'd broken away and had run down the hallway laughing, her brown hair streaming out behind her, like gold in the sun.

In silence and from a long way off, desperately, hopelessly, J.P. guessed that he had loved her. But in the end, it was Danny who got the girl. Not that J.P. held that against him. After all, there's only one Lena for every Ole, as the saying goes. Anyway, he went on to find Emmy and they had fallen in love, but sometimes he missed those carefree days of high school, with nothing to worry about except the next big football game, or where the party was that weekend.

He didn't finish watching the movie. He felt buzzed enough now. Instead, he turned off the TV and went up to the bedroom. Emmy was lying on the bed, facing the wall, with the sheets pulled up to her chin.

J.P. went into the bathroom and slipped into his pajamas and brushed his teeth, staring at himself in the mirror. Putting on a little weight, he thought. His wedding ring was too tight these days.

He flipped off the bathroom light and glanced at the digital clock on the table beside his bed. Jesus Christ, it was almost two in the morning. He was already regretting staying up so late and drinking so much; he knew he'd pay for it in the morning.

Chapter Twenty

He woke up feeling better than he had in a long time. Maybe the fresh air and the open spaces of the North Shore were cleansing him somehow. He wasn't coughing up a lung and his brain wasn't fuzzy. And he wasn't craving a cigarette or coke either—not yet. But it was still early. He knew it would come later. That restless craving. It always did.

He took a cold shower and shaved. He was hurrying, nicked his chin with the twice-used disposable Bic and spent several minutes stopping the dot of blood with a Kleenex.

Then he suddenly remembered the dream last night and something glimmered—something that might have been the spark of an idea. He couldn't say exactly what it was. It wasn't concrete or defined enough to be called a suspicion or even intuition. Just a stray thought; entering his mind through a dream, and acted upon by reflex.

A grin moved across Danny's face.

Since he started this case, it had felt like there had been a mist behind his eyes, everything moving at a mercurial pace, and now everything was slowing down for the first time...

†††

J.P. was in the midst of uneasy dreams when the phone rang, startling him awake.

"What is it?" Emmy whispered.

"Nothing. Go back to bed."

J.P. reached across the bed and picked up the phone.

"This better be important," he grumbled into the receiver.

"We're you sleeping?" Danny asked.

"Yeah, it's five in the morning. I was sleeping."

"I know what happened."

J.P. sighed and tried to clear his brain. He had only been asleep for less than three hours.

"What the hell are you talking about, Danny?"

"Did you ever check Palisade Head?" Danny asked, his voice practically doing somersaults.

"What?"

"Palisade Head. Did you ever check it?"

"We checked it once."

"I mean in the water."

"No," J.P. said. "It's pretty fucking deep down there. We don't have the capabilities for that."

"I think maybe he threw her off the cliff. I think maybe he fucking threw her off the cliff into the lake. Can you meet me there?"

"Yah. I'll meet you there in an hour."

J.P. hung up the phone. He needed a cigarette to open his brain. Switch on the old "vacancy" sign.

"What is it?" Emmy asked.

He looked at her. God, he loved her.

"It's nothing. Go back to bed."

Emmy yawned deeply and tried to rub the sleep from her eyes.

"Who was that on the phone?"

"Danny."

"Is it a break in the case?" she mumbled.

"I don't know. Maybe."

"God, I hope so."

She didn't mean it as an insult, and J.P. knew that.

Emmy blinked her eyes and looked at him. She yawned again and rubbed her face with the palm of her hand.

"I'm sorry about fighting last night," she said.

"Yah. Me, too."

She moved her body up against his.

"I love you, J.P. Garski. You know that, don't you?"

She kissed him. He could smell the sweet morning breath on her lips. He ran his hand through her long burgundy hair. She kicked the covers off and rolled over on top of him.

He lifted the T-shirt off her and pulled the panties down her slim hips. She still had a killer body, even after having the twins. She reached under her legs and put him inside her. They moved together in unison and she came before he did.

"God, I love you," she whispered into his face.

He got out of bed and slipped his boots on.

"Gotta go. I'll see ya later."

He started walking out of the bedroom.

"Love ya, hon," Emmy called out to him.

"Love ya, too."

"Oh—" she said. "Can you do me a favor before you leave?"

"Yah. What is it?"

"Can you take the butter out of the fridge so it's soft enough to spread on the toast when the girls wake up for school?"

"Sure thing, Emmy."

He went down into the kitchen, took the butter out of the fridge, and slipped on his parka. It was going to be a cold one today. At least that's what the meteorologists had predicted on last night's news.

He went out back to the garage and got in the prowler.

It wouldn't start.

He swore under his breath and lit a cigarette. He tried starting it again, but it just wouldn't turn over.

He went back in the house and up the stairs. Emmy turned over on the bed.

"What is it?"

"Prowler needs a jump."

Chapter Twenty-one

By the time Danny got to Palisade Head, the wind had picked up and clotted blankets of charcoal clouds were hovering above the lake.

The air was fragile and the water far below was rumbling with eleven-foot rollers. There was nothing to see for miles but the distant lighthouse out on Marblehead Island flashing through the gray dawn sky and the limitless haze of water. The lake was like a living, breathing thing, crashing against the granite fangs below. The breadth and bigness of it, which had lifted Danny's spirit when he first saw it again a few short days ago, began to frighten him now. It spread out, went on so uncontrollably.

A few minutes later the sun rose in red, painting the lighthouse pink, turning the lake from gray to dazzling blue. There was spray in the air. An arrow of mallards pointing south honked overhead, signifying the end of autumn. The snow would be here soon, Halloween in a few days, Thanksgiving, the hysterical countdown to Christmas as the days darkened and gave way to long, tree-cracking nights.

J.P. walked up behind him. The wind flattened his orange parka against him. He looked like an orange version of the Michelin Man.

"Mornin'," J.P. said, taking out his pack of smokes. "Want one?"

Danny grimaced.

"Oops, sorry. I forgot you quit."

"Go ahead."

J.P. took out his Zippo and set fire to the cigarette. His face was red from the wind whipping against it.

The air was salty and fresh and bitter cold. Danny walked to the edge of the cliff. J.P. followed.

"Whoa, it's far down there," J.P. said.

Danny stared off into the vast horizon. For the first time since being called up here on this case, he felt balanced. He felt calm. He felt things were finally falling into place just as they were destined to.

"This is where it happened," he said. He had to talk loud to be heard over the wind on the surf. "I can feel it."

"If Dale threw Rose off here, we'll never find her," J.P. said, after a silence. "Unless she's still hooked up on the rocks down there."

Danny looked down at the crashing lake and turned his head into the wind and closed his eyes. The water on his face felt like tears.

J.P.'s voice became sepulchral. "Me and my boys will make a grid of a thousand square yards in each direction. If Dale was here, he must have left some traces—some clues—and we'll find 'em. We'll sift through every piece of trash we find."

"What about the lake?" Danny asked.

"I can get a team up from Dulut' to check it out, but if she's not on the rocks, then the current pulled her out, and we won't find her."

"Why's that?"

"It's autumn and the water temperatures are droppin' rapidly. When the lake's core temperature reaches thirty-two degrees, the water becomes a refrigerant and a human body does not produce gas to cause it to rise to the surface. The scientific word for it is *refloatation*. If she's in there, the body isn't likely to float to the surface until mid-or late May, when core water temperatures reach more than forty degrees and refloatation conditions occur. Superior is vast, but it does give up its dead eventually."

"Well, it's worth a shot," Danny said. "When can you get this team from Duluth up here?"

"Probably take 'bout two hours. Two or three hours."

"How long will it take you to search the grid?"

"I've got two deputies. I'll pull 'em out here, but it'll take at least a day, maybe more."

"Alright," Danny said. "I'm going back into town. I'll call you later this afternoon."

Chapter Twenty-two

Dale didn't sleep well, he did not sleep long. The chair in front of the TV was old and uncomfortable. There were dreams he didn't remember. At seven o'clock he woke up, his sleep-swollen face bent discordantly into the plump muscle-hammock of his right shoulder. He stretched miserably out of thick, rubbery sleep, and for a moment he sat heavily upright, rubbing his eyes with the clenched backs of his fingers.

He got to his feet with one determined motion and stumbled down the dark cold hallway to the little dirty bathroom where he quickly showered and shaved.

The fat whale was still sleeping in the bedroom. He smiled when he thought about what he did to her last night, then he went into the kitchen, poured himself a glass of orange juice, swallowed three Advil to still his headache and a Nexium to quell his aching stomach.

He didn't want to go to work today, but he knew that it might draw more suspicion from that slick city cop and that Andy Griffith buddy of his if he didn't.

Still, the thought of sweating away eight hours in that dungeon of a factory didn't do anything to improve his mood.

His arm still ached where that fat fuck bartender had hit him with the baseball bat last night.

He hiccupped and almost threw up.

Shit.

He walked out of the trailer and got in his pickup and put the Stones' *Exile On Main St.* in the truck's CD player. Old Mick started singing about getting his rocks off. What a life. All that fresh pussy every night.

It was a half hour drive up to the taconite factory in Croftville and by the time Dale got there, Mick had moved on to Sweet Virginia. Yeah, what a life. Some life.

†††

The alarm clock started buzzing at six. It went through Sadie's brain like an SOS. She had exactly an hour to get the kids up and ready for school.

She reached over the bed and hit the snooze button. What the hell, it wouldn't hurt to get a few more moments of precious shut-eye.

Ten minutes later the alarm went off again.

Onk, Onk, Onk, Onk.

She swore under her breath, slammed her hand down on the clock, and rolled out of the protective cocoon of the warm bed.

It was cold in the house. Her father didn't believe in turning on the heat until after Thanksgiving, no matter how far the mercury in the backyard thermometer dipped.

Sadie turned on the television and clicked on the local weather station. A funny computerized voice came on over the map of the state and announced it was going to be cloudy today.

What's new, Sadie grumbled. Cloudy, with a cold front moving in, a high temperature of forty-five.

She turned off the TV and went into the bathroom. When she turned on the light, it pierced her eyes. She yawned heavily and rubbed them with the meaty part of her hand below the thumb. She turned on the shower to let the water warm up, slipped out of her pajamas and stood naked before the mirror.

She smiled. Not bad for an old lady. Thirty-seven and she still had a nice figure. Not as nice as it was when she was seventeen, but still, not bad after having three kids. Her stomach was flat, just a tiny surplus right below the belly-button, but not bad. At least she didn't have any cellulite anywhere. She could thank her mother for that. It was hereditary. She'd heard that on Oprah the other day.

She pirouetted a little to the side and looked at her ass. It was right where it should be.

The room was filling with steam now. She had forgotten to turn on the fan. She turned it on and stepped delicately into the shower. The water burned her. She gasped and turned it down until she got the temperature just right and then she let the tiny warm pellets just beat against her back.

Ten minutes later when she stepped out of the shower, she instantly froze. She saw in the mirror her big pink nipples pointing straight out. God, they could cut diamonds. That was the one thing she hated about her body—her nipples. They were huge and just didn't seem to fit in with rest of her rather small breasts. She'd had to wear bras with extra padding since high school to prevent anyone from getting a glimpse at her *NHO's*.

She reached for her bathrobe and snuggled deep inside it. Then she went through her usual morning routine—brush teeth, put lotion on legs and tummy, blow-dry hair, clip toenails, and get dressed. Today she felt like wearing her extra big sweater, the one she got from Kyle a few years back. It was going to be cold today. She threw the sweater over her head and picked out her favorite jeans, some warm socks, and her black mid-heel Thom McAn's.

Time to wake up the kids. Every day it was like World War III. She went down to Jeffrey's room first. He had been getting better about waking up for school. This morning he got up with just a slight grumble and went down the hall to the bathroom to take a shower.

The girls were the tough ones. Sadie was lucky today though, she only had to wake Kimberly. Leah was in Kindergarten and had every other Friday off.

Kimmey woke up with a bawl like a lion cub. "I don't want to go to school today!"

"But it's Friday today, honey," Sadie whispered, trying to keep her cool. "It's the last day of the week."

"I'm not going!" Kimmey whined stubbornly.

"You have to, honey. Now, c'mon, up and at 'em."

"No!"

"Do you want me to pick out your clothes, or do you want to do it?"

"I'll do it," Kimmey said reluctantly. "But I'm still not going to school today."

"Mom!" Jeffrey called from the shower. "What time is it?"

Sadie looked at the *100 and One Dalmatians* clock on Kimberly's dresser. "It's six-twenty-eight."

"Tell me when it's six-thirty-four," Jeffrey called out. "I want to get out then."

"Okay," Sadie said. Then to Kimmey: "C'mon, start getting dressed."

Kimberly screamed.

"Sssh," Sadie whispered. "You'll wake Leah."

Leah, amazingly, was still sleeping soundly and snugly in the other bed.

"It's not fair that she gets to stay home," Kimberly said.

"Leah's still in Kindergarten," Sadie whispered. "When you were in Kindergarten last year you got to stay home on Fridays. Now get dressed."

Kimmey rolled out of bed and rummaged in her dresser for some clothes. When she was finally dressed, she followed her mother down the hall to the bathroom.

"Jeffrey, it's six-thirty-four," Sadie called out.

Jeffrey turned off the shower and stepped out. When he saw his little sister standing there, he threw a towel around his naked waist and scowled at her.

"What are you looking at, fatty?"

"Shut up," Kimmey fired back.

"Knock it off, you two," Sadie said.

Jeffrey stormed off to his room and Sadie started combing the nest that was her daughter's hair. Kimberly had Sadie's beautiful long hair, but it was a pain in the ass to deal with every morning.

"Ouch!" Kimmey screamed. "Don't pull so hard!"

"I'm not."

"Ouch! You are, too."

Sadie suddenly thought about a quote she read in last month's Good Housekeeping: *I regard (parenting) as the hardest, most complicated, anxiety ridden, sweat-and-blood producing job in the world.*

She didn't remember who said it, but she couldn't agree more. Being a mom, there were so many highs and so many lows, tearing your hair out wondering if you're doing it right, if you're a good parent; what your kids are going to turn out like when it's all said and done. The doubt ringing in your ears, the happiness and the pain, the struggles and the little victories. Not all women are cut out for it, no matter what the bible says.

When she finally got Jeffrey and Kimmey downstairs and into the kitchen, the daily battle about what to eat for breakfast began. Despite Sadie's wishes, Jeffrey demanded Capn' Crunch. She gave in today and let him have it. Kimmey liked fruit, which was fine with Sadie. She dished her up some fresh strawberries and blueberries and gave each of them a vitamin C.

Sadie's father came down the stairs already dressed for the day.

"We gonna carve pumpkins tonight before you run off to the big Homecoming game?" he said jovially.

"Uh-huh," the kids replied in unison.

Sadie's mother came down in her robe and started a pot of coffee. She kissed the kids and asked how Sadie slept.

"Fine," Sadie lied.

"Want some coffee?"

"Yeah, that'd be good."

The kids finished eating and bussed their dishes to the counter. Sadie never got a chance to finish her coffee.

"Did you do your homework last night?" she asked Kimmey.

"Yep," Kimmey said, slinging her backpack over her shoulder.

Sadie didn't have to worry about Jeffrey's schoolwork. He was doing just fine in school and he always did his homework as soon as he got it. He was a worry-wart just like his father had been.

"Love you, Mom," Kimmey said, kissing Sadie on the lips.

The kids went out the door with a flutter of coats, hats, mittens, and goodbyes and Kimmey followed her big brother down the long driveway to the bus stop.

"Go get 'em, kids!" their grandfather called out.

Sadie went to the window and stood there watching them at the bus stop. They lived in a good neighborhood with lots of kids and the bus stop was always packed, but still she worried just a little bit whenever Jeffrey and Kimmey were out of her sight. Especially with the whole Rose Violette thing. Sure, everybody in town who wasn't a Johnny-come-lately believed Dale Jacob did something to his little girl, but what if he hadn't? What if there was a monster out there waiting to prey on the next unsuspecting child?

"Don't worry about the kids so much, Sadie," her father said from over her shoulder, seeming to read her thoughts. "They're fine. When I was a kid we walked to school. By ourselves. Heck, we walked everywhere. Nowadays parents don't let their kids go anywhere by themselves, they're smothering their own children and don't even know it."

Nice, Sadie thought. She hated when her father tried to tell her how to parent her own kids, but the worst part of it was, deep down, she knew he was right.

She looked out the window again and watched Jeffrey and Kimmey get on the bus, and then they were gone, absorbed in a multi-colored stream of school-age children.

Chapter Twenty-three

The wind was whistling like a screaming bullet, spilling the loose cornstalks across the highway from picked-out fields where frost now glittered like diamonds on the fence posts.

Danny stopped at a diner just outside Devil Track Lake and used the drive-up payphone in the parking lot.

O'Malley answered on the fourth ring.

"How's it going, Pierce?" O'Malley said in his thick voice.

"Peachy," Danny replied.

O'Malley was a hallowed, hyper-intelligent man, an eternal student of something. He had a son who was a cop in Minneapolis and a small daughter named Bobbie who had Down syndrome and a wife who was a high-buck lawyer in Saint Paul.

"You gotta get a cell phone, Pierce," O'Malley said. "I've been trying to get a hold of you up there all morning."

"Fire me."

"I can't fire you. Or else I already would have. What's going on up there?"

"She's dead."

O'Malley's voice dropped a notch. "The little girl?"

"Uh-huh."

"Can you prove it?"

"No. Not yet."

"The heckya mean? Got any leads?"

"Couple."

"No body?"

"No. But I think she may have been dumped in the lake. We got a team from Duluth checking it out."

"Well, you better find a body, Danny Boy. No body, no case."

He hung up with O'Malley and threw another thirty-five cents in the payphone. There was black smoke rising above the tree line and the smell of smoked fish. Far off in the hills came the crackle of guns. Deer season. When he was a kid it was one of his favorite times of the year, sneaking off into the woods with his father before the sun came up, the silence of the forest, the kill and their freezer in the garage heaped with meat.

J.P. answered his cell phone and said hello in his buoyant way.

"Did you find anything up there yet?" Danny asked, skipping any pleasantries.

J.P. sighed heavily, all the buoyancy gone from his voice, and Danny knew what the answer was.

"Not much," J.P. said. "But the good thing is there's not a lot of foot traffic up here at the Head. Especially this time of year. Not too many tourists know about it. It's not like there's a stand on the side of the highway sellin' T-shirts. The few things that we found; a gum wrapper, a few cigarette butts, a used condom. That's about it. We'll run 'em all through the lab just the same."

"What about that water team from Duluth?" Danny asked.

"They're still out there on the lake. I'm lookin' at 'em now. Done a couple dives; haven't found anythin' yet."

"What about on the rocks?"

"Nothin'. No blood; nothin'."

Danny heard another gunshot and a train whistle in the distance—the ten-fifty to Silver Bay, he imagined.

"I still think he did it up there."

"Yah, me, too," J.P. said.

"It's just a matter of proving it."

"Yah," J.P. said. "There's always that."

Chapter Twenty-four

Danny was craving a cigarette. Being off nicotine was like being in a daze. Almost like being high. Colors stood out more sharply, but everything else was gray, like being stuck in a cloud. His head was spinning. Everything was moving too quickly. He needed to stop and think things through.

It was lunchtime and downtown Temperance River was busy, its stores overrun with tourists, the streets wet, brown leaves in the gutters. He waited at the stoplight on Minnesota Street and then turned left. There was a little park up on 2nd Avenue and he pulled the car over and watched a mother playing with her little girl. The girl was climbing the blue monkey-bars and hanging off them, doing gymnastic routines, soft and smooth and almost weightless.

It was nice to see kids playing in the park. Sadly, you hardly saw that anymore. The girl's mother was sitting on a bench nearby with an open paperback novel in her lap.

Danny got out of the car and the cool breeze hit him like a tonic. He walked across the grass to the play area. When he approached the bench, the woman reading the paperback looked up at him.

She swallowed hard when she saw him, and stood up from the bench. She was wearing faded blue jeans and a bright orange down coat leaking feathers at the seams. The cold had brought a rosiness to her cheeks, striking against the downy whiteness of her skin.

"What are you doing here, Danny?" Sadie asked in a shrill, accusatory voice.

"I was just getting some air," Danny said, his voice stuttering.

Sadie looked like she didn't believe him.

"Is that your kid?" he asked, nodding to the little girl on the monkey bars.

"Yes."

After a wordless pause of several moments, she started to move away from him.

"Wait," he called out. "Sadie, wait."

She turned back and faced him again.

"Is this just another coincidence, Danny?"

He put his hands in his pockets, hunched his shoulders. "I was just driving by and I saw the girl playing and it was nice. I didn't know it was you at first. Sitting here on the bench."

She stared hard at him. The new skin over his bruised eye was pink. Those eyes. Boring into her.

She wondered if she should be angry, but it was a drifting thought, and she discovered that she was somewhat flattered and pleased by his presence.

"I'm sorry I was so rude to you the other night," she said in a voice that was not quite steady, as if she was not sure if she should feel happiness or fear or wonder or guilt. "I had no right to be. It's just—it's just I've had a pretty bad time of it lately."

"I know," Danny said. "I heard about what happened. With your husband. I'm sorry." He was trying his hardest to be sympathetic; consolatory, in a gruff sort of way, which was the only way he knew how.

"Figures you would know," she said. She moved her hands finely, precisely as she spoke, her fingertips grazing her neck. "Everybody in this town knows." She let out a humorless laugh. "This town. You'd think I'd be used to it by now." She looked up into his eyes again. "I was happily married with three kids, Danny. My life was torn apart when my husband died."

"I'm sorry, Sadie."

She wiped away little tears with the heels of her hands.

The girl climbed down from the monkey-bars and ran over to them.

"Are you okay, Mommy?" she asked, pulling at the pocket of Sadie's jeans.

She was wearing Oshkosh overalls, a fluffy pink coat, cowboy boots and a wool stocking cap pulled over her head; a tiny blonde head that had the advantage of dimples and naturally curly hair.

"Mommy's just fine, honey," Sadie said, wiping away the tears. "I was just talking to an old friend of mine. This is Danny."

The girl held out her tiny hand. "Hello, Danny. I'm Leah. Did you make my Mommy cry?" Her singsong delivery blunted the edge of her interrogation.

"I hope not." Danny smiled down at her and shook her hand. "What a pretty name. How old are you, Leah?"

"I'm five." Her eyes sparked and she pushed her bangs away from her face. She turned away from Danny and addressed her mother. "Mommy,

Mommy, can we go to the bakery now?" she asked, pulling on Sadie's sleeve. "You promised. You did."

Sadie looked up at Danny. "Leah's in Kindergarten. She has every other Friday off. I take her to the bakery. It's our little tradition." She smiled and rubbed the little girl's head. "Isn't it, pumpkin?"

"Uh-huh," Leah said. "You can come with us if you want to, Danny."

A faint flame trembled on Sadie's cheek. "I'm sure Danny's much too busy, honey," she said, trying hard not to catch Danny's eyes.

"Well—" Danny looked at Sadie for any sign of affirmation.

"Can he come with us, Mommy?" Leah pleaded. "Can he? It'll be fun."

"Sure."

She smiled one of her old smiles then; breathtakingly resplendent and genuine. And it was almost the old Sadie. So very close to the old Sadie.

Leah skipped on ahead of them and they walked without speaking, the only sound the dry rustle of fallen leaves under their feet.

"So you're a mom," Danny said, because he had to say something. "What's it like?"

"It's like nothing I ever dreamed," Sadie said heartily. "It's the best feeling in the world. And it's pretty scary, too. They grow up so fast. Everything you do with your kids lives on in their memories as well as yours. Everything's more valid because it's shared. A hundred years from now, it won't matter what car you drove or what house you lived in, but it will matter how you raised your children."

"She's a cute kid. Takes after her mother."

Sadie smiled at him out of the corner of her mouth. "You're a smooth smoothie, Danny Pierce. You always were."

There was another long silence.

"I heard you lived in Hawaii for a while?" he asked. "On a military base?"

"Yeah."

"What was that like?"

"Nice. Real nice. But I missed the cold and snow while I was there. There's something about Minnesota winters, you know? We like to complain about them, but when you're away, they're like a siren calling you back home. So when my husband died I came back, to Temperance, and then I sank back into the warm, safe ooze I used to call home, like a monkey in a zoo. I'm living with my parents over on Benjamin. It's okay and I'm thankful to them for taking us in, but when I was young I always had to fight so hard to be independent. It's hard to surrender that again."

Sadie asked him why he became a cop. It was the inevitable question. Everyone asked him sooner or later.

"It pays the bills," he said. "Like being a dentist or fixing shoes. That's all it is."

Sadie listened intently, watching his face, soaking him in, as if her eyes were acting on their own accord. That little something from long ago still responded to him—his voice, his self-possession, the scent of him, the same after all these years—surprised her. Even Leah faded a little, she was concentrating so hard on him, and she could almost pretend that they were the only two people in the world. Like it had been in high school.

The afternoon had a crisp, leafy smell. A lawn mower droned a few houses down and the air was cool and charged. A brisk fall Friday, and the sidewalks were crowded with people. Sadie waved to all the neighbors who were out raking their front lawns and there was a fragrance of burning leaves. It was like a picture out of a Norman Rockwell painting.

They drifted down Main Street, pausing now and then to inspect the shop windows which were decked out with Halloween displays and poster board signs cheering on the high school football team. The Hi-Quality bakery was down on Third and Main. They went in and were greeted by the warm scent of fried dough. The floors were wood and creaked comfortably underfoot, a throwback to the bakeries of the 1950s.

An abbreviated woman with a tangle of gray hair called out to them: "Sadie, honey, how the heck ya doin'?"

"I'm doing real good, Marian," Sadie said with a big smile. "How are you?"

"I'm really doing super there, thanks." Marian Van Campen looked down at Leah who was scoping out the baked goodies in the big display cases. "And how's my favorite girl?"

"Good," Leah said, all business. "Can I have a cinnamon twist?"

"Good choice," Marian said, and she reached under and pulled out the biggest twist in the case. "Here ya are, honey."

Leah took the twist and almost started jumping up and down in anticipation of sinking into it.

"You goin' trick-or-treatin' tomorrow night?" Marian asked her.

"Uh-huh."

"Watch out for all those ghosts and goblins," she said, making faces at Leah, popping her eyes, making a clownish O of her mouth.

Leah laughed. "There's no such thing as ghosts and goblins."

Marian was shocked. "There's not?"

"Nope. My Mommy told me."

Marian smiled at Sadie and Danny. "Who's your friend there, Sadie?"

"This is Danny."

"Father God and Sonny Jesus! You're not Nancy Pierce's little boy, are ya?"

Danny nodded.

"My, have you grown up. Me and your mom go way back. A lot of years. How she doin' anyway? Haven't seen her round much. The last I heard you moved down to the cities. You back visiting, or are you plannin' on stayin' a spell?"

"He's up here to help find Rose Violette," Sadie put in, almost apolitically.

"You a cop or somethin'?"

"Yeah," Danny said with a smile, "or somethin'."

Marian looked at them conspiratorially. "That whole thing just frosts my butt!" she said, clicking her tongue in her mouth after she'd said it. "And you wanna know the worst part? The absolute cat's pajamas? Dale and Michelle still walk round town like nothing happened. That just steams my bean!"

An old guy in a blaze orange hunting jacket tapped on the display case. "You finished yacking down there, Marian? I'd like a jelly if ain't too much trouble."

"You just cool your jewels down there, Mike," Marian scolded him. "I'll be down there in a sec. Those jellies ain't goin' nowhere."

Sadie and Danny smiled at each other and Marian let out a loud laugh. It was a good laugh; a country laugh, ebullient and deep.

"Now what can I get 'cha, Sadie?"

"I'll take one of those crème-filled long johns."

"How about you, dearie?" Marian asked Danny.

"One of those chocolate-covered doughnuts will do."

Marian rang them up and Danny paid.

"It was real nice seeing you again," Marian said. "Say hi to your mom next time you see her. Tell her to stop in once in a while."

"I will."

They took their doughnuts and went into the back room where Leah took charge like a drill sergeant.

"We always sit in the same spot," she said, pulling out chairs for Sadie and Danny.

They sat and ate their doughnuts and Sadie kept sneaking proud little glances at her daughter.

Danny watched both of them and he felt good. It felt like he was part of something secret and special.

Suddenly, Sadie was pointing a finger at him. He leaned forward. Leah was busy stuffing her mouth full of sticky doughnut.

"Your gun," Sadie whispered.

The butt of the Sig Sauer was sticking out of his coat. He looked down and pushed it back toward his ribs and pulled the coat over it. He was sure Leah hadn't seen it.

"Sorry," he lip-synced to Sadie.

When they finished eating they went out on the street again and started back to the park. The afternoon was large and empty.

"Can we go to the lake, Mommy?" Leah asked. "Can we? Can we?"

"Okay," Sadie said. "But only for a little bit. We got to get back before your brother and sister come home from school."

"Can Danny come too?"

Sadie looked at Danny. She was hoping he would say yes.

"Okay," Danny said, and they started walking toward the lake.

It was a glorious day and the sun was still hanging around making it feel warmer than it actually was. A promenade had been built along the waterfront, with park benches as box seats to watch the freighters and boats out on the lake. Danny bought them popcorn from a vendor near the breakwater and Leah giggled in unrestrained glee as she fed the seagulls and watched them cluster and squawk for more.

Danny and Sadie sat on a bench and watched her, simultaneously dipping their fingers into a bag of popcorn. It was like the old days, back in high school, when they went to the movies at the Apache 6 Theater and shared a big tub of greasy corn.

The waterfront was rich with the smell of fish and the sound of bells and horns and lapping water. They sat in silence for a few crimson moments, watching the lake and laughing at Leah as she chased the gulls. The sun was over the lake, sweeping across the water, and the waves broke it up like pieces of gold.

"When I was a little girl," Sadie said in a voice so low it was hardly more than a whisper, "my dad used to tell me it was gold out there on the water, and that sometimes mermaids came up and stole it." She smiled. "I've never seen one though."

"It's beautiful out there," Danny said.

He made her nervous and unsure and dreamy as a teenager. She thought back to their first date—*Top Gun* at the Apache—way back in high school and tried to remember what it was like at the beginning. Was it love at first sight, if there is such a thing? Was it like that when she had first met Kyle at that dance on the Army base? She couldn't remember anymore.

She looked out at the lake again. The wind started to move the water as a current pulled the waves to the windward shore of Little Marais Island.

The breeze had a chill to it. Sadie hugged herself, and Danny, without making anything of it, moved to block the wind. They sat in that crimson silence for a few soft minutes, listening to the bells and horns and lapping water, until finally Sadie called Leah over.

The girl protested about having to leave, but Sadie explained to her that they had to get back before Jeffrey and Kimberly got home from school. Jeffrey had his heart set on going to the football game tonight.

"You going to the game tonight?" Sadie asked Danny.

"What game?"

"The big homecoming game. Didn't you see all the poster boards in the shop windows?"

"Is that tonight?"

"Can ya come with us, can ya?" Leah practically begged him.

"Leah!" Sadie said, flicking a glance back over her shoulder at Danny. "Danny's probably busy tonight."

"Are you busy tonight, Danny?" Leah asked.

Danny looked at Sadie, trying to gauge her.

"You don't have to work at the Wells tonight?" he asked.

"Nah," Sadie said. "I get every other weekend off. Keeps me sane."

"Do you mind?"

Sadie looked away. "Sure, you can come if you want. The game starts at seven."

"Well, if you don't mind."

"I don't mind, Danny."

"Okay, I'll pick you up at a quarter to."

"You remember where my parents live?"

"How could I forget?"

They stumbled toward a clumsy goodbye and Danny stood there and watched as Sadie and her daughter drifted down the ruddy street until the afternoon shadows swallowed them whole and they disappeared into the leafy silence.

Chapter Twenty-five

Sadie got home just before the bus dumped Jeffrey and Kimmey off at the end of the driveway. They came blasting into the house and threw their coats and backpacks on the floor and sat down in front of the TV in the living room to watch cartoons.

"How was school today?" Sadie asked.

"Good," Kimmey said.

Jeffrey was already lost inside *SpongeBob SquarePants*. The little yellow Nazi annoyed Sadie to no end.

"Did you eat lunch today, Jeffrey?"

He didn't answer. He was sitting on the floor, cross-legged, hunched forward, as if the TV was sucking him in.

"Jeffrey, what did you have for lunch?" she asked him again.

"Hot ham and cheese," he murmured, without looking at her.

She should send them outside to play. It'd been getting dark so early these days. But when the first SpongeBob ended, Jeffrey and Kimmey wanted to watch the second one, already coming on, and Sadie yielded.

"After that one I want the TV turned off."

Her father came into the room. "I thought we were gonna carve pumpkins?" he asked the kids.

"Yeah, yeah," they replied.

"Well, listen to your mother then," he said, in a low tone. "Ya can't carve pumpkins with that TV set blaring alla da time."

Sadie left the kids with her dad and went upstairs and took a shower. Then she got dressed and put on make-up. It wasn't perfect, but it would do. She had over three hours to kill before Danny was supposed to pick her up for the game. She felt like she was in high school again, getting ready for a big date. She went back downstairs and the kids were in the kitchen with their grandfather. Her mom had gone to the IGA to buy Halloween candy for tomorrow night. Her father was at the kitchen table, busy carving a jack-o'-lantern. Jeffrey and Kimmey were helping him, sticking their little arms into the top of the pumpkin and pulling out the guts. Leah was bored already and lobbying for Dr. Pepper.

"What time's the game?" Sadie's father asked her.

"Seven."

Leah finally got her way and popped the top off a can of Dr. Pepper. "Danny's coming with us," she said, proud to know something her brother and sister didn't.

Sadie's father stopped carving.

"Danny who?"

"Pierce."

"Who's Danny Pierce?" Jeffrey asked suddenly.

"He's Mommy's friend," Leah said.

Sadie's father was watching her quizzically. "Isn't that the boy you used to run around with in high school?"

Sadie knew her father remembered Danny. How couldn't he?

"Yes," she said calmly.

"We saw him in the park today," Leah added.

"Why does he have to come?" Jeffrey said, letting out a tense breath.

"He's nice," Leah said.

"I don't care, fatty," Jeffrey shouted. "I'm not going to the game if that man's coming!"

"Jeffrey!" Sadie said. "You don't even know him."

"I don't want to know him! I'm not going!"

"We've been talking about going to this game for weeks. You're going."

"Am not."

"Why do you always do this? Huh? Every time we get halfway excited about something, you have to ruin it."

"Maybe I should go live someplace else!"

"Don't say that, Jeffrey."

He was crying now. "No! Get away from me. I want to go live someplace else!"

He ran out of the kitchen crying and went upstairs to his room.

Sadie looked around. The girls were just sitting there, quiet, not looking anywhere or saying anything. Her father looked sad.

"I guess I better go talk to him," Sadie said, knowing she'd handled her son badly.

†††

He was sitting in a beanbag chair in front of his TV playing Madden on his Xbox. There were tears stuck to his cheeks and his eyes were red.

"Can we talk for a sec," Sadie said, sticking her head inside the door.

Jeffrey turned off the game. "Sure."

Sadie went in and sat down on the floor beside him. Whenever she looked at her son she saw her husband in the boy. She missed Kyle very much. She missed his smile, his laugh; his dark green eyes. Jeffrey was a carbon copy.

"I'm sorry, Jeffrey."

"For what?"

"For making you feel bad."

He looked up at her and swiped at his eyes with the inside of his wrists. "Are you going to marry that man?"

The question shocked her. "No. No, I just ...he's just an old friend I knew from high school. Before I met your dad."

"Mom?"

"Yeah?"

"Are you lonely?"

She felt like crying. The tears almost came.

"Yes, Jeffrey. I am kinda lonely sometimes."

"But you still have us," Jeffrey said, and it almost broke her heart. She felt her eyes getting watery and there was an actual pain in her stomach.

"I know I do, Jeffrey. And I love you and your sisters more than anything in the whole world. I hope you will always remember that. No matter what happens."

Jeffrey saw the tears in his mother's eyes and his little face scrunched up and he started rubbing his own eye, trying to hide the tears.

"Hey, it's okay," Sadie said, squatting down next to him so her eyes were level with his. Suddenly he looked far younger than his nine years, and the sadness in his eyes tore at her. "I know you miss Daddy, Jeffrey. So do I. But we have to be strong—together."

Jeffrey's jaw trembled. "I'm okay, Mom."

Chapter Twenty-six

It was only quarter to four and Danny had the rest of the afternoon before the game to kill so he drove over to Apache Wells. The same bartender from the other night was working. Every move he made behind the bar was quick and agile despite his large size. There was a vivacity about him, a cheerfulness. He acted as if he was so habituated to his work that he never gave it a thought, even actually enjoyed it.

The rest of the place was almost deserted, except for a pair of old purple-noses soaking up their social security checks at the far end of the bar.

A George Jones tune was playing out of the box in the corner. *Never Bit a Bullet Like This.*

The big bartender came down the bar. "What can I get 'cha, pal?"

"Bud," Danny said.

He reached under the bar and set the bottle down in front of Danny. "Weren't you in here the other night?" he asked, wiping the bar with elaborate indifference.

Danny nodded his head and took a sip of beer.

The bartender spoke more aloud to himself than to Danny. "You're the guy that was bugging Sadie."

"I was just talking to her."

"You from Temperance? I haven't seen you around."

"I lived here when I was a kid."

"What do you do now?"

"I'm a cop."

"No shit?"

"No shit."

"You up here on business or pleasure?"

"Business."

The bartender flashed Danny another suspicious glance. Then he understood. "Jacob?"

"Yeah. What can you tell me about him?"

"A real prick."

"Does he come in here a lot?"

"Alla the time. He comes after work and starts drinking beer and double-shots of whiskey and bothering people. Thinks he's a real ladies' man."

"Is he?"

"Nah. Most of the girls are afraid of him. 'Specially after all this business with his missing girl. You want another?"

"Not yet."

Danny reached into his coat pocket for a smoke, then he remembered he quit.

"Lookin for something?" the bartender asked.

"Nah. What's your name?"

"Jake. What do people call you?"

"Danny."

"Nice to meet ya, Danny. I didn't mean to get on your case about Sadie, but someone has to look out for her. 'Specially in a dice like this. It gets a little rowdy in here sometimes."

Danny nodded. "I'll take another now."

Jake reached under the bar again and came up with a fresh Bud. "On the house."

"Thanks. So what about Jacob? How can I find out more about him?"

Just then, the door swung open and a tall, raw-boned bald guy walked in. He went down the bar, and looked at Danny suspiciously out of the corner of his eye.

Jake pointed down the bar at the bald guy. "You want to know more about Jacob, ask him. As far as I can tell, that guy is the only friend Dale Jacob has left in this town."

The bald guy called out from the other end of the bar: "Pour me a pitcher of Leinie's, will ya, Jake?"

"Excuse me," Jake said to Danny.

"No problem."

After a few seconds Danny picked up his fresh beer and went down the bar.

The bald guy already had his mitts into the free peanuts and he swung another glance at Danny. "Do I know you, pal?"

"I don't think so," Danny said, taking the stool on the bald guy's left, facing him dully.

"You a fag?"

Danny laughed. "No, I'm not a fag."

"Whatta want then?"

"I'm a cop," Danny said and took a sip of his beer.

"I didn't do nothin'," the bald guy stammered defensively.

"I didn't say you did."

"Well, what do you want then?"

"I want to ask you a few questions about Dale Jacob."

"Ah, man, I don't know nothin' about Dale's kid, man," the bald guy said.

"There was a party at Dale's place the night before his daughter disappeared. Were you there?"

The bald guy didn't answer.

"What's your name?" Danny asked.

"Stevie," he replied, his eyes fixed on the top of the bar. "Stevie McIntire."

"Got any warrants, Stevie McIntire?"

Stevie winced. "What the fuck you talkin' about, man?"

"Look," Danny said, popping a handful of peanuts in his mouth. "We can make this easy or we can make this difficult. It's your choice, Stevie."

"Easy's my middle name," Stevie said, with a gentle drunken unction.

"Good." Danny finished his beer and set the bottle down on the bar. "Mind if I mooch a beer?"

"Help yourself, man."

Danny nodded to Jake for a glass and then poured himself one from Stevie's pitcher.

"So—were you there, Stevie?" Danny asked. "Were you at Dale's trailer the night it happened?"

Stevie nervously lit a cigarette from the pack in front of him on the bar. "Suppose you want to mooch one of these, too?" he asked, holding up the cigarette.

Danny shook his head.

Stevie gulped again at his beer. "Yeah, I was there that night, but nothing happened, man. I swear it. I swear on my mother's eyes."

"I don't know your mother."

"What?"

"Nothing. So you were there at Dale's trailer?"

"Yeah. We were just drinkin' a few brews and gettin' a little high." Stevie looked up at Danny nervously—stupidly. "You ain't gonna arrest me for that, are ya?"

"Go on, Stevie."

"Go on with what? Man, I already told you nothin' happened."

"Did you see Rose?"

"Yeah, she was there. Dale and Michelle kept yellin' at her to go to bed. Then she did and I didn't see her again the rest of the night."

"How late were you there?"

"One. Maybe two."

"When you left the trailer that night, did you see anyone hanging around outside?"

"Nope."

"You think they're good parents; Dale and Michelle?"

Stevie laughed. "I wouldn't say that. But what do I know? I don't got no kids."

"You think someone took her?"

"Shit, man, I don't know. What the fuck do I look like, Sherlock fuckin' Holmes?"

"You look like a piece of shit to me," Danny said. "What do you know about Michelle?"

"I don't know, man," Stevie said. "I know her parents live in some new development up by the overlook. That's all I know."

"You're not holding out on me, are you, Stevie?"

"Man, I'm workin' with ya on this thing, but I...I just don't know. I drink a few beers with Dale once in a while. What the fuck ya want from me?"

"There's a little girl missing, Stevie; maybe dead. And if I find out you had anything to do with it—if you helped Dale in any way—I'm going to fry your fucking hillbilly ass."

"Man, I told ya all I know."

Danny stood up and scraped back the bar stool. "See ya around, Stevie."

"Hey, man, do me a favor and don't tell Dale that I talked to ya. He'd be really pissed and I'm not looking to get my teeth kicked in for nothin'."

Danny put a ten on the bar. "You better stop worrying about Dale so much, Stevie, and start worrying about me."

Chapter Twenty-seven

Michelle Violette's parents lived out in a newer development at the base of the Cedar Hills Overlook. It was a nice house, a neat little Cape Cod, which surprised Danny. He was expecting something a little more in the vein of their daughter's run-down trailer.

He went up to the front door and rang the bell. A few moments later the door opened and a young girl answered. She was about fifteen or sixteen and very pretty, with blonde hair fluffed up and wearing a blue and gold Temperance River High cheerleading outfit.

"Your mom or dad around?" Danny asked the girl.

"Hold on," she said and left the door open.

Danny could smell something cooking inside the house. A moment later a middle-aged woman about fifty came to the door. She was wearing an expensive velour lounge suit and her hair was dyed a nice shade of blonde.

"Yes?" she asked, her eyes blank, her round face grinning uncertainly. The man at her front door was a stranger to her, and strangers in

Temperance River were rare once the fleeting summer was over. "Can I help you?"

"My name's Danny Pierce. I work for the BCA."

"I beg pardon."

"The Bureau of Criminal Apprehension. Do you have a minute, ma'am?"

Danny heard a voice call out from somewhere inside the house. "What is it, Linda?"

Linda Violette looked over her shoulder. "It's a policeman, Frank. At least I think he is."

"Well, let him in."

"Come in, please," she said to Danny.

"Thank you. Should I take my shoes off?"

"No, that's alright," Linda Violette said.

She led him to a well-furnished living room with windows opening on the strip of lawn between the house and the quiet residential street, except all the shades were drawn down, giving the windows a suggestion of lifeless closed eyes and making the room seem withdrawn from everything.

A short stocky man was sitting in a well-worn expensive leather chair watching the History Channel. He clicked the television off when Danny came into the room.

"Yes?" the man said to Danny. "How can I help you?"

Linda Violette went and stood behind the leather chair and never took her eyes off Danny.

"My name's Danny Pierce—"

"Yes, yes," the man said, cutting him off. "I heard you at the door. What is it, Mr. Pierce?"

"I'd like to ask you a few questions about your daughter," Danny said, trying to keep his voice even.

"And about Rose?" Linda asked.

Danny nodded. "Yes."

Frank Violette drained what was left in his highball. "Would you like a drink, Mr. Pierce? I was just about to have another."

"No, thank you."

"Sure?"

"No, thank you."

"You're not a teetotaler, are you? I've never trusted teetotalers."

Danny smiled. "Well, maybe one then."

"Okey-doke," Frank Violette said. "Linda..." He gestured with his glass. "Would you be a dear and get us a couple drinks, hon?"

She took his glass and disappeared from the room. A few seconds later she returned with two drinks and handed Danny his. Then she resumed her post behind her husband's chair.

"Thank you," Danny told her.

"Sit down, Mr. Pierce," Frank said, waving his hand toward a chair opposite his.

Danny sat down and took a sip of his drink. It was made well.

Michelle's father took a long pull on his scotch, rattled the ice cubes against the rim of the glass. "May I call you Danny?"

"Sure."

"How can we help you then, Danny?"

The room had an aspect of scrupulous neatness and comfort. An old-fashioned piano with a stool in front of it, the floor covered with a dark carpet. In the center of the room there was a clumsy, marble-topped table. On the table, a large china lamp, a bulky bible, and a little photo album grandparents carry around to show off their grandchildren.

"Your daughter..." Danny began, leaving it out there for them to take the lead.

"What about her?" Frank said; a strength about his expression, a ruthless self-confidence in his eyes.

"She may be in trouble."

Linda Violette made a small noise in her throat.

"You think she had something to do with Rose's disappearance?" Frank asked.

"Yes, I do."

"Why?" Linda Violette almost screamed. "Why would she do something like that? What you're suggesting? Why would Michelle do something like that to her own child?"

"I'm more concerned that Dale..."

"Dale Jacob is a low-life," Frank said. "Always has been. I told Michelle not to get involved with someone like Dale. But she wouldn't listen. They never do. That's the bane of parenthood. Our curse as parents. You try to raise your children to the best of your ability and in the end they turn their back on you. Think they know more than you. Michelle came from a good family and from a nice home. Then she met Dale and moved into that trailer with him. Pretty soon she started walking around barefoot like a hick and didn't wear any makeup. I told her Dale was no good for her, but she didn't listen. Then she went and had Rose, out of wedlock. Do you have children, Danny?"

"No, sir, I don't."

Frank sipped his drink and stared at him. "What do you think happened to our granddaughter?"

"I don't know for sure, sir."

"Do you think—" Linda Violette asked, but couldn't finish—her eyes gleaming with tears.

"C'mon, Linda," Frank said, grasping for her hand, hoping she wouldn't throw another fit. "We don't know anything for sure yet. Ain't that right, Danny?"

"Have you stopped searching for Rose?" Linda asked. "I mean...alive?"

Danny didn't answer her. He didn't know how to answer her.

"You'll find her, won't you, Danny?" Frank said. "You'll find our granddaughter?"

Chapter Twenty-eight

It was a good night for a football game. The air was clear and cold and so clean it almost sparkled. The moon wasn't out yet but the stars lit up everything.

Danny parked the car in front of the Petersen house and just sat there for a minute, a flash of memories racing through him. His first date with Sadie. Picking her up, just like this, nervous, his mouth dry, his hands clammy. Too much cologne.

He got out of the car and walked up to the front door. He took a deep breath, rang the doorbell, and waited. It was quiet except for the scraping sound of leaves blowing across the street.

The door opened and Sadie was standing there. They looked at each other in silence for a moment. Then Sadie smiled. He would have paid a thousand dollars for that smile.

"Would you like to come in," she said. "The kids are still getting ready."

"Sure."

The house was exactly as he remembered it. It even had the same smell. The smell of Downy fabric softener and apples with just a touch of cinnamon. The hallway boasted a huge coatrack, and a grandmother clock that still appeared to be keeping perfect time. Its loud ticking echoed throughout the house. A flight of carved mahogany stairs led up to the second floor, and to the left was the living room, furnished with a dependable leather couch and loveseat. There were photographs on the mantel and on the walls, one of them featuring a man in a soldier's uniform.

Sadie led Danny into the kitchen where her father was sitting at the table among a circle of carved pumpkins.

"Dad," Sadie said, "you remember Danny Pierce?"

Her father stood up from the table, shook Danny's hand, and said, "Howya doing, Danny" friendly enough—as friendly as any father ever greets the man who's taking out his daughter. There was a quality about Russ Petersen of a likable, affectionate boy who has never grown up.

"I'm doing fine, sir," Danny replied.

"It's Russ. At this stage in our lives, it's Russ."

Just then a gaggle of kids ran into the kitchen. Little Leah smiled when she saw Danny.

"Hi, Danny!"

Danny kneeled down so he was eye-level with the little girl. She was so pretty and so alive, that for a brief moment he touched the thought of having a kid of his own someday.

"Hey, kiddo," he said. "That's a nice sweater you have."

Leah beamed proudly. "Mommy gave it to me."

"She did, did she?"

Sadie's father was wrestling around with the other kids. "Goin' to a football game, huh, kids?" he said, putting Jeffrey into a headlock.

At that moment, Sadie's mother came into the room, calling her grandchildren to come and give her hugs goodbye. When she saw Danny, she smiled politely.

"How are you, Daniel?"

She was one of only two people who ever called him Daniel. The other was his Aunt Esther and she had been dead for twenty years. He wasn't used to being called Daniel. It made him feel like he wasn't wearing pants or something.

"I'm doing great, Mrs. Petersen."

Sadie packed the kids up in heavy coats and mittens and pushed them toward the door. Danny said goodbye to Sadie's mom and dad and followed Sadie out the door. He tried to make eye contact with the boy, but Jeffrey kept his eyes solemnly on the floor, his head down and the long blonde bangs hanging in his eyes. They went out into the street and Danny held the car door open for them. Jeffrey's face seemed to perk up a bit when he saw the Caddy.

The kids sat in back and Sadie took the front passenger seat. Danny went around and got behind the wheel. Sadie smelled good in the closeness of the car. Fresh and clean, no perfume, just skin not long out of the shower. It was feeling more and more like a date; except with kids. Weird.

The high school football field was over on Seven Bridges Road by the harbor. There were hundreds of cars and pickups parked on the street surrounding the field and illegally in the IGA parking lot across the street. Danny found a spot about three blocks away up on Primrose Lane. He parked the car and the kids ran on ahead and Sadie called out to them to watch out for cars. The rumbling of a high school band could be heard faintly in the distance, getting louder as they got closer to the stadium and they could smell popcorn and hot dogs and hot chocolate. It brought back memories of when Danny played and Sadie was on the sidelines cheering him on in her blue and gold cheerleading outfit.

They got to the gate and Danny paid for them. The crowd was huge and he couldn't help wondering if the crowds for his football games were this big when he played. When you're on the field you never notice.

A lot of people on the sidelines and in the stands remembered him, and asked him how he was doing. He smiled back at them, and couldn't help feeling a touch of weird forgotten pride. The old quarterback who'd finally come home like the Prodigal Son.

Sadie smiled at him and they found a spot in the upper bleachers and squeezed in. Even before the first kickoff Leah started begging for snacks. Sadie tried to hold her off, but then Kimmey started in on her, too. Jeffrey was watching the field intently. His deep-blue eyes were keen and sharp and seemed to bore into everything around him in a way that was habitual.

"Would you mind if I took the girls to get some snacks?" Sadie asked Danny.

The thought of being alone with the boy was almost painful, but he told her he didn't mind.

The boy wouldn't even look over at him.

"You like football?" Danny asked.

Jeffrey gave him a hard nod.

"I used to play, you know."

The boy turned and looked at him questioningly.

"What position did you play?"

"Quarterback."

His brows lifted. "Any good?"

"Pretty good."

"Did you play in college?"

Danny winced. "Nope. I hurt my knee my senior year."

"Could've you? If you hadn't hurt your knee."

"I suppose."

For a moment, Jeffrey forgot the barrier he'd put up, and he looked at Danny eagerly. "Wow, you must have been good. My grandpa says you gotta be good to play football in college."

"Your grandpa's right."

"I want to play for Colorado College when I grow up."

"Why Colorado?" Danny asked. "Why not the Gophers?"

"Gophers suck. I want to play for Colorado and then the Broncos. I like Colorado. My dad—" Jeffrey paused for a minute, then went on in a shakier voice. "My dad used to live in Colorado when he was a kid. He's dead now. My dad."

"Yes, I know."

They sat in silence for a minute; then Jeffrey got excited again when the Temperance running back broke free for a thirty-yard gainer.

"What position do you play?" Danny asked the boy.

"Running back and strong safety."

"Good positions."

Sadie and the girls were returning now. Their arms were full of goodies—popcorn, licorice, hot dogs, nachos—you name it, they had it. Jeffrey grabbed a hot dog and practically shoved the whole thing in his mouth. Then he saw a few of his friends on the sidelines and asked Sadie if he could go with them.

Sadie looked worried for a moment. "Just be careful," she said. "Don't talk to strangers and don't leave the stadium."

"I won't, Mom."

Jeffrey hopped down the bleachers and got lost in the large crowd that was roaming the sidelines.

Sadie looked at Danny and shrugged. "They grow up so fast," she said, a little too sadly. "I'm sorry he's so reluctant."

"No, it's fine."

"Ever since his dad died—"

"I got him to open up a little bit," Danny said. "Just started talking about football."

Sadie smiled. "That'll do it. He loves football. Ever since he was a baby. Just like *you* did."

They sat close in the bleachers. With the large crowd, they didn't have a choice. Kimmey and Leah quickly devoured the snacks and demanded more, but Sadie held her ground this time.

There was a thin sliver of moon and a sharp-edged wind sprang up, with the feel of cold rain in it.

"I don't remember it being so cold up here in Temperance," Danny said, his shoulders hunched forward and his face tucked into his collar.

"The wind comes up off the lake every night about this time," Sadie said. "You get so you like it after a while."

The Temperance Tommies ended up beating the Two Harbors Agates 23-7. After the game most of the locals were headed over to Apache Wells or the C&M to celebrate and Danny had to swerve the Caddy in and out of the honking cars and revving pickups. You could feel the energy coming off things, even the cars and the buildings. The kids were excited in the backseat. Danny drove them home and pulled the car up in front of the house. Jeffrey and Kimmey made a mad dash to the front door, racing to see who was the rotten egg. Leah stayed behind with Sadie and Danny.

"Do you wanna come trick-or-treating with us tomorrow night, Danny?" the little girl asked.

The question hit him off-guard. He looked at Sadie for support and she just shrugged her shoulders and smiled at him. "How can you say no to that face?" she whispered to him.

"You're right, I can't," Danny said. Then to Leah, "I'd love to come trick-or-treating with you tomorrow night."

The girl seemed content with that. Danny got out of the car and walked them to the front door. Leah ran inside, but Sadie held back for a moment.

They stood on the front steps, in the shadows cast by the moonlight, trying to draw to themselves anything that was familiar.

"It was a good game," Sadie said, slowly.

"Yeah, it was. I had a real nice time tonight, Sadie. Your kids are great."

"Thanks. But I think Leah has a crush the size of a pickup truck on you."

"Can you blame her?"

Sadie rocked forward on the tips of her toes, holding his eyes with her own.

He wanted to kiss her. The evening had brought them closer, rekindling some of those old high school feelings, but any acknowledgment of this, he knew, would only frighten her right back into her shell again.

She took a little step toward him and raised her head, and for a fleeting second he thought *she* was going to kiss him, but something quickly caught her and she stopped. It was like when they were teenagers, wanting to give in but having to push away.

"I can't," she said, ending the communion. "I mean—don't kiss me, Danny. Not tonight. This isn't the night for it."

She glanced away and caught her breath awkwardly. With a sudden movement she turned and went up the steps and opened the front door. Still looking at him to the last, she slowly drew the door closed past her face, very slowly and very softly.

Chapter Twenty-nine

"So—" her father asked, a little smirk curling the corners of his mouth.

"What are you smiling about?" Sadie asked.

"Oh, nothing."

"I think it's nice," her mother said. "Daniel coming around. Are you going to see him again?"

"Yes," Sadie said. "In fact, he's agreed to help me take the kids trick-or-treating tomorrow night. And then we may go have a cocktail afterward."

"Great."

"Can you watch the kids, Mom, if we decide to go out?"

"Sure, honey, sure."

"What does Jeffrey think about all this?" her father asked.

"He seems fine," Sadie said. "He was happier tonight than I've seen him in a long time. This last year's been really hard on him. On all of us."

"You know, I never did like Danny much when you were in high school," her father said. "I thought he thought too much of himself—being the big-shot football player—but—it seems like he turned into a decent man."

"Well, I'm glad you approve, Daddy," Sadie said, a little too sarcastically. "I'm tired. I'm going to bed."

She kissed her father and mother on the cheek, left them in the kitchen, and went upstairs to prepare for bed even though she knew she would be awake for a long time thinking of this night and of Danny Pierce again.

†††

Danny woke up early the next morning. Everything felt different. His first thought wasn't of cigarettes and booze and regret as it had just yesterday and every day before that for the last fifteen years. Today he was thinking about Sadie, and only of Sadie. For the first time in a lot of years he felt good about himself.

He wondered if Sadie was awake yet. Maybe he should call her?

Nah, he didn't want to push it. Not just yet. Hell, they weren't in high school anymore.

He got out of bed and turned on the television. The local news station out of Duluth was talking about Rose. They had a picture of her up on the screen behind a beautifully sterile anchorwoman.

"...the search continues for six-year-old Rose Violette," the anchorwoman was saying. "Rose has blonde hair with blue eyes, and her hair is longer than it is in this picture. If you have any information regarding Rose's whereabouts, we urge you to call the Temperance River Police Department or this station." Two phone numbers were flashed on screen; then the phone numbers were replaced with the face of the anchorwoman again. She clucked with sympathy for a moment, but then—as if magically—her expression shifted quickly back to bubbly enthusiasm. "And now let's check weather with..."

With no fresh information, the news reports were already getting shorter. Soon something else would happen, and Rose would be forgotten.

Danny turned off the television.

†††

Dale was busy loading taconite pellets into the hull of a tanker when he got the call over the intercom. That cunt of a boss wanted to see him ASAP.

He was led to the second floor meeting room, the same room Danny Pierce had harassed him in. Dale paced around the room waiting for his boss Laurie Jackson to come in. He wanted a smoke real bad. He almost risked it and lit one, but he knew if the cunt busted him she'd have a fit. Instead he stood at the window looking out at the lake and woods beyond. Two miles away, a church-tower stood on Skunk Hill, the houses of the little town of Croftville climbing assiduously up to it.

Then Laurie Jackson walked in, looking very smart and businesslike, and carrying a manila folder under her arm.

"Sit down, Dale," she said.

"What's this all about?"

She opened the manila folder and started shuffling around some papers. "Dale, I'm going to give it to you straight," she said, never letting her pretty little eyes meet his. "We can no longer tolerate your kind of behavior here at Reserve Mining."

His mind went kind of blank. There was something about Laurie Jackson that made his mind go kind of blank.

All of a sudden he realized what she was doing.

"What?" he said; his voice a wet and sticky thing. "You're firing me? *Me?* I work harder than any of those fucking spics and niggers you got working down there."

"I don't appreciate that language, Dale."

"My kid is missing," Dale said. "And you're firing me?"

Laurie Jackson shuffled some more of her precious papers. "We're very sorry about...your *predicament,* Dale, but over the past year you've continuously shown up late for your shift—hungover and God knows what else. We simply can't tolerate that kind of behavior on the job. I'm sorry. We're prepared to give you two week's severance, but we'd like you to clean out your locker this afternoon."

Dale stood up from the table and glared at her. "You're nothing but an affirmative action cunt, you know that? I don't give a flying fuck about your job."

He reached over the table and took her stupid little manila folder with her treasured papers inside and threw it across the room.

"Happy fucking Halloween," he said, and walked out.

†††

Danny drove over to the Public Safety Building and found J.P. sitting behind his desk, smoking a cigarette and drinking coffee out of a thermos. His friend looked tired.

"Did you find anything up at Palisade?" Danny asked, skipping any greetings or salutations.

J.P. looked up. "My guys are still working on it," he said, his voice heavy and weary. "How was the game last night?"

"Good," Danny said.

"They win?"

"Yep. 23-7."

"How's Sadie?"

"Fine."

"Tell her I said hello...next time you see her."

There was something in J.P.'s voice that Danny didn't recognize.

"I will."

"Babe Gorman stopped by to see me again this mornin'," J.P. said. "He wants to know when we're gonna break this thing. Says the townsfolk are gettin' real anxious."

"Is it an election year?" Danny asked, his voice leaking with sarcasm.

"Every year's an election year for our fair Mayor. He goes up and down Main Street shakin' hands and smilin' that gold-toothed grin of his; got a good word for everyone he meets, never forgets a name; but he's such a hick he don't even know it."

"Maybe he'd like to take over the case? See if he can do any better."

"He'd probably jump at the chance," J.P. said. "Babe's family has lived in Temperance River since it was a fur trading post. One of the founding families. If he had his way he'd put together a lynch mob and have himself a little hanging party right in the middle of the town square. Dale and Michelle would be his honored guests."

Danny shrugged. "At this point, that doesn't sound half bad."

Chapter Thirty

It was Halloween night. Trick or Treaters all happy-fouled and tangled under the street-corner lights. Little goblins and ghosts and vampires prowling the leafy streets.

Danny drove over to the Petersen house and parked the Caddy out front. Jack-o'-lanterns and a bulging straw scarecrow in bib overalls had been set out on the front porch. Sadie answered the door, wearing a sunset of purple and blues and a khaki Stone Island coat. She looked as beautiful as a sunset.

"Come in," she rushed him.

Danny followed her down the hall and into the kitchen. Jeffrey and Kimmey were sitting around the table fighting because they didn't want to have to go trick-or-treating together.

"You walk too slow, fatty," Jeffrey was shouting at his sister.

"You always run ahead and try to lose me," Kimmey cried.

"Knock it off you two," Sadie's mother said to the squabbling children.

"Hola, Danny," Russ said. "You ready for All Hallow's Eve?"

"As ready as I'll ever be."

Leah came running down the stairs and into the kitchen dressed as a princess. She hugged Danny around the waist.

"Hey, cutie," Danny said. "All set to get lots of candy?"

"As ready as I'll ever be," she said, copying him with one of her patented smiles.

"Mom, can I go with Paul and Austin?" Jeffrey asked. He was dressed as Randy Moss. "Their moms are letting them go trick-or-treating by themselves. I'll be real careful."

"Oh, Jeffrey, I don't know."

"Ah, let the boy go," Russ Petersen said. "He's old enough now."

"Thanks, Dad," Sadie said contemptuously, then sighed and nodded. She turned to Jeffrey and examined his costume. "Are you going to be warm enough in that?"

"Yeah, Mom," Jeffrey said. "You worry too much. I'm not a little kid."

"Okay," Sadie said. "Just be careful."

Jeffrey started toward the door.

"Hold on a minute," his grandfather said. "You forgot your afro."

"Grandpa, I can't wear that," Jeffrey said. "It's prejudice."

"Oh, what the hell? Howya gonna be Randy Moss if you don't have an afro?"

Sadie's mother said, "Let him be, Russ."

Jeffrey ran out the door without the afro.

"Let's go, Mom," Kimmey cried, putting her witch's hat on her head. "My hat won't stay on!"

"Sure it will," Sadie said, pushing her toward the door. "You're the prettiest little witch in town."

"Witches aren't supposed to be pretty, Mom."

Danny and Leah followed them out.

"Have fun, kids," Russ called after them. "Watch out for all the ghosts out there!"

"Don't eat any unwrapped candy!" Sadie's mother said in a low warning voice.

They went out the front door and down the driveway. The abounding streets were filled with little kids dressed as Raggedy Annies, Spiderman, Batman, and Darth Vader. Cars lined the side of the road, their headlights shining in the inky-blue night.

"Everybody from town comes out here to trick-or-treat," Sadie explained to Danny. "They think this neighborhood gives out the most candy."

They went house to house, collecting popcorn balls, suckers, chocolate, and every other candied good that had been stocked this year down at the Wal-Mart in Two Harbors.

Kimmey and Leah were grabbing everything they could get their hands on, and pretty soon their pillowcases were filled to the brim. At one house, a fat bald guy asked Sadie if she would like to have a beer. Sadie politely declined and moved on to the next house.

"Who was that guy?" Danny asked her.

"That's just Pat," Sadie said. "He's the neighborhood bachelor. He asks all the single young mothers if they want a beer. It's sort of a tradition."

Danny followed her to the next house, and the next, and the next, pumpkins aglow on every porch, tiny footsteps rustling through fallen leaves. It was almost nine o'clock before the girls tired out and decided it was time to call it quits.

When they got back home Jeffrey was already there, sitting in front of the television and reaping the rewards of his booty. Sadie's father tried to get his mitts on the girls' pillowcase, but they only gave him the Milky Ways that they didn't like anyway.

"Want to go get a beer?" Sadie asked Danny, her voice weary and need of relief. "Mom, can you watch the kids?"

"Sure," her mother said. "You two go and have a good time."

Sadie went into the living room and had to bend down to kiss Kimmey and Leah, both now too absorbed in the TV to get up and kiss her goodbye.

"Jeffrey, brush your teeth before you go to bed," Sadie said. "I don't want all that candy to rot your teeth."

"Where you going, Mom?" Jeffrey asked.

"Me and Danny are going out for a while," she said. "I want you in bed at ten, okay?"

"Don't worry about 'em," Sadie's father said. "We'll get 'em to bed."

†††

Apache Wells was packed with the adult trick-or-treaters—vampires, sexy French maids, pirates, cheerleaders, and clowns. Danny and Sadie had a hard time finding a place to sit at the bar. Music was pumping out of jukebox: Sam the Sham & The Pharaohs singing *Lil' Red Riding Hood.*

Jake was behind the bar furiously working the taps like a Chinese vase juggler.

"Hey—" he greeted them with boisterous affection when he saw Sadie. "What can I get 'cha?"

"Couple of beers," Sadie said.

Jake came up with two bottles of Harp. "That's your favorite, right, Sadie?"

"Yep."

"On the house," Jake said when Danny tried to pay him.

They didn't know it, but Dale Jacob was sitting at the other end of the bar, a pitcher of Budweiser and a pack of Marlboros in front of him. He'd been there since noon, ever since he learned that he was unemployed. He'd been drinking heavily, but there was no lift to his jag; his disposition was mean and sullen. He didn't like the big crowd. Fucking Halloween. Biggest bar night of the year. Who gave a fuck?

Stevie McIntire was sitting next to him, his own pitcher of Bud in front of him. "You gonna watch the Vikes this week?" Stevie was saying. "They're on *Monday Night Football.*"

"Yeah, probably," Dale grunted. That was the one thing he hated most about Stevie—the way he rambled on at the mouth like a little old lady.

"They're playing the Packers," Stevie said.

"My ex-boss is a Packer's fan."

"She is?"

"Yeah," Dale said, thinking about Laurie Jackson's tight little ass. "She's from Milwaukee. Fucking Milwaukee!" The words came out in a guttural slur. His lips were dry and he tried to wet them, but his tongue was dry, too. "Can you believe she fired me? Me, of all people. I worked harder than any of those wetbacks down there!"

"Forget about it," Stevie said. "You'll find another job. Take it easy, Dale."

"You take it easy," Dale said slowly, clutching his beer tightly for balance. He had to consciously make himself relax his grip before he broke the glass. "Have you found a new job yet, you fuckin' bald bastard! What is it with you guys that shave your head anyway?"

"Whatta mean?"

"You're all over the fuckin' place," Dale said, his voice and manner getting thicker by the minute. "Is it because you're losing your hair? Is that why you shave your head?"

"No, it's not 'cause we're losing our hair."

"Then what is it? You think women dig that?"

"Whatta talkin' about?"

"Women don't dig that. You ain't gonna get no pussy with a bald head. Women like men with hair. They like to run their fingers through it when you're eating them out. But you wouldn't know anything about *that,* now would'ya, Stevie."

"Fuck you, Dale. You're a real asshole when you're drunk."

"You sayin' I'm drunk?"

"Yeah," Stevie almost whined. "I'm sayin' you're drunk!"

Dale picked up his pitcher and smashed it across Stevie's forehead.

Fragments of glass went flying everywhere. There was a big bloody crack down the center of Stevie's forehead, the white glimmer of bone. Blood was dripping down his face and onto his shirt.

From the other end of the bar, Danny made a move toward them, but stopped when he saw Jake jump over and forcibly restrain Dale. Jake didn't need any help—it looked like he had seen this kind of thing before—and Danny felt he should stay by Sadie's side. She'd covered her face with her hands and was trembling.

"'the fuck off me!" Dale was screaming at Jake.

"Get out of here before I call the cops," Jake shouted back, dragging Dale toward the door.

"Fuck you and your fuckin' mother!" Dale hollered back at him.

Jake casually released one of his hands and smacked Dale across the face with it. "Fuck my mother, is it?"

"Yeah, fuck your mother, and your grandmother, and your..."

Jake slapped Dale again and drove him toward the door.

Dale was kicking and screaming; then he saw Danny and Sadie, and his eyes went across them like skates across a frozen pond.

Sadie did not move, but sat with her face in her hands, unseeing, apart. Only Danny turned round and glared back at Dale.

Jake threw Dale face first out the door. "Don't come back here, Dale, ya gobshit ya!"

A cold wave of wind washed across the room. Jake came back in and shut the door. He looked around the place, briefly apologized to Sadie, and then went down to where Stevie was sitting, half-concussed and bleeding all over the top of the bar.

Stevie's eyes were wide and blank—double zeros. His mouth was opening and closing, opening and closing, like the mouth of a fish in a fish bowl.

"What did he do that for?" Stevie asked in a weak and watery voice.

Jake took a hanky out of his back pocket and started dabbing it at Stevie's forehead, Stevie yelping slightly in pain.

"Ouch!" he cried. "There better not be any of your moldy old snot on that boogerrag, Jake."

"Don'tcha be worryin' about that, Stevie. I think we need to get you to the hospital."

"I ain't goin' to no hospital. Hospitals are for homophiles that can't stand the sight of a little blood."

"There's quite a bit more than a little blood ya got there, Stevie. A bang on the head like you got can be awful serious if not looked at."

Stevie stood up, and was overcome with dizziness. He swayed round the room on weak legs and only managed not to collapse by clinging to the bar.

"Em, I ain't going to no damn hospital, Jake."

He took a deep breath, then staggered across the room, swaying, just making it out through the door, which he pulled closed behind him.

Chapter Thirty-one

Sadie's unsteady eyes looked up at Danny. They walked out into the cold damp night and hurried to Danny's car. The fog had gathered in a ghostly cloud that crawled around and under the car. Danny didn't see Dale anywhere, but he had a nasty feeling that he was somewhere in the shadows watching them. He kept thinking he saw something move, out of the corner of his eye, but every time he turned around, it was just a shadow lying black against a doorway. He wished he had his gun, but he'd left it back at the motel.

He started the car and pulled out of the parking lot, not sure where to go.

"You want to go back to my parents' house?" Sadie asked in a low voice. "My dad usually has a bottle of Kessler's lying around."

"Sure."

When they pulled up in front, the house was dark.

"Looks like everyone's sleeping," Sadie said.

Danny followed her inside. She went to the kitchen and poured them two tumblers of whiskey and cracked a can of Coke. She poured the Coke in and stirred the whiskey and then licked the fork.

"So, what now?" she asked.

Danny shrugged. "I don't know."

"You want go downstairs and watch TV?"

Memory washed over him again. When they were in high school they used to always go down to the basement to watch TV. It was the only place they could truly be alone to do whatever seventeen-year-olds do, mostly make out on the couch in the soft blue glow of the television as Sadie's father paced the floor above them like distant thunder.

He followed her down the stairs and into the cool gray corner of the basement. She sat down on an old battered couch and flicked on the TV. Danny stood there, not sure if he should sit next to her on the couch or if he should sit in the chair against the wall.

"Sit down," she said. "You're blocking the TV."

He sat down beside her on the couch and felt her warmth seeping against him. She smelled good. The volume on the TV was turned low and he could hear her deep little breaths.

They sat and watched TV for a while in silence. The room was dark, except for the glow from the screen.

"Do you remember our first date?" she asked him.

"Yeah. I took you to see *Top Gun* at the Apache."

She laughed. "God, what a horrible movie. But it was my favorite back then because we were together. That's all that mattered...being with you." She looked up at him and for a second he saw the girl she once was back in high school.

He didn't know what to say. He was fighting back an urge to take her in his arms. She scootched up closer to him, wedged herself against him, and let all her weight rest on him. With her in his arms, he felt that he had suddenly become strong and fearless and sure of himself again.

After a while, she spoke. "When we're like this, I can't think of anything but you. This feeling between us—it's like the lake yesterday. It never seems to go away."

Danny wasn't really sure what happened next. Whether it was he or Sadie, or a little of both. He was leaning forward at the same time that Sadie was. They were closer than either had intended. With a sudden movement he bowed his head and joined his lips to hers and it was as though time had melted in that kiss, in their lips.

Sadie went stiff and made a mousy little sound deep in her throat. "I didn't want this to happen, Danny." He saw tears form in her eyes, but she kept them back. She looked as scared and confused as a kid in a thunderstorm.

"It has to be real. It has to mean something. It has to..."

He kissed her again, crushing her closer. Suddenly she could barely breathe. There was no turning back. She moved her hands slowly over his chest, then across his face and offered her lips to him again. He kissed her harder and their mouths broke loose once more, long enough for him to pull her sweater over her head. Her arms were cold despite the fever running through her, the blonde hair on them light as milkweed fluff. He ran his fingers over the gooseflesh and she shivered.

It was like they were in high school again. That feeling of innocence. That's all they wanted now. The innocence of their first love.

Sadie reached around her back and undid the clasp of her black lace bra and used both hands to slide it off her breasts as if she was shedding a second skin. Her nakedness yielded to him, radiant, warm. He ran his fingers lightly over her downy skin, so delicate that he could see the traceries of blue veins lying just beneath. Her skin, with the moon angling in from the egress window, was polished platinum marble. Her breasts were small and firm and perfect.

He brushed the taut nipples with his fingers and she made a sound, a sad sound straight out of the heart without any voice, like a moan, like a cry from one lost animal to another. Her face floated there, in angel-blue light, in front of his face and then she brought her mouth down on him again. She let it touch just the corner of his mouth, then envelope him, as if she was trying to swallow him. She used her hands to lift his shirt over his head and her fingers swung madly down to his belt and unbuckled his jeans, slipping them over his thin hips, using her foot to push them down. Her right hand reached into his boxers and she took him in her fingers. He was hard and she could tell that her touch made him even more rigid.

He made a sound deep in his throat. It was all going so fast. He took her face in his hands.

"I love your face," he said, his voice quavering. "You have the most beautiful face."

She reached up and pulled his hair and told him, "No more compliments."

She put her hand on the front of his face and covered his mouth and started to squeeze her fingers together. Was she trying to hurt him? Did it feel good? She didn't know anymore. Finally she took her hand away. His cheeks had deep red marks where her fingers had been.

They locked themselves to one another, but after a while Sadie began to weep in large, flat sobs that made her whole body shake.

"What's wrong?" Danny whispered.

"I can't," she said, suddenly resisting and pushing away, her eyes bewildered and humbled by dark penitence. "I just can't. I'm not ready yet, Danny."

He backed off, knowing if he pressed her he'd lose her. He never wanted to lose her again.

She looked at him and put out her hand. He looked at her hands, but he did not touch her hand with his.

"I'm sorry," she said, "if you don't understand."

"I'll understand all the time. Every day and every night, I'll understand. You don't have to worry about that. You don't have to worry about anything anymore."

Chapter Thirty-two

Stevie's head hurt so goddamn bad he figured he probably should go to the hospital and have it checked out. He didn't know why Dale had hit him. Sometimes he just got like that. Dale was a decent guy overall, except when he got drunk and angry like that, then there was no telling what he might do. Stevie started wondering if all that stuff people around town were saying about Dale was true. If he really killed his little girl. But it was so weird and scary to think about that, so he pushed the thought out of his heavy head.

Since getting clobbered with the pitcher, everything looked funny. He wondered if he had damaged his brain somehow. The cut on his forehead was really pumping. He could feel the gash with his fingers and it felt deep, like a river.

The hospital was over on Fireweed Lane. Stevie thought the Emergency Room might be empty this late at night, but it was crowded with lots of whining kids still dressed in their Halloween costumes.

Stevie hated hospitals. He'd watched his little brother die of an overdose in this very hospital.

Whenever he entered the big glass doors out front and got a whiff of the unnatural, antiseptic smell in the corridors, he thought of Mikey and how he died snorting some bad coke that Dale had sold to him. When Stevie had confronted Dale about it, he went on to deny the whole thing. He even showed up at the funeral, but Stevie never forgave him. Yeah, Dale Jacob was a *decent* guy alright. Sometimes it made Stevie feel like a real shitheel for never being able to stick up to Dale.

A little girl was staring at him, making a face like she was grossed-out looking at all the blood on his face. God, it smelled like vinegar in this place.

He had to wait over an hour to see a doctor and he started wondering if they had forgotten about him. Hell, he was bleeding all over the place. How the hell could they forget about him? Then a fat old wrinkly nurse called out his name and brought him to a white room in back. She started asking him all kinds of questions and he told her he just wanted to see the doc. She left with a puff and a few minutes later the doctor came in. Christ, he was just a kid. Stevie couldn't believe he was a real doctor. He looked like he was still in high school. Stevie gave him some real shit about it, calling him Doogie Howser, but the kid was a good sport.

"What happened, Stevie?"

"I fell down and bumped my head," Stevie said in a cracked voice.

"I guess you did," the young doctor replied.

He washed off the side of Stevie's head with some green stuff that smelled awful and burned like hell.

"That's a fairly nice gash you got, Stevie," he said, taking out a bunch of shiny sharp things that were wrapped in soft blue paper. "You 'bumped your head' pretty hard." He grinned down at Stevie like he knew he got in a fight somehow, like he'd seen it a million and one times.

The doc took out a long needle.

"This might sting a little," he said, leaning over Stevie and sticking the needle in the gash on his head.

He wasn't kidding when he said it might sting a little. It felt like being stung by a pack of hornet bees, but after a while Stevie didn't feel nothing up there.

The doc took out another needle and leaned in real close and Stevie could smell his good cologne. It helped him relax a little for some reason he didn't quite understand. He couldn't see what the doc was doing up there, but it didn't hurt anymore, so he just lay there and didn't give him any more trouble.

When it was all said and done, Stevie walked out of there with seven stitches in his head and a checkbook that was sixty bucks lighter. He knew his old lady was gonna give him hell when he got home. And he knew he was gonna have one hell of a headache in the morning. Some Halloween night it turned out to be. Some friend Dale Jacob turned out to be. Yeah, Dale was a *decent* guy alright.

Chapter Thirty-three

J.P. was sleeping soundly when the telephone rang.

"Damn," he groaned, even before he woke up.

"What is it?" Emmy moaned from her side of the bed.

"Phone. Go back to bed." J.P. picked it up, and said into the headset, "Yeah, what is it this time?"

Davina Watson, his dispatcher down at headquarters, practically blew his ear out. "J.P., we got a call from Apache Wells. It seems Dale Jacob assaulted Stevie McIntire down there tonight."

"Hell, I thought they were friends."

"Yeah, but you know Dale," Davina said. "Jake down there at the Wells called it in half an hour ago."

"Can you find anybody else to cover it? Where's Bobby?"

"At home with a sick kid."

"Again? Are his kids ever not sick?"

Davina let out a long breath. "I don't know, J.P. What do you want me to do with this one?"

There was some unfilled time before he said, "I guess I'll go down to the Wells and have a private chin with Jake. See what happened."

"Okey-doke. Thanks, J.P."

He hated this part of the job. Getting out of bed in the middle of a cold night and rousting drunks. He was getting too old for it. He only did it because he still liked being a cop. And he liked being a cop in Temperance River. He liked the town because he knew the town, every last person, every dark corner, every nasty secret. He simply couldn't imagine himself doing anything else or living someplace else. He was as much a part of Temperance River as Temperance was a part of him.

He got out of bed, threw on a pair of wrinkled Levi's and a gray sweatshirt with TEMPERANCE RIVER PD stenciled across the front of it.

In his stocking feet, trying for silence, he moved out of the room without waking Emmy. He went down to the dark kitchen and made a pot of coffee and went outside to the driveway where the prowler waited for him. It almost didn't start again it was so damn cold. The wind was kicking off the lake something terrible and freezing everything in sight. But he eventually got it started and drove it through town, its police flashers turning lazily in the sallow darkness.

Apache Wells was still roaring and packed when he got there, despite the fact that it was well past midnight. The state had passed a new law about a year ago that let the bars stay open as late as 2:30 on the weekends. It just made J.P.'s job that more difficult.

He went in and was greeted by a bunch of loud drunks standing at the bar. He knew all of them—grew up with most of them—dropouts from high school who were still looking for the next party at forty years old.

Jake was behind the bar with a sour look on his face.

"What happened, Jake?" J.P. asked him.

"It was that goddamn Jacob again. When you gonna lock his ass up, J.P. Bring him in and keep him there as far as I'm concerned."

"Bring him in on what, Jake? You know we're doin' the best we can to try to find Rose."

"I know, J.P. But nobody cares anymore about procedure. Just bring Dale in and lock him up. Throw his ass in the county stir where he can't hurt nobody no more. Rid this fuckin' town of him."

"You wanna tell me what happened here tonight, Jake?"

"Dale clobbered old Stevie over the head with a pitcher. Cut him open real good and Stevie wasn't doin' nothin' neider! I threw Dale out after that. Told him not to ever come back."

"Where's Stevie now?"

"I don't know. He left. I told him to go to the hospital, but he started snortin'. I don't know if he went or not."

"I reckon I'll go find him," J.P. said. "Make sure he's alright. Happy fuckin' Halloween, huh, Jake?"

"You got that right."

†††

J.P. walked out of the bar and got back in the prowler. He'd left it running while he was in the Wells, so it was nice and warm now. It was still freezing and nasty outside. The waves on the lake were crashing high against the pilings, throwing spray. The houses on the far side of the street were misty, as if seen through a veil.

J.P. drove over to the hospital. That young doctor from Minneapolis was working the night shift in the ER. Doc Godfrey was skinny; sand-blond, with a thin mouth and a child's amused eyes. Hell, he looked like he was barely out of diapers and here he was pulling down over a hundred g's. That was more than twice what J.P. was making and he'd been sheriff for almost ten years now.

"Yeah, I sewed him up," Doc Godfrey told J.P. "He left about an hour ago. I practically had to prop him up so he wouldn't fall on his nose. I threw him in a cab. Had to pay for the fare out of my own pocket."

"That's mighty white of ya, Doc."

Godfrey looked up at him with steady eyes. "Is it true what they're saying about that Jacob fellow? That he killed his own daughter?"

"That's what we're tryin' to find out, Doc. But without knowin' what happened to Rose we don't have much of a case."

Godfrey frowned. "It's not at all like one of those crime shows you see on TV, is it, Sheriff?"

"No, Doc, it ain't," J.P. said; but he was thinking that it *did* remind him just a little bit of a *CSI* episode he'd seen once. Only given the circumstances, he didn't think Gil Grissom was going to show up to solve this one.

"He seems like a real animal, you know," Doc Godfrey was saying. "I was finally able to get it out of Stevie that Jacob was the one who did this to him. Can you at least arrest him for that, Sheriff?"

"I'm gonna try, Doc. I'm gonna try."

†††

Stevie McIntire and his wife Melanie Jane lived on the west side of town, over by St. Pius Catholic Church and My Sister's Place tavern. It was a small box of a house with rusted gutters, a discolored and flaking roof, dirty windows and two famine-stricken dogs full of disease and spite, nosing obscenely in the garbage cans at the front door.

J.P. pulled the prowler up behind Melanie Jane's rusted-out Ford Explorer. The Ford used to be purple at one time, but you couldn't tell that no more.

Stevie and Melanie Jane had been married for six years now and most people in town were surprised as shit that they had made it that long. Melanie Jane was always harping on Stevie. She was a big woman and meaner than a gut shot bitch wolf with nine suckling pups. More than once J.P. and his deputies had been called out here to stop Melanie Jane from busting Stevie's skull in. Poor Stevie, if it wasn't Melanie Jane kicking him around, it was Dale. He was like some poor lost puppy out in the rain.

J.P.'s trooper hat was on the seat beside him, next to his holster and gun—a good Smith & Wesson .45-caliber revolver with a 6-inch barrel. He put the trooper hat on top of his head and glanced down at the gun. He decided to leave it there. Then he opened the door and climbed out of the prowler and walked up to the front porch.

"Get on out of here," he said to the two famine-stricken dogs, but he could have easily been saying the same thing to himself.

He took off his glove and knocked on the front door. He thought everybody might be sleeping, but a few seconds later, the door swung open and Melanie Jane McIntire stood there in all her glory, looking and smelling like Sasquatch itself.

"Bout time you got here, J.P.," she said in a rough, loud voice.

She was wearing a T-shirt with "GUILTY" printed on it and huge baggy *Zubaz* shorts. She reeked of Mad Dog 20-20 and vomit waiting to happen.

"You gonna let me in, Melanie Jane?" J.P. asked. "I'm freezin' my tookus off out here."

She held the door for him and he followed her inside. The twilight stank and was loud with flies. The squalor of that little house made him want to retch. In greasy bags on the floor were the remains of a fast-food meal, perhaps several meals. The light from a streetlamp was coming in the window and J.P. could see Stevie clearly. He looked bad, like something lying in the gutter that no alley cat would lower itself to drag in. He was sitting in a chair in the shadows, pointing a remote control at the TV and flipping through the channels randomly.

Melanie Jane stepped across the threshold and stood looking at J.P., staring incredulously, her mouth open. J.P. noticed with disgust that two of her front teeth were missing. And the color of the ones that remained...he shuddered.

"You gonna arrest that bastard, J.P.?" Melanie Jane said, crossing her arms and grasping her fat elbows with nicotine-stained fingers. "Just look what he did to my Stevie!"

Stevie just sat there in the threadbare chair staring at the TV. He was covered in dry blood. He was in a pitiable state, his face pasty, haggard with sleeplessness and raw nerves, his eyes sick and haunted, like a mangy animal waiting to die.

"What happened tonight, Stevie?" J.P. asked in a thick and tired voice. All he could think about was getting home and getting back into bed.

"Nothin'," Stevie said.

"Nothin'!" Melanie Jane shot back at him, bristling with anger. "That beerfuck Dale Jacob slaps you upside the head with a pitcher and you just sit there and say nothin'?"

"Mind your business, woman," Stevie said, a little sheepishly.

Melanie Jane's eyes snapped with anger. "Don't get cheeky with me, mister."

J.P. sighed. Goddamn, he was tired. Too tired. He wondered how many years this fucking job had eaten off his life already.

He stepped over the greasy bags of discarded food and stood in front of the TV. "Listen to me, Stevie. I got to know if you was plannin' on pressin' charges against Dale?"

Stevie chuckled. "Yeah, right, and get myself kilt? You're crazy, Sheriff. I ain't itching to get my head kicked in permanently."

Melanie Jane stormed across the room. "Oh ...you're pressing charges all right," she shouted at him. Then to J.P. "You can count on that, Sheriff. Stevie might be scared shitless of that child-murdering bastard Dale Jacob, but I ain't." She squinted her eyes at him. "How come you haven't got that bastard off the street yet, anyway?"

J.P. stared back at her. "We're working on it, Melanie Jane." To Stevie he said, "So whatta ya say, Stevie? You gonna help me get Dale off the streets so he can't hurt anyone else?"

Stevie turned his blood-stained head and looked up at him. "Can you promise me that he won't hurt me no more, Sheriff?"

J.P. exploded. "Fuckin'-A, Stevie! Dale probably killed his little girl, and I'm bustin' my ass tryin' to prove that, and all you can think of is yourself? You little piece of shit! You fuckin' disgust me, you know that?"

"Listen to the sheriff, Stevie," Melanie Jane put in.

Stevie grimaced and stared at the TV. After a long, sad pause, he said, "Y'know, after Dale cracked me tonight, I was scared stiff. I thought I was dyin', I was so scared. I really felt weird. How come things always happen like that? I didn't do nothin' wrong to Dale. Seems like you let your defenses down for one second and, man, you get it. Give a fuck about another person and you get cracked over the head. How come it's like that?" He looked up at J.P. "Okay, Sheriff, I'll do it. I'll do whatever you say."

"You'll press charges?"

"Yeah, I'll press charges.

†††

When the sheriff left, Stevie went into the bathroom and puked. He was sick. For a moment he really thought he had dreamed the whole thing. A nightmare he only vaguely remembered. It seemed like forever before it finally got through to him what had really happened. Then he got sick again, and he wondered why people didn't die from being so fucked-up.

He stumbled out of the bathroom and down the hall to the bedroom. Melanie Jane was lying out on the bed, like a big dog, snoring and twitching her fat legs.

Stevie sat down on the edge of the bed, holding his head in his hands. It felt like his head was going to explode.

Why'd he do it? Why'd he turn Dale in? He tried to justify it by telling himself Dale deserved it. He deserved everything he got. But he knew that if Dale ended up going to jail, it would kill him. Dale was a tough bastard, the toughest guy Stevie had ever met; but he wasn't cut out for jail. It would kill him.

Chapter Thirty-four

He lay for a long time looking at her. At her face and body in the reflection of the streetlight through the egress window, admiring the smoothness of her neck and shoulders; the tiny wrinkles at her eyes, and the two peculiarly webbed toes on her right foot. She was sleeping on the couch with his arm under her. He was frozen there, and he couldn't have been more content to be that way. It didn't seem real to him that Sadie was actually under his arm and he was still actually on this earth.

Sadie stirred, raised herself up slowly, and it was then that Danny realized how completely numb and dead his arm had gone. He hadn't moved it from that spot around her for almost two hours.

She looked up at him and smiled; her eyes half closed in a dreamy contentedness.

"I was dreaming of us, that we were back in high school," she said in a moaning little whisper.

He looked down into the blue of her eyes, and it was almost as if they'd never been apart.

"What time is it?"

Danny looked at his watch. "Quarter to five. Should I go?"

Sadie's mouth went into a tight line, as if she were trying to keep something from slipping through. "Yeah, maybe," she finally said, "before anyone wakes up."

She moved her head and kissed him on the lips.

"Can I call you later?" he asked.

"Yes."

He got dressed quickly and Sadie walked him upstairs to the kitchen door. She locked it behind him and hustled upstairs to her bedroom. When she got there she went over to the window and pulled back the blinds. It had snowed during the night and she saw Danny down on the street, cleaning the snow off the windshield of his car. He was beautiful, with his disheveled hair and his cheeks full and red. Clouds of white steam were leaking out of his mouth like a train whenever he breathed.

She watched him until he got in the car and drove off, then she glanced at the clock. It was almost five. The kids wouldn't be getting up for another hour or two. She lay on the bed, with the smell of Danny still on her. She was hoping for another hour of sleep before the kids woke up, but with all the excitement of last night, she knew it would be difficult. She couldn't stop thinking about him; that was part of it. Well, most of it. She felt almost girlishly giddy whenever she thought of him touching her.

The room was in shadows and the sleeping house was tranquil and euphonious. She heard, from just below the bedroom window, a snowplow lowering its shovel and the soft beep, beep, beep as it backed up.

Finally, she gave up on sleep. It was useless. All she could think about was Danny and how much they had been in love back in high school. They were so young then. Seeing him again and being with him again had restored some long-broken line to a self of twenty years ago. She felt as if her body had begun to exist again. For the last year her body had been ineffectual, almost dead. What happened last night was good, but she couldn't help feeling a little guilty, too. She was afraid of erasing the line between real and unreal.

†††

The morning broke, brutally cold. The sun wasn't up yet and the sky was a blanket of stars. Danny had the heater in the Caddy turned all the way up, but it was still freezing and the windows were clouded over. He had to pull over once to get out and scrape the ice off the windshield with his credit card.

The plows were out, scraping the main roads. The fog off the lake was thick enough to carve with your hands. He drove through the Sunday-shuttered town, made the turn onto Limestone Road—still not plowed, rutted with a few tire tracks, and pulled into the parking lot of the Aurora Bora.

Millie Hjermstad was behind the front desk.

"Foggier'n a drunk's head out there."

"Yeah," Danny said, "and cold."

"Sheriff's been lookin' for ya. Left pert near a dozen messages. He was getting a might frickin' pushy, pardon my *François*."

As he walked down the hall to his room he wondered what was so urgent, why J.P. was trying to get a hold of him all night.

Had they finally found Rose?

He hoped to hell they had.

But what if they had and she was dead?

Would he be relieved?

He sat on the bed and dialed up J.P.'s cell number. J.P. answered on the first ring.

"Where the hell you been? Tryin' to get a hold of you all night."

"What's up? Did you find anything at Palisade?"

"No, we didn't find anythin' up there," J.P. said, a rasp catching at his throat. "But Dale Jacob beat up some local loser last night. I'm going to pick him up."

"You think that's wise?" Danny asked. "Bringing him in on some bullshit misdemeanor?"

"No choice. The guy he assaulted—or I should say, the guy's wife—wants to press charges."

"And you'd like some company?"

"That's what I was thinking."

"Where are you?"

"About ten minutes away."

"Okay."

Danny hung up the phone. He was tired, he hadn't slept at all, but he knew he wasn't going to be getting any sleep for awhile. Hell, he didn't even have time to shower. Instead, he slipped out of his jeans and shirt and put on a fresh pair of jeans and slipped the Sig Sauer in its holster under his shoulder.

Ten minutes later he was waiting in the parking lot for J.P. The prowler pulled up slowly and Danny got in. J.P. handed him a big Styrofoam cup of coffee.

"It ain't Starbucks, but it ain't bad either."

"Thanks."

"You don't mind me sayin' so, but you look like hell, my friend."

"This coffee will help," Danny said, unable to reign in a big yawn.

J.P. pulled out of the parking lot and they drove in silence, the expectancy being stretched again, tauter, tauter, almost to the tearing point. This whole case had been nothing but shadows you couldn't quite catch hold of.

The sky overhead was grayer than ever. The lake, visible in the background, was alive with gray chop, oblivious to anything but its own monolithic beauty.

"Think there's any chance we'll ever find her alive?" J.P. asked, his mouth smiling bitterly and alone.

Danny turned his head to look at his old friend sitting there beside him on the cracked leather seat.

"I don't know, J.P. I don't think so. Not at this point."

J.P. looked up at the sky. It was the color of an old wound, with a fist-sized cloud on the horizon, no more than that, but a fist-sized cloud up here can mean a storm is coming, predestined and ferocious. It's coming, all right. A big one.

"I don't like this weather much. Feels like somethin's gonna happen. Somethin' bad. Babe Gorman put a sign-up sheet on the door of the town hall Friday afternoon, and yesterday he fielded a search-party of twenty or thirty men to find Rose. They formed up a line by Naniboujou and worked their way down to the Caribou Trail. I seen 'em crossin' the Gunflint around one o'clock, laughin' and jokin' and passin' the bottle around, just like it was a big party."

"Did they find anything?"

"Nope."

J.P. pulled the prowler into the Big Timber Trailer Court. They got out and crossed the plotted driveway to Dale and Michelle's trailer. The first thing Danny noticed was that Dale's pickup wasn't parked in the driveway. The trailer itself was dark and quiet. Whoever was in there was probably still asleep.

"Do you think he's armed?" J.P. asked in a whispering voice.

"If he's here, he's armed," Danny whispered back.

Darkness moved within darkness.

"All right, let's do it. Just like we talked about. Quick and simple."

They drew their service weapons and Danny took a position on the side.

J.P. pulled back the screen and gave the solid door a rap.

Nothing happened.

J.P. rapped on the door again.

Nothing.

He rapped a third time.

Michelle's weary voice: "Dale? Is that you?"

She opened the door a crack, but left the chain on. Her beady little eyes latched onto Danny. Her mouth twitched in the beginnings of a little smile, but when she saw J.P., the smile collapsed. Her voice was nasal. "What do you want, J.P.?"

"Open up, Michelle. We're lookin' for Dale."

"He ain't here. Jesus, it ain't even seven o'clock in the mornin' yet."

"Open up, Michelle. I have a warrant authorizin' me to pick up and detain Dale for questionin' in connection with the assault of Stevie McIntire."

Michelle let loose with a string of snarled curses, then the chain on the door clicked and she pulled it open.

"What the fuck, J.P.?"

"You sure Dale ain't here, Michelle?"

"I just told you, he ain't here."

"We need to come in."

Michelle held the door wedged between them. "I already told you everything, J.P., so I guess there's no need to reheat that hash, is there?"

"We're comin' in, Michelle."

J.P. pushed Michelle out of the way. Danny brushed past her and followed him inside the trailer. He immediately noticed that it no longer had that awful ripe smell. The kitchen was clean and the sink was cleared and scrubbed, the walls scoured, the floors vacuumed. Almost like Michelle was trying to hide something.

She was hanging back in the shadow of the trailer, smoking a Viceroy. She stared at J.P., then at Danny, as if she didn't quite understand their presence.

A large bruise marred her face, a purple silhouette along the high bone of her right cheek. Her bottom lip was puffy and crusted with blood.

"What happened to your face, Michelle?" J.P. asked.

Her hand went automatically toward the bruise but stopped before she touched it. "I fell."

"Did *he* do that to you? Did he beat you up, Michelle?"

She kept her bloodshot eyes steady on him. "I fell."

"He beat up Stevie last night. Did you know that?"

She didn't answer him.

"Stevie's pressin' charges. I'm bringin' Dale in. The game's over, Michelle. You weren't lyin' to me when you said he weren't here?"

"I ain't lying."

"I'll check out the bedroom," Danny said, slowly moving down the dark hallway.

There was nothing but shadows. He got to the threshold and stuck his head inside the bedroom.

Nothing.

The bed was made and everything looked tidy. He couldn't understand it. The last time he was here the place looked like a tornado had hit it. Now it looked like it could be on one of those home makeover shows on *HGTV*.

"All clear," Danny called out.

Michelle was in the kitchen.

"How often do you think of her?" J.P. was saying.

Michelle was standing in front of the stove watching the blue flames beneath a kettle of water she had on for instant coffee.

"Every day," she said. "Every minute. Every second. She possesses me."

"Do you feel guilty, Michelle? I see you've been bitin' your nails. You're nervous, aren't you, Michelle? Do you sleep okay at night?"

"That's no concern of yours," she snapped.

"I'm afraid it is," J.P. said. "Everythin' you do is a concern of mine until we find Rose."

"I know what you're doin'..."

He raised his hand and cut her off like a knife-blade. "What you want to do right now isn't talk but listen, so we can put this shitmiserable business behind us once and for all and find Rose."

Michelle rubbed her face—her nose was oily, her hair a wreck, but it was too late to fix any of that.

"Jesus, J.P., I told you everything. Don't you think if I could help find Rose I would?"

"You're gonna talk to us," J.P. said. "You're goin' to tell us everythin' we want to hear. Twice, if that's the way we want it."

Michelle's lips were pressed together so tightly they were white. Her breasts heaved as she opened her mouth and drew in breath. "I told you everything. Honest, J.P., I did." She took the kettle off the stove. "I feel like I'm coming down with something. I have a pain behind my eyes, like something's fighting to get out. I better lay down for a while."

"We can charge you right now, Michelle," Danny said.

She took a breath. "Charge me? Charge me with what?"

"Manslaughter and reckless endangerment."

She eyed him suspiciously. "I know what you're doin', too. I know what both y'all are doin'. I think it's sad what you're tryin' to do."

Danny slammed his fist into the wall. "Who gives a fuck what you think!"

Michelle was trembling now, like a puppy that's been mistreated by mean kids, and her face had gone white as a dirty sheet.

"You're going to tell me where she is, Michelle, or I'm going to beat it out of you."

"Get out! Get out of my house."

"You think it hurts when Dale beats you? That pussy. You haven't felt pain like I'm gonna give you."

Danny grabbed her by the arm and dragged her into the living room.

"What are you going to do to me?" she cried.

He threw her on the couch so hard she almost bounced off.

"Tell me where she is!" Danny screamed, his face bright red and puffed up like a fish. "You like killing little kids, Michelle? Huh?"

"NO—that's not what happened!"

"Your own daughter. You let him kill your own daughter."

"No—"

A small strangled sob erupted from her throat. How could she tell them what she was feeling? How could she tell anyone? How could anyone understand the guilt she felt every day?

"I do feel guilty," she said, crying and putting her hand up. "But sometimes it's almost like it never happened. Like I was never here."

"Tell us what happened to Rose," J.P. said. "You have to tell us, Michelle."

She drew the hair away from her eyes and nodded slowly. "Dale, he—" she stuttered, struggling against another sob that was threatening to strangle her.

"He what!" J.P. said, more harshly now.

There was this shroud of guilt that seeped into Michelle's face, finally a resolution that she had done something terribly wrong. She couldn't hide it any longer. "He took her. He took her and I never saw her again. Oh, God, I never saw her again."

Danny and J.P. drew beads on each other. So there it was. Laid out like a Royal Flush. Dale Jacob had killed his own daughter. His own little girl.

Danny stared down at the pitiful, blubbering mass on the couch. "How could you let it happen, Michelle?"

"I'll testify against him! I swear I didn't hurt her, I swear. I just didn't know what to do. God, I didn't know what to do. I was so scared."

"Where is he?" Danny asked. "Where's Dale?"

"I don't know. He didn't come home last night. I haven't seen him. He—" She wiped the tears from her eyes with the front of her T-shirt. "He won't come back here if he finds out you've arrested me. He'll leave town. He'll leave town and never come back."

Danny was considering his options. Michelle was the little fish in the big pond. He wanted Dale. Dale was the trophy.

"I want you to stay here," he told Michelle, and he could see J.P. give him a look out of the corner of his eye. "Don't go anywhere, Michelle. Don't go for a walk. Don't go down to the store for cigarettes. Don't go anywhere, you here?"

"Yes."

"Do you have any idea where Dale might be?"

"No."

"What about his parents?"

"His mother died last year. Lung cancer. She used to smoke like a factory."

"What about his old man?"

"Moved to Arizona after Dale's mother died. But Dale wouldn't go there. He doesn't talk to his father. They haven't spoken for almost a year."

"Any other family? Or friends? Someplace he can go and hide?"

Michelle chewed the insides of her cheeks. "His dad had a hunting cabin up at Baptism Lake."

"Up near the Boundary Waters?" J.P. asked.

"Uh-huh. Dale used to like to go there when he was a kid."

†††

The windshield wipers were clapping back and forth rapidly, but the glass was still snowing up.

J.P. and Danny sat in silence for a long time, just staring out the window of the prowler at the falling snow and the gray, unplowed streets.

"You got a smoke?" Danny asked, breaking the silence.

"I thought you quit?"

"I did. But right now I need one more than ever."

J.P. took his pack out of the inside pocket of his down parka, lit one, and handed the pack over to Danny. When he moved, the frozen leather of the seat made a cracking sound like bones breaking.

Danny shook out a cigarette and lit it. The smoke caught hard in his lungs and he started to cough. It had only been a few days since he quit, but he could already feel the nicotine going to his head. He felt dizzy and hot in the closeness of the car. Soon, smoke filled the cab and J.P. rolled down the window a notch, despite the cold.

"I'll put out an All-States bulletin on Dale," J.P. said. He looked across the seat at Danny. "You sure we shouldn't bring Michelle in, too?"

"No. Let's use her for bait. Fatten the frog for the snake, as the saying goes."

"What if somethin' happens to her?"

"That's the chance we gotta take, J.P. She's not exactly innocent in this thing, you know."

"I know, Danny," J.P. said, a bit touchily. "I know."

"Can you put a couple of your deputies on the trailer around the clock?"

"It'll mean more overtime, but yeah, we can do it."

"Good."

"What about Dale? You think he's at Baptism?"

"Only one way to find out."

J.P. was staring out the window at a morning whose arrival he had barely noticed. Out on the lake the sky tangled in threads of gray and snow fell like feathers shaken from a pillow.

"This is goin' to be one bad mother of a storm when all's said and done," he said. "They're talkin' maybe six to eight inches."

Danny didn't answer. He didn't have to.

Chapter Thirty-five

Winter came on like a white beast shaking its fur. It had been raining, and then, just before dawn, it turned to snow, blanketing everything in a sheath of crystal white. Dale woke up naked; an uncased pillow smelling of stale whiskey and cheap cigarettes cradling his head.

The room was dark and full of shadows. He got up and went over to the window, pulled open the blinds, and looked out at the white shores and gray waters of Baptism Lake shining coldly amid the frozen snow.

He remembered coming up here with his dad a lot when he was a kid to hunt deer and ducks, but when his mom died last year and his dad ran away to Arizona, the cabin was abandoned, like an old battlefield or a country cemetery. No one came here anymore. It was isolated and cold. Looked like it was haunted with the windows all cracked. The weeds had grown up and there were birds in the chimney. Dale could hear them, rustling around like ghosts.

When he tried to think of something nice, his thoughts kept returning to Rose and a restless feeling of guilt covered him like a soft, vaporous cloud. He thought of the little red bow of her mouth, her teeth when she smiled, her little body. He remembered how he felt when Michelle got pregnant. Christ; was he pissed. He was too young to be a dad, too shiftless. He didn't want a baby, didn't want to have to get a job to support the baby. Then, he got stuck with both.

Now, he had neither.

He had seen a kid on a school playground yesterday, standing all alone and it made him sad, made him think of his lost little girl. He felt crazy like that sometimes. He couldn't stop it and he couldn't let it out. The anger came on him; he wore it like a stigma. The causes were many; remote and near. He was angry at Michelle, angry at losing his job, angry at that cop Danny Pierce, angry at that stuck-up cunt Sadie Petersen, angry at his mom for dying and his father for running away, angry at this whole fucked-up world. The anger was always there—a buzzing, pulsing tone under everything else. Angry at everything, angry at...everything...

He was tired, too. He was *always* tired now.

Dale wiped his face with his hand and stumbled over to the kitchen and stuck his lips under the faucet. His mouth was dry and tasted like burnt hair. He caught sight of himself in the mirror above the sink. At first he thought he had spotted someone in the reflection of the mirror, and he turned around sharply to see who it was.

But there was no one there. Of course there was no one there.

He turned back to examine the mirror more closely. He didn't like the person that was staring back at him. He didn't like what he had become—a drunk and bitter man in a harsh and resentful world of death and sorrow. He went into the bathroom and stood at the toilet and took a long piss. It smelled like blood and booze. He thought about what he did to Stevie last night. He felt bad about that. But Goddamn, Stevie just didn't know when to shut the fuck up. He just kept going and going and going, like that fucking *Energizer* bunny on TV.

Dale hadn't eaten anything since yesterday afternoon. His stomach was telling him it needed something *now,* despite how lousy he felt. He glanced around the cabin. He knew there was no food here. Hell, nobody had even been in the place since his old man took off for Arizona. Fucking cocksucker.

He had to get organized. Or as De Niro said in the *Taxi Driver:* O - R - G - A - N - E - Z - I - E - Z - D.

Tighten up. Straighten out. Focus. He knew he needed to come up with a way to get some money, and then get the hell out of Temperance, but there was something else he needed to take care of first.

He went to the couch and crouched down low and felt under it with his hand. It was his father's favorite hiding place. Dale knew about it since he was a kid. At first his hand touched nothing but dust and carpet. But then he nudged it with his thumb and grabbed on to it and pulled it out from under the couch. The gun was wrapped in a piece of torn bed sheet with the grease spots from the barrel still bleeding through. The smell of gun oil made him reminiscent.

He lit a cigarette and sat there for a while, just looking at it. A steel-blue .44 with a 6 1/2 inch barrel still loaded full with Oregon Trail True Shot 310 Wide, a flat cast bullet with a gas check.

Dale held the gun, almost lovingly, and thought of an old Tom Waits lyric: *A .44 will get you 99.* He almost smiled at the thought of that.

He looked out the window at the falling snow. It was coming down hard now, with the wind driving it into slanting lines. Ordinarily, this would have pissed him off. He didn't like the snow and the cold, but today it was like a balm, passing over his senses, hiding from his eyes the feverish succussion inside his blood.

It was a glorious day.

A good day to die.

Chapter Thirty-six

As they pulled away from town, a snowplow rumbled past in the opposite direction. J.P. exchanged a wave with the driver as Danny settled back in the passenger seat and gazed out the window. The flat white wilderness seemed to stretch on forever. The Minnesota winter was on.

The goofy weatherman on the local radio station was forecasting a foot of snow in some places and a thirty-mile-an-hour wind to pile up the drifts: "A real humdinger. One of those storms you'll be telling your grandkids about...and they probably won't believe you. Expect closures of roads and government offices. Expect power outages. Use flashlights, not candles. Don't even think about the shovel until the plows have come by. And make sure your kitchen is stocked with plenty of Hormel SPAM. When the weather turns cold, nothing warms your cockles like SPAM. Now back to you, Bob..."

Danny took the Sig Sauer out of its holster and checked it over carefully. It was fully loaded—six .40 caliber hollow points—and its chamber spun smoothly, free of lint. At ten feet it could reduce a man's skull to splinters.

J.P. brought the prowler to a complete stop by the dead tree on the low hill at Injun Creek Road. A dense, unbroken forest extended for miles in every direction. He eased a cigarette out of his shirt pocket and punched in the lighter on the dash and waited for it to pop back out.

"You think Dale's up here?" he asked Danny.

"I don't know."

J.P. cracked the window a bit to let the smoke out. Then he turned off Route 12 and went up Injun Creek Road, toward the old Jacob cabin. It was a little dirt road, one of the millions that run along the lakes up here and through the woods surrounding them. The prowler dipped and swayed on the slippery ruts, and then they saw the Jacob cabin, with its aged front porch, the paint peeling and fading like old skin. It was just an old cabin, but it looked mean and intimidating.

J.P. turned the prowler onto the dirt driveway and drove through the snow to the front porch. He threw the prowler in park, killed the engine, and looked around.

The place freaked him out.

It seemed to him that the place was being wrapped in a strange vaporous fog, rising from the trees and the nearby lake until it swallowed the cabin whole. He stared at the vacant eyelike windows and at the white bare trunks of the birch trees surrounding it.

From the glove compartment he took out a flashlight and headed toward the cabin. Danny got out of the prowler and followed him, both men drawing their guns and holding them at their sides.

It was so quiet, nothing but the low hum of wind in the trees and the crackling of snow as it fell on the branches.

J.P. looked hard into Danny's eyes as they cautiously approached the front door. Something in the appearance of the place made Danny shutter. When he first became a cop he'd have this recurring dream of an abandoned cabin in the woods. He would approach the door. A metallic slide of a rifle being cocked. Then a blast and he'd be sent flying backward, a huge gaping hole in his chest. *Déjà vu?*

J.P. put his ear to the front door, listened for a full thirty seconds, and then stepped back. Danny flanked the door to his right.

J.P. gave a perfunctory knock. No movement from inside. His heart was beating hard and fast. He drew a deep breath and knocked again.

Nothing.

On the count of three he kicked open the door and crashed into a shuttered twilight. The place had a musty, unlived-in smell, dank and oppressive, a brittle, hollowed-out aura.

Danny flicked on a light. The kitchen had a wooden table, two wooden chairs, and an old cast-iron stove. Cobwebs were in the corners of the walls, hanging from the ceiling like strips of rotting lace. The only sign of life was a nearly empty bottle of Wild Turkey sitting on the table and an overflowing ashtray sandwiched between a *Hustler* magazine and an empty deck of Camels. Dale's brand of cigarettes.

"Looks like the chicken has flown the coop," J.P. whispered.

Danny looked at him reflectively. "Was this place ever searched after Rose disappeared?"

"We didn't know about it."

The cabin had two bedrooms. In the bigger one, a crucifix was nailed to the closet door and the bed was unmade and greasy. A dark oak dresser matched the nightstand. There was no mirror or pictures in the room. The smaller bedroom had a twin bed with sheets so tight it looked like it had never been used. They went through every closet and drawer, but found nothing, not one piece of clothing, nothing.

"I can get a hair and fiber team from the Cities up here tomorrow morning," Danny told J.P. "Maybe Dale brought Rose here."

"Even if we did find somethin', Dale can just say he took Rose up here in the summer to go swimmin'."

"We might find traces of blood."

"We ain't gonna find anythin' up here."

Danny looked hard at J.P.'s face, searched his eyes. "Let's check out the perimeter."

Outside, white pine surrounded the back of the cabin. From there, they could see the long stretch of darkness that was Baptism Lake. Down by the dock and the boathouse there was a path, what had once been a logging trace that went around the lake and into the woods.

"The lake's not completely frozen yet," J.P. said, blowing into his hands and shifting on his feet as if he were freezing. "Dale could've dumped her out there on the lake."

Danny's voice was monotone. "He could've."

They followed the path over a knoll and to the edge of another small wooded area. There was the sound of crows in the trees, frogs barking on the edge of the lake, and a small stream babbling somewhere close by. The lake was making an eerie popping sound, freezing in parts, getting itself ready for the long winter ahead.

They immediately made a grid of the area, stretching a cord from one tree to another, so that the entire ridge was marked off into a series of small squares. Then they searched each section of the area for any evidence, such as loose fibers, gum wrappers, cigarette butts, anything that might have a relevance to the case.

"Hey, Danny," J.P. called from the edge of the woods. "Somethin' here you ought to see."

"What is it?" Danny shouted back.

J.P.'s voice was solemn and distant. "Looks like a grave."

†††

Danny followed the direction of J.P.'s finger and felt a sinking—not just of the belly, but of the heart.

"Over there," J.P. said, looking away from the lake, craning his neck at something in the distance.

It was a mound of dirt and rocks underneath a big pine tree. Danny could just make out the large black smear over the frosted ground. It was the size and shape of a small child and looked badly out of place among the thick white drifts. If you were going to bury a body where it wouldn't be found, this was the perfect place.

Danny plodded through the snow, and as he approached the ugly black stain, he realized what they were looking at.

J.P. hooked his thumbs into his wide gun belt, looking at nothing in particular. "I'll go get my shovel."

He climbed up the hill and seemed to vanish into the dark. Danny waited in the cold silence and the evening shadows drew long through the trees. A brunet crow issued its grim laughter from the top of a scrub tree. There were no human sounds. Flecks of snowflake landed on Danny's eyelashes and melted there. He peered deeply into the places where night and shadow already met, where the snow divided itself into clusters over the dock and boathouse.

A few moments later J.P. returned, his flashlight cutting arcs through the falling snow. He stood there with the shovel in his hands and for the moment, neither of them spoke.

Is this the end of it, then? Danny was wondering, almost speaking out loud. Was this going to be the end of everything?

He had never felt so drained, so completely used up and unreal. Maybe it was going to stop now. Maybe it could just end.

J.P. planted his foot on the shovel and stamped it fiercely into the cold ground and fell to work. He drove the shovel in again, and again, and yet again. The only sounds were the thuds of earth as it dropped from the shovel. After about a half hour, he had reached the depth of two feet, but there was no sign of anything. He lifted another shovelful of earth. He was sweating despite the cold.

"Maybe nothin's down here," he said, making an effort to speak in an ordinary tone.

Danny insisted that they enlarge the circumference of the circle. He relieved J.P. and took the shovel. Still nothing turned up. The shovel struck against a stone; he stooped to pick it up. He dug some more, until finally, the shovel turned over something brown and soft.

"What is it?" J.P. said, shining his flashlight into the hole.

"I don't know," Danny said, falling to his knees and turning over the earth with his bare hands.

"What the *fuck* is it?" J.P. said. "Is it—"

Danny stood up, wiped his hands on his jeans, his fingers pink from the cold, the nails packed with black dirt.

"Danny, what is it?" J.P. asked again.

Punctured, utterly deflated, Danny knelt into the hole and came back up again holding something small and brown in his red, raw hands.

It was a child's teddy bear. *Mr. Honey.*

Chapter Thirty-seven

The streets were empty and ivory in color. Nothing moved. The snow muted everything, slowed everything down. The snow was magic.

How sad...and how beautiful the snow was.

Dale wanted to cry, but not for himself.

For Rose. So beautiful and sad.

The pain inside him was like a cancer. He'd been having sweaty ugly dreams about it. Dreams of being woken up by a peal of thunder and finding her gone.

Oh, Rose. Beautiful, sad little Rose.

The drive through the blanched, snow-shrouded town and the thought of the bare cheerless trailer made his heart heavy, filled him with an aberrant terror, as though it could harm him.

As he turned onto Eighth Avenue, he immediately knew something wasn't right. It was no more than an intuition, but he felt it in the very marrow of his bones.

On the other side of Eighth, behind a row of fallow pines, he saw a car—one that he had never seen before. He could barely make it out, but he thought he saw two people sitting in the front seat. It was one of those nondescript Fords or Chevys that the cops are always using for stake-outs. He knew right away they were cops.

The trailer stood by itself, and could be easily watched, but Dale knew a way to get to it without being seen. He turned down an alley and parked his pickup behind a dilapidated garage only dimly illuminated by a corner lamppost. He got out of the truck and went out the other side of the gray alley on foot. It was cold and the snow was bitter as it slapped his face, but he felt warm inside. It was like he had some kind of purpose at last. For once in his miserable little life he had a purpose.

He climbed over a fence, and hiked his way up one side of Sweetheart's Bluff and down the other. From here he could see the back of the trailer but there was no way the cops up in the Ford could have seen him.

As he got closer to the trailer he could hear the television blaring inside. Michelle always kept it loud. She was probably watching one of her stupid reality shows.

Dale crouched and stooped around to the front door, trusting that the cops hadn't seen him. The screen door was half busted off, so he opened it as quickly and quietly as he could and as he did so he reached around and felt for the .44 in the waistband of his jeans. Then he pushed open the door and went inside.

†††

Simon Cowell was on the TV savaging some poor blonde surfer kid who was on stage singing like a rusted gate. "If your lifeguard duties were as good as your singing," the loud-mouthed Londoner was saying in his pompous Brit accent, "a lot of people would be drowning."

Ordinarily, Michelle would have been busting a nut laughing—after all, *American Idol* was her favorite show of all time—but tonight she was too shaken up.

The phone rang and it startled her.

The phone rang again. She struggled out of the recliner.

"Yeah, yeah, hold your freakin' horses."

She waddled over to the phone and breathed a heavy hello into the receiver.

"*Get out of Temperance, Child Killer!*"

"Who is this?" Michelle asked, feeling wary. "Joey Dalton, if this is you and your little freakin' friends, you'll get yours!"

"*You won't get away with it! If the law doesn't get you, we will! We don't have to live with murderers like you in Temperance, Michelle Violette.*"

Michelle slammed the phone down and stood there for a second. She closed her eyes and wanted to cry. Not just cry, she wanted to bawl.

Outside the wind howled and the naked fingers of the big elm tree tapped and lashed at the window.

Michelle ran her hands over the kitchen table and imagined that Rose was sitting across from her again, sitting in her highchair, throwing her green beans all over the floor. She could almost see her in every room just as she used to be. Her baby. Her sweet, precious baby.

She closed her eyes and Rose was there. She could smell her. She was there in the kitchen, beside her, in front of her, inside her, and she felt the overwhelming urge to reach out to her, to take her in her arms, protect her.

But she hadn't protected her. Instead, she had failed Rose; failed her only child, and as long as she lived, that failure would haunt her.

She buried her face in her hands and started crying, crying with all her trembling body, crying with whimpering lips: "Forgive me. Please forgive me."

The front door clicked open with a soft snick of the latch and Michelle's heart bounded in her breast.

"*Dale!*"

His face was inside the grating; then his whole body followed, slipping into the trailer like a slithering snake.

He was holding a gun in his hand and he was looking at her—looking through her—with a weird, faraway shimmer in his eyes. He looked oddly like Jack Nicholson in that movie *The Shining*. Michelle half expected him to say, "*Heeeere's Johnny.*"

For a moment she thought it was almost funny.

But Dale didn't say "*Heeeere's Johnny.*" He didn't say anything at all, which almost made it worse. He just stared at her with those faraway, empty eyes.

Finally, he said, "Hello, Michelle."

"Dale, what are you doing here?" she said, opening her mouth like a seal expecting a fish to be thrown to it. "The cops are all over the place. If they find you here...they're looking for you, Dale. They know you beat up Stevie."

"What else do they know, Michelle?"

He was inching closer to her and she backed defensively into the corner.

"What did you tell them!" he shouted, turning on her with a flash of rage and indignation. "What lies did you tell them?"

"Nothing, Dale. They don't know nothing. I swear I didn't tell them nothing. I swear it."

"I'll bet you didn't, you lying bitch!"

"Dale—"

"Shut up! Just shut the fuck up. Don't say a fucking word, Michelle."

He lifted the big gun in his hand.

"Dale—" Her eyes pleaded with him in a burst of futile mercy, her hands reaching out to him.

"I should have killed you a long time ago," he said in a low voice, knocking her hand angrily away.

She fell whimpering to the floor on her hands and knees. Something cloudy passed briefly across her face.

"We're gonna burn in hell for what we done, Dale," she said. "We did a horrible thing, Dale. Do you know what I think? I think we deserve to die for what we've done. It's fucked-up how you've got to bluff alla time and keep bluffing even when screaming 'Help!' is all you really want to do."

Dale slowly lifted the .44 and placed it on Michelle's temple and squeezed the trigger.

Her head jerked violently and her body lurched over onto the linoleum floor; her wide, shocked eyes rolling upward, begging a God she never really believed in for a succor she knew would never come.

Chapter Thirty-eight

They had no more proof than when they started. The weight of circumstantial evidence was impermeable; the last straw floating down to the camel's back, but they needed to find what Dale had done with Rose. Danny remembered reading of a case where a husband had been convicted for the murder of his wife without a *corpus delicti*. The court had accepted what it had called reasonable proof of death. But it rarely happened like that.

"I'm gonna see if my dispatcher's heard anythin' else," J.P. told Danny, reaching inside the prowler for the radio mike. "Unit One to Dispatch. Over."

"...is...patch," a crackly voice came over the line. "Go...head...John...e..."

"You're breakin' up on me, Davina. What's the word from Montgomery and Jackson?" J.P. asked, referring to the two deputies who'd been posted overnight at Michelle and Dale's place.

There was some more static before Davina's voice returned. "Nothing. No...one's come...in or..out of the trailer since you left. Over."

J.P. took out his smokes and lit one, struggling to light it against the wind and snow.

"Anythin' else happenin'? Over."

"Did Sadie Peter..hold of..up there, Sheriff?"

"That's a negative."

"She's…trying to…you all day…your cell, but…must be out of range way up there. She just called…here not ten…ago looking for ya. She…real worried."

"What is it?" J.P. said into the mike. "What's wrong? Did she say? I'm barely picking you up, Davina. Go slow!"

"It…seems…someone been calling…to her…parents' house…leaving threatening…"

The last word, at least, came through clearly.

"Does she know who it is?" J.P. asked.

"No…but she thinks…might have…idea who it is."

J.P. looked over at Danny, and Danny could tell something was wrong.

"What is it?"

"Just settle down a sec—"

"Don't tell me to settle down. You look at me like that and then tell me to settle down. What the fuck's going on, J.P.?"

"It's Sadie."

"What about her? What's wrong?"

"She's been getting some strange calls at her parents' house."

"From Dale?"

"We don't know for sure." J.P. spoke into the mic again. "Listen, Davina, can you send somebody over to the Petersen place and have them check it out? Make sure everythin's okay?"

"Sorry…J…can't…that unless…pull Montgomery and Jackson off…trailer."

"What about Bobby? His kid sick again?"

"No, he's over...Moose Lake...a fishin' trip. I can call...but he won't like it. Besides, it'd take...half...night just to get home."

J.P. threw his cigarette away. "Forget it. I'll head over there myself. Radio me if anything comes through."

"Okay, J.P. Be care...hear?"

"I will, Davina. I will."

†††

J.P. turned the prowler around and had it headed back toward town before Davina even finished giving them all the facts.

He switched on the cherries and the red taillights of the cars ahead of them moved to the right; the gray headlights of the oncoming ones edged to their left.

"Do you think he's going after Sadie?" Danny asked in a voice that was barely recognizable.

J.P. took a deep breath, and, even though his voice was normal, he was gripping the steering wheel so hard his knuckles were white. "I don't know."

He had the speedometer buried at seventy-five, careful on the wet turns so they wouldn't go flying off into the ditch. The headlights stabbed at the night, illuminating a wilderness of snow. The prowler came out of the growing gloom of the highway, crunching through drifts and chewing through crests in the streets. It was dark when they got back into town. Banks of snow were already beginning to pile up against the storefronts.

Main Street was white and glittering; muted sounds, sterilizing shadows. The town's storm emergency signal began to howl: one long, two shorts, a pause, and then once again. The shrieking of the whistle rose and fell, rose and fell. Its sound was terrifying and dreamy.

J.P. took out his cell and tried calling over to the Petersen place. The phone rang four times before the answering machine picked up...

Chapter Thirty-nine

She was a fairy-tale princess, lying on the bed, her small delicate hands folded across her chest, her long brown hair flowing over the white sheets like spilled root beer. The long white curtains on the open window billowed like ghostly arms.

He only wanted to watch her. He didn't want to hurt her.

He stood over the bed and watched her measured breaths, her chest moving up and down, her large dark nipples showing softly through the silk nightgown that she wore.

†††

Something stirred inside of Danny. He tried to will the prowler to go faster, speed seemed essential, but it was like being in one of those dreams where you're trying to run from something—or to something—and your legs feel weighted down like lead.

A steady grist of snow was still blowing, sending sheaths down Main Street and continuing to build up in drifts.

When they turned the corner on Benjamin Street and neared the house, he saw instantly that something wasn't right. All of the lights were turned off, including the outside porch light over the front doors. Sadie's car in the driveway was little more than a snow-covered hump. The thing stirring inside him crept into the pit of his stomach and coiled there, hot and hissing.

J.P. slid the prowler into the driveway and they got out. A gust of wind struck them, rocking them back on their heels. The wind moaned. Branches clacked against the front porch, wallowing under the drifts like a slowly sinking ship.

Danny took out his handgun and struggled up the snow-burdened steps. He looked around, nervous. It was too quiet; too quiet and too still...

†††

Dale slipped the clear plastic bag over her head. Her eyes burst open and bulged out. Her face, stifled under the plastic, contorted like a face photographed under water or from behind a plane of glass and her mouth formed a terrified orb, stretching in a silent scream.

The first thing that came to Sadie's mind was that she would never get to see her kids again. Then the visualization that he might have gone to them first struck her and she struggled madly, kicking at him with her bare feet and grabbing out with both hands. She tried screaming but the only thing that came out was a muffled frightened cry.

Her nose was trickling blood now and her face was turning an ugly shade of blue. Spittle was flying out through the open screaming circle of her mouth, trapped within the clear plastic.

Dale held the bag tightly, almost lovingly, around her head. She tried reaching out with her hands to scratch at his face, but it was no use. She stopped struggling and her body finally slumped against his upon the bed.

†††

The bedroom door crashed inward. Danny paused in the threshold and saw Sadie on the bed, lying unconscious. He tasted the bright steel of panic in his mouth and felt a foamy nausea rising up inside him. The front of his brain was swelling, locking up, and all he could think was, *She's dead. Oh, my God, she's dead!*

Dale was on his knees on the bed beside her. His eyes were as cold and cadaverous as ice flows.

"Get away from her!" Danny shouted, pushing his gun up toward Dale.

Dale didn't move. There was no sign of emotion.

"Dale—get off the bed," J.P. said calmly.

Dale smiled once, a sick, yellow smile. Then he slid off the bed like a ghost in an old black-and-white movie.

J.P.'s calmness exploded into rage. "On your knees!" he ordered Dale. "Put your hands behind your back. I swear to God I'll shoot you!"

Dale moved in slow motion, as if drugged.

Danny rushed over to the bed and held Sadie's lolling head in his hands.

J.P. grabbed the walkie-talkie off his shoulder and paged dispatch.

"Davina, we got a situation out here at the Petersen place. Get an ambulance out here as soon as you can."

Chapter Forty

She woke to blinding light.

At first she thought it was that light you see when you die, but she never believed in all that before, so why should she start now.

Then she saw the girl in the perfectly-starched white dress and white stockings sitting in the corner of the room. When the girl saw that Sadie was awake she stood up, smiled and walked over to the bed. She put her hand on Sadie's arm.

"Am I in Heaven?" Sadie said through dry, cracked lips.

"No," the girl said in a comforting, syrupy voice. "You're in the hospital."

"The hospital?"

The nurse smiled again and nodded her head. "You almost didn't make it. Do you remember?"

"My children? My mother and father? Are they..."

"They're okay. They've been waiting for you to wake up. I finally sent them home to get some rest. You're going to be just fine. Thing's didn't look too good at first but you're a fighter. There's someone outside who would like to see you. Want me to bring him in?"

Sadie nodded. A few seconds later the door opened again and Danny came tentatively into the room. He was wearing a gray Brooks Brothers suit and his dark hair was off his face.

He was carrying a little white teddy bear in his hands.

"Who's your friend?" Sadie asked.

Danny looked down at the stuffed animal and smiled.

"It's for you," he said, holding it out in front of him. "It's all I could find in the store downstairs."

He put the bear down by Sadie's feet.

"You okay?" he asked.

She seemed to let out a little sob; then she smiled.

"I thought you were going to die," Danny said and his eyes shone.

Sadie tried to smile again but it came out all crooked. "What happened to Dale?"

"We arrested him. He killed Michelle."

"What about Rose? Did you find Rose?"

"Not yet. But we will."

"Did he kill her?"

"He hasn't said."

She was solemn for a moment, her head still spinning from the morphine drip in her arm. Everything was falling into place and still she couldn't really grasp it. She was tired and her whole body ached. She yawned cavernously.

"I should go," Danny said. "You're tired."

"Don't go."

He sat down on the edge of the bed and the shuffling of his suit sounded like gentle rain.

"Don't go," she said again, and reached out for him.

"I'm not."

"My ears are ringing," she said.

He bent toward her and touched her face with the palm of his hand. She kissed him. His tight lips held back at first, then yielded until there was only softness and his breath became naked.

"Don't go," she said again. "Don't you go. Don't go away ever again."

Chapter Forty-one

They had Dale in a long, bare room with iron bars in front of the narrow windows. The cell was secured by a door cleaved from a single slab of oak that was hung on iron hinges and bolted by an iron bar padlocked through two iron hasps. It still had bullet holes in it from a lynching back in the 40s when two black men from a traveling circus were accused of raping a white woman from Temperance.

The air was repulsive. A patterning of graffiti and smeared blood decorated the fading yellow walls. Muffled moans and shouts escaped from the other cells lining the corridor. Above the sounds inside the cell Dale could hear a milling mob outside on the street through the narrow window.

Ignore the sounds, he told himself. Ignore the smells. Clear your mind. Relax. Go away to that private place in your mind. Your sanctuary. It's always there in your mind. It's where you went when you were a kid and things got bad. It's always been there for you.

†††

As Danny came down the hill to the Public Safety Building he saw the mob. A screaming throng, electric with vengeance, crowding everything, swarming over the sidewalks, surging like a riptide against the glass front doors. Some of them carried big signs and others sat on the curb or leaned against parked cars, shouting at anyone going in or out. Hungrily they gathered, talking excitedly and asking questions and finding out some of the facts and most of the fiction and passing them on to others. They all felt a death now, and wanted a part of it. Grief and remorse, compassion and accountability—all were forgotten now and consumed into an intense overpowering hatred.

"They'll kill him," Danny thought as he got out of his car. *"They're going to kill him."*

A great shout suddenly went up from the crowd, a wave of movement driving it threateningly closer to the solid double doors of the Public Safety Building.

Danny halted and, with dazed and horrified eyes, stared round at the mob, in the midst of which, overtopping it by a full head, Babe Gorman appeared.

He had on a straw cowboy hat, a loud suit; tie and shirt, and snakeskin cowboy boots. His eyes were clear and he looked strong as a bull.

"It's a good day to die, isn't it, Pierce?" Gorman whispered, smiling menacingly, his voice as rotten as his politics. "A very good day to die."

"You're crazy!" Danny shouted back at him. "You're all fucking crazy."

"Dale Jacob will atone for his sins!"

"Only God can forgive sins," Danny said, his eyes growing hard.

"But that doesn't change the responsibility of his flock to atone for those sins," Babe said with an impatient flick of his hand. "Soon Dale will be pushing up grass and feeding the worms."

Danny left Gorman there in the middle of the throng and pushed his way up the steps toward the entrance of the Public Safety Building. He recognized the deputy on the other side of the glass doors.

"Let me in!" Danny called out to him.

The mob trailed him, screaming and pushing and clawing. The deputy looked uncertain for a moment. Hell, he looked terrified. Then he pushed the clip into the shotgun he was holding and unlocked the door. As the crowd pushed forward, he raised the shotgun into the air and they were forced to reluctantly fall back. Danny slipped inside and the deputy locked the doors again behind him.

†††

Danny saw Dale sitting in a faded yellow cell, his legs drawn up so that the heels of his stocking feet were on the edge of the cot. His legs were bent and he was peering at Danny through his slightly spread knees.

J.P. was sitting at a desk in the corner of the room and another deputy armed with a 12-gauge stood uneasily at attention against the wall. The ashtray on the desk in front of J.P. was past the point of overflowing and a freshly lit cigarette dangled from the corner of his mouth.

"A charming bunch out there in the street," Danny said, his face convulsed with detestation. "Gorman's got the whole town worked up into a mob."

J.P. stood up and Danny followed him into the squad room in back. He went to the big silver coffee pot, poured two Styrofoam cups full of Folgers, and handed Danny one.

"Has Dale come forward with anything yet?" Danny asked.

"Nope," J.P. said with slow contempt. "He'll get a lawyer. Maybe plead innocent."

"Maybe," Danny said. "But at least we've got him for Michelle's murder."

"Will there be enough to convict him?"

"I think so."

"You think so, but you're not sure."

"Hard to tell these days. I've seen enough courtroom dramas to know that murder in the first degree doesn't always stick."

"You mean he'll plea bargain?"

Danny shrugged. "There's always that possibility."

"She was just a little girl!" J.P. burst out. "A helpless little girl. The thought of Dale alive when that little girl—" he couldn't even bear to say her name—"when that little girl is dead, is too much for this town to live with." He paused and went over to the window and looked out at the milling crowd in the street. "Every day we will know that she is dead and the man—if you can still call him that—who killed her is still alive."

"What are you saying, J.P.?"

"When I became a cop I never thought of the harsh red realities I would have to face. The time is past for doing what's mandated, Danny. It passed when Dale killed Rose and buried her somewhere in the woods, all alone where no one would find her. A person who could do those things doesn't deserve to be defended and sent to jail for what—maybe five years at the most? No, what he deserves, hell, the courts just aren't the ones to deliver. You think maybe this once there's going to be a little justice…a moment of justice to make up for all the shit."

"Justice isn't bringing the dead back, J.P. You'll never bring them back. There is a process in place. There is a system of justice. It's flawed, and it doesn't always work the way it should, but it's the best we have. You cannot carry out acts of evil in the name of the greater good, because the good always suffers."

"Is it better to let evil go uncurbed than to sacrifice a little of the good to resist it?"

"And who decides that? Who decides what is an acceptable level of good to sacrifice?"

Chapter Forty-two

The interrogation room was small and sachet-like. Its walls were stained with decades of stale cigarette smoke and the air had a tightly packed feel, compressed and tenuous.

Dale sat sideways at the table and J.P. took the other chair. Danny was standing in the shadows in the corner of the room.

J.P. reached over the table and pressed the start button on a battered tape recorder.

"Where's Rose, Dale?"

Dale looked up at him. "Aren't you supposed to lead up to that question, pig? Build the tension? Put me off guard? Can I smoke, or is this one of those dumbass Clean Air buildings?"

J.P. took out a fresh pack of Marlboros and threw them on the table in front of Dale. "Go ahead. Smoke up."

Dale started peeling the cellophane off the pack.

"We got you for Michelle's murder," J.P. said. "Why not tell us what happened to Rose. What's the harm?"

"I killed Michelle, but I didn't kill Rose."

"Why'd you kill Michelle?"

Dale bowed his head a little, his voice filled with a strange exhausted relief. "Michelle needed killin', so I killed her. Like a dog with its guts ripped out that you'd put out of its misery."

"Where's Rose, Dale?"

"I don't know."

"We can do this all night, Dale."

Dale shrugged. "I ain't goin' nowhere."

"What was she like? What was Rose like? I didn't get the chance to know her. Was she energetic? Feisty?"

"Yeah. Ain't they all?"

J.P. let out a forced laugh. "Yeah, mine sure are. Did you love her?"

"Of course I loved her, man. What's wrong wit 'chou?"

"I mean really love her? Like you can't explain it. You love 'em so much it actually hurts. That's how I love my kids."

"Yeah. I loved her."

"Isn't it true that Michelle was afraid for Rose when she was around you?"

"Michelle was a stupid bitch."

"Is that why you killed her?"

"I already told you why I killed Michelle."

"Is that why you killed Rose?"

Dale looked up at him. "I didn't kill Rose. I already told you that, too."

"Is it cold in here?" J.P. asked. "Are either of you cold?"

"Why did you kill Rose?" Danny said.

"I didn't kill her."

"You're a drunk, aren't you, Dale? Michelle was afraid you might hurt Rose when you got drunk, isn't that right, Dale?"

"That's a fucking lie. I never laid a hand on Rose."

"You go to church, Dale?"

"No. I haven't been to church since I was a kid. What the fuck does that have to do with anything?"

"What do you suppose God would do to the man who killed Rose?"

"Who said she's dead?"

"Do you think God might punish that man for what he did to Rose?"

"I don't know. You'll have to ask God. Maybe you can set him down in this room and give him the third degree." Dale looked steadily up at Danny. "You think I don't know what you're doing, pig? You don't scare me."

"Was she sweet, Dale?" J.P. asked.

"Who?"

"Rose. Was she sweet?"

"Yeah, she was sweet."

"Was she very sweet?"

"Yeah."

"Very, very sweet?"

"Yeah."

"Did you hear any screams that morning?"

"No."

"You didn't hear anything?"

Dale raised his eyebrows slowly and nervously. "No."

"Listen to me," Danny said, leaning close in Dale's ear. "You're lying to us. You know where Rose is. You know what happened to her."

"I don't know anything."

"Yes you do! Say her name, man. Say her name."

"What?"

"Her name. Say her name."

"*Her name?*"

"Yeah, her name. Say it. Say Rose. Say her name." Danny took out a photograph of Rose and held it inches from Dale's face. "Say her name!"

Dale stared at the photograph. "Rose," he whispered. "Rose. My little Rose."

After a long, dry pause, Danny said, "I think you did it. I think you killed your little girl. Your own little girl. You took her life away."

"I didn't."

"You took her life away and I think you should have the decency to tell us what you did with her."

"I don't give a fuck what you think."

Danny slammed his hand on the table. "Do you hear that mob down there?" He went to the window. "Do you hear them? They want us to hand you over to them, Dale. That crowd down there. They want to rip you limb from limb. Should we do it, Dale? Should we give you to them? Should we?"

J.P. lit a fresh cigarette and handed Dale the pack. "I think you should have the decency for once in your life to do what's right, Dale. Do what's right. Tell us where Rose is. Tell us what happened to her."

"I don't know anything."

"Yes, you do," Danny said.

"I didn't kill her."

"Tell us the truth, Dale. For once in your miserable little life, tell the truth. Why did you kill her, Dale?"

"I didn't kill her and that's the truth."

"You were late for work that morning, Dale, and that's the truth. Now, why don't you tell us what's the truth? What is the truth? The real truth. Answer me. Answer me."

"I...didn't...kill...her."

"We already know the truth, Dale. The real truth. We know you killed Michelle. We know you attacked Sadie. Why did you go to Sadie's house? Why did you try to kill Sadie? That's the only part I can't understand."

"I didn't want to kill her. I—I only wanted to *watch* her."

"Watch her?" Danny sucked in his breath with a fierce sound. "Bullshit. That's bullshit, Dale. You wanted to kill her because she pissed you off somehow. Just like Michelle. Just like Rose. Just like every other woman in your life."

"You don't know. You don't know."

"I know everything, Dale. I know everything. You killed Rose, Dale."

"No."

"She was your daughter. She made you angry and you killed her. It's the only way it could have happened."

"No. I didn't kill her. I don't know."

"You want to take a polygraph test?"

"Yes."

"Really? You're willing to take a polygraph test? A lie-detector test?"

"Yes. Right now. I didn't kill her."

"You're nothing, Dale. You understand me? You're nothing. I feel like handing you over to that mob down there. You killed her, Dale! You killed her."

"I didn't do it."

Danny grabbed Dale by the neck. "Look me in the eyes and tell me you didn't do it."

"I...didn't...do...it."

"You did it! That's not the truth! Tell me the truth!" He yanked Dale out of the chair and threw him up against the wall. "Tell me the truth! You tell me the truth! Tell me the truth."

"Get your hands off me!"

"Tell me the truth!"

"Get your hands off me, man!"

Danny held Dale's face in his hands. "Tell me!"

Dale faltered, his face becoming distorted into an ugly mask of grief, his eyes watering. "I didn't kill Rose! I'll look you straight in the eye and I'll say it all night."

"We've got all night, Dale. We've got all night and all fucking day."

"I didn't kill her! Why can't you believe that?"

"Tell us where she is, Dale. Tell us what you did with her."

"I didn't kill her."

"You got a block in your mind telling yourself you didn't do it. But we can see that you did do it. You killed her, Dale."

"I don't care what you believe. Why won't you listen to me?"

"You killed her, Dale. You killed her."

"I didn't kill her!"

"You're just holding back that little bit, Dale," J.P. said. "Tell us. Tell us what happened. I'll believe anything you say. Tell me what happened. Tell me what happened. I want to know your side. Dale, I really do. Tell me what happened."

Dale blinked hard. "I—I—I—"

"Tell me, Dale. Tell me—"

"I didn't kill my little girl."

"Okay, fine. You don't care. Okay."

"I cared about Rose. I loved her. I didn't kill Rose."

"You've never loved anything in your life."

"I loved Rose. I didn't kill her."

"Tell us the truth."

"I've been telling you the truth, except you ain't been hearing it. The truth? Which truth? Would you know it if you heard it? The truth? The truth? I loved her. I loved Rose. I loved my little girl." Dale's face convulsed with self-loathing. "Sure I got mad at her sometime, and I spanked her, but I still loved her. She wanted to be a singer when she grew up. Like Hannah Montana. She could have been. She always asked me to play my CD's and she'd sing and we'd laugh. We'd laugh. I didn't kill her. I spanked her sometimes, that's all. I spanked her that morning but I never killed her. She was my little girl. I loved her. I spanked her, that's all."

"Tell us what really happened, Dale—"

"Michelle killed her! She killed Rose. She said Rose was the reason I never loved her. But that's not the truth. The truth? I never loved Michelle, but I loved Rose. She was the only thing I ever did love. A little girl. My little girl. Michelle took Rose from me that morning and slammed her against the bathtub. She hit her head. I don't know if she meant to do it. She said she didn't. She panicked. She said she didn't mean to kill her. But I think she did."

J.P. and Danny locked eyes.

To Dale, J.P. said, "What happened next?"

"She told me I had to get rid of her. I didn't want to do it. God, I didn't want to. But I didn't know what else to do. So I wrapped her in a blanket and drove her to the woods. The Devil Track Woods. I carried her out to the old Indian trails in the woods. She was so small. I carried her into the woods and buried her up by Cutface Creek. It seemed so quiet out there, so smotheringly still. Almost as though a heavy blanket had fallen down all over me, muffling everything. My ears couldn't seem to get used to it. They almost seemed to be ringing with the emptiness. And the trees; the trees. They were like my judges, shaming me. Oh, God! Oh, God; Rose! Rose."

Chapter Forty-three

The Devil Track Woods were located halfway between Temperance River and Croftville; a four-hundred-acre windfall-tangled amplitude of pristine woods, water, sky and forest. Danny and J.P. were in the prowler now, heading north on Highway 61. Overhead, a pale gray sun burned without heat, the afternoon slowly tilting toward shadows.

No snow, Danny was thinking. At least there was that.

"Do you think Dale was telling the truth?" J.P. asked, breaking the heavy silence.

Danny looked over at him. "I don't know. I don't know anything anymore."

The headlights of the prowler showed a white nothing up ahead, snow piled up on the side of the highway on both sides. Fifteen minutes later, J.P. turned the prowler onto a side road that lead to the entrance of the Devil Track; nothing but a dirt country road winding back into the forest, thick with birches and pine, in the middle of nowhere.

They followed the dirt road for a quarter mile, slowly bumping over the uneven earth, then turned north through the deep forest until they came to the old fire tower.

J.P. put the prowler in park and killed the engine. They'd have to hoof it from here.

"You ready?" J.P. asked. His eyes held on Danny, grim and gray in the dashboard lights.

"Yeah."

They got out of the prowler and made their way into the Devil Track. The snow cracked under their feet and in some places that were moderately protected from the overhang of tall trees they had to wallow through mud and dirt. J.P. was wearing a pair of insulated boots, but Dale didn't have such comfort and his feet immediately froze inside his thin city shoes.

"I should have lent you a pair of my boots," J.P. said.

Danny shrugged it off. "I'm alright. Let's go."

They crossed an old footbridge and followed a stream that bubbled along off to their right. The woods freaked Danny out a bit, but he was struck by the sensation that Rose was somewhere close by. The walking was hard on his pavement-trained feet. Not to mention that they felt like two bricks of solid ice.

Overhead, branches moaned and creaked in the wind, and Danny looked up uneasily. The leaves above him resembled little brown hands, rubbing in the white wind like a ghostly applause. A half moon was up now, pale and cold. The night seemed to wrap itself around them. It was a raw night, and they could see their own breaths snatched away by the wind, little gusts of silver vanishing into the darkness.

They passed an old wooden deer stand rotting among the trees and a gray weathered No Trespassing sign; naked birches, green spruces, barbed wire, and blue shadows, strips of rotting fence and sterile soil long unaccustomed to the plow.

Then they came to the old Indian trails and just over the ridge, surrounded by birch and pine was Cutface Creek. Dale had told them that he buried Rose on the north face of the creek, and they immediately saw a mound of rock and dirt that scarred the snow-covered earth. For maybe a minute the two of them just stood there, looking down on the creek like mourners. A minute can be an awful long space of time under such circumstances, as if that mound of rock and dirt was an alter and they could pray Rose back to life.

They both fell to their knees and began digging like two drifters searching for lost gold. The ground was frozen and progress was slow, but it was a shallow grave, and in less than ten minutes, Danny's raw fingers struck something.

It was a foot.

Immediately, Danny noticed the familiar stench. The smell of death. He stared at the remains, sickness rising in his belly. The smell of rot and decay was nearly palpable.

J.P. made a tortured gagging sound in his throat and twisted his head involuntarily.

Danny covered his face with his hands. It was the ugliest, foulest thing he had ever seen in his entire life. What happened to little Rose was an offense, to the eyes and the soul and the heart.

She was stiff with death. A slowly disintegrating diaper and rubber pants still hung on her bony hips. Her neck was broken, her eyes wide with accusation.

Danny crouched by the twisted body, and he touched Rose's cold, bony hand gently with his fingertips.

"I'm sorry."

Chapter Forty-four

MURDER SUSPECT MISSING

TEMPERANCE RIVER—A capital murder suspect who escaped from a Cook County jail center earlier this month is still missing.

Dale Jacob was being held in connection with the murder of his live-in girlfriend and their six-year-old daughter.

Jacob shot Michelle Violette and was suspected of killing Rose Violette, putting her in his vehicle and driving to a rural area where he buried her in a shallow grave, reports say.

He has not yet gone to trial for the murder.

"We don't know if he's still in this area," Temperance River Police chief J.P. Garski said. "But we're assuming that he is and we're searching the area."

Jacob escaped from the Temperance River jail on December 12. He is 34 years old, 5 feet 8 inches tall and 175 pounds.

Garski said Jacob is considered dangerous, but did not know if he was armed.

"We don't have any information that he has a weapon and we don't know if he has a vehicle."

Jacob has been featured on "USA's Most Wanted." His profile can be viewed on the television show's website at www.usasmostwanted.com.

Garski urged anyone with any information or anyone who thinks they may have spotted Jacob to call the Temperance River Police at 763-441-6075.

†††

The story was on the front page of the Temperance Daily News. Danny scanned through it one final time, looked at the photograph of Rose, then rolled the paper up and threw it into a trash bin on the promenade along the waterfront.

"They got away with it," he muttered to himself. "Goddamn, they actually got away with it."

He sat there for a moment, along the breakwater, watching the ships in the fog go sailing by. Shipping season would be over pretty soon, once the big lake froze up entirely.

He wondered what they had done with Dale's body after they had exacted their small-town version of justice.

†††

Danny got in his car and drove out to the cemetery, the one out by Belle Creek. Snow slanted over the black iron gates and drifted back over the marble headstones and the names of the dead.

He hadn't gone to Rose's funeral, but he knew where she was buried. He stood in front of her grave. The ground was still scarred where she lay.

"I'm sorry, Rose."

He took Mr. Honey out from underneath his coat and placed it against the gravestone and then he just let himself drift away.

Epilogue

Danny picked up Sadie and the kids and they drove through the empty market square. The snow was thick on the road and on the roofs of the surrounding houses. Pretty colored lights on Christmas trees winked in the windows.

It was a beautiful morning. The countryside was glistening and white under the thick layer of new snow. Each storefront had a Christmas wreath in the window and one on the door. Before long it would be Christmas Eve. In a few days Santa Claus would be starting out on his annual ride over the roof-tops.

Sadie looked across the seat and smiled at Danny. Jeffrey was in the backseat listening intently to his Walkman; Kimmey was staring out the window dreamily and Leah was humming her favorite song, *American Pie*.

They were headed to the annual Moose Stomp Festival; Temperance River's snowy version of Mardi Gras. The three-day festival featured polka music, ethnic food and drink, a fish toss, ice fishing contest, motorcycle ice races, an ice shanty pageant, and, of course, a black-tie dinner Saturday evening out on the lake.

The whole town was out, and after the heavy dread of the past few weeks, it felt good to be doing something normal again.

At five minutes before noon, a recording of the National Anthem was piped through the stereo speakers attached to poles dug into the ice. The townsfolk stood in respectful silence with gloved and mittened hands over their hearts. At noon a cannon shot fireworks into the sky, a loud cheer went up from the crowd, and the baited hooks were dropped into holes. The ice fishing contest had officially begun.

Danny and Sadie and the kids found an open spot of ice near shore and dropped their lines in a hole. Jeffrey started complaining about his line getting tangled and Danny went over to show him how to unravel the mess. Sadie watched him and when he returned she leaned over and kissed him on the cheek.

"Thank you," she whispered.

"For what?"

She smiled again. "For being here."

Leah started screaming and they both went over to her.

"I've got one!" she said, all bubbly excitement. "I've got a fish."

"Okay," Danny said, "go slow. Pull him out of the hole nice and gentle."

Leah bit down on her lower lip and started cranking the reel.

"Here, hold it like this," Danny said, showing her how to wrap her left hand around the cork handle.

He closed his own hand over Leah's; strengthening the grip, and gave the reel a small crank until the drag clicked on the line.

"Now reel. Reel him in."

He snapped her wrist and the rod came alive with the fish fighting on the other end. A few seconds later the head popped out of the hole and Leah almost dropped the rod into the lake.

"Hold on to him!" Danny called out. "You've almost got him."

Leah reeled harder and the body of the fish slipped out of the hole. Danny grabbed it and held him out in front of her.

"Look, Mommy," Leah said, beaming proudly. "I got a fish."

It was a trout, with beautiful markings and purple stripes along its side.

"Can we keep him, Mommy," Leah cried out excitedly. "Can we keep him, Mommy? Can we?"

Sadie stared off into the white distance; at the lake, at the river, at the town and its people.

"What do you say we throw him back?"